CONTEMPORARY AMERICAN FICTION

BEING INVISIBLE

Thomas Berger has been called "America's wittiest, most elegant novelist" (*The Village Voice*), "an exquisitely subtle artist" (*New Republic*), and "a master of the American language and experience" (*Ross MacDonald*). He is the author of fifteen novels, among them *Little Big Man, Neighbors, The Feud,* the quartet that constitutes the celebrated Reinhart Series, and, most recently, *The Houseguest.*

BEING
INVISIBLE

THOMAS BERGER

PENGUIN BOOKS

PENGUIN BOOKS
Published by the Penguin Group
Viking Penguin Inc., 40 West 23rd Street,
New York, New York 10010, U.S.A.
Penguin Books Ltd, 27 Wrights Lane,
London W8 5TZ, England
Penguin Books Australia Ltd, Ringwood,
Victoria, Australia
Penguin Books Canada Ltd, 2801 John Street,
Markham, Ontario, Canada L3R 1B4
Penguin Books (N.Z.) Ltd, 182–190 Wairau Road,
Auckland 10, New Zealand

Penguin Books Ltd, Registered Offices:
Harmondsworth, Middlesex, England

First published in the United States of America by
Little, Brown and Company, 1987
Reprinted by arrangement with Little, Brown and Company
Published in Penguin Books 1988

The characters and events portrayed in this book
are fictitious. Any similarities to real persons,
living or dead, are purely coincidental
and not intended by the author.

LIBRARY OF CONGRESS CATALOGING IN PUBLICATION DATA
Berger, Thomas, 1924–
Being invisible.
I. Title.
[PS3552.E719B4   1988]   813'.54   88-4075
ISBN 0 14 01.0871 8

Printed in the United States of America by
R. R. Donnelley & Sons Company, Harrisonburg, Virginia
Set in Garamond

To Richard Schickel

BEING
INVISIBLE

1

FRED WAGNER BEGAN HIS CAREER OF PUBLIC INVIS-
ibility in a large midtown post office. Until that time he
had only experimented with the technique in the privacy of
his home (where he lived alone at the moment), before the
full-length mirror mounted on the back of the bedroom
door, for especially when starting out, one does not become invisible without carefully studying one's reflection.
No human being can otherwise see much of himself, the
corollary of which state of affairs is that other people, even
strangers, are therefore greater authorities on one's exterior
than the owner thereof. From the first, through being invisible Wagner learned many truths that otherwise would
have been inaccessible.

On the day in question he had written an unusually long
letter to his sister, who lived across the continent from
him, on the subject of his failed marriage. He had written
it at work, but he could not get away with mailing it there,
where lately management had instituted a stern new program of economy, which included the interception of any
attempt to charge private postage to the firm. Paper-clip
and rubber-band allotments were policed as well, and telephone calls were sometimes monitored so as to ascertain in

whose interest they were being made, the company's or personal.

In the vast lobby of the post office, a grandiose architectural relic, were several machines that provided stamps on the application of coins. But as it happened Wagner was not at all sure that, though the letter seemed heavier than an ounce, it really needed more than one basic stamp, and having a low opinion of the postal service he was not eager to overpay it for what he believed, perhaps unfairly, was a job that had been performed ever more inefficiently as the rates continued to rise.

Thus for moral reasons he joined the end of the long queue at the only one of the many First Class windows in operation, though the postal workers were not away at lunch: a dozen or more were either casually conversing with one another, hooting occasionally with laughter, or wandering aimlessly about, carrying no burdens, en route to noplace. Several were puffing on lighted cigarettes, usually just under the bold signs that prohibited smoking. At least one of these men displayed a holstered revolver at his belt; he wore no upper garment but a dirty T-shirt. He looked less like a guard than like the kind of malefactor the gun was presumably intended to deter.

The line had not moved since Wagner joined it. There were seven persons ahead of him, and now the clerk, shaking his bald head, left the window. The pudgy woman in front of Wagner exhaled loudly, and the young man who was third in line turned to show an unshaven grimace to the others. Grumblings were heard, and there were those who pointed indignantly to the sequence of nonoperating windows.

Time was, Wagner would have joined the others in the impotent display of negative emotion, but no longer. He was getting on, had passed the midpoint of the slide towards forty. He suspected there was a hopeless look in his eye, but could not himself catch it in the mirror: it was as if that organ had a pride of its own, vis-à-vis the man it served. He sometimes wondered whether he was not a unit but rather a collection of disparate parts which, finding themselves thrown together, made the best of what easily could have been seen as an unfortunate accident.

In time the clerk returned, and eventually the woman just ahead of Wagner reached the window. She briskly asked for a roll of stamps and was quickly furnished with one and departed, but as Wagner stepped forward, the postal employee, whose tinted eyeglasses were taped at the nosepiece, replaced himself with a handmade sign that was not even decent enough to contain a word: a crudely drawn arrow, in what would seem from its color (orange) a child's crayon, pointed to the left. But all the other windows in that direction remained unmanned as Wagner plodded from one to the next, in the assumption he was the leader of a delegation. When he reached the end of the counter and turned back, he saw a new clerk in attendance at the window immediately next to the one he had left, and the queue was in place before it. He had been too impatient. Once again his age was inhibiting. As a younger man he might have taken his just cause to the persons in line. It was by no means certain he would have been rejected: kindnesses, little decencies were not unknown in the city, despite the received idea that man when crowded is necessarily callous. But nowadays he could not risk being turned away. He had exiled himself from this temporarily cohesive group: why should they forgive him?

Later, looking back on himself as he had been during this era, he wondered at his reluctance to use his marvelous gift.

But he had not been at all sure it would work. Becoming invisible in the sanctuary of a private bedroom was one thing: that he could not see himself when alone might be an optical illusion. If reality were to be respected — and except in this case he had never known its principles to have been abrogated his life long — it was impossible to become invisible simply as an exercise of the will. He might well be insane: to act publicly on his madness might result in his being committed.

However, a failure to become invisible would hardly be detectable and would leave one no worse off than at the outset, unless of course one was so foolish as to assume the process was working when it was not, which would be easy enough to ascertain. Then too, Wagner recognized that in his current situation he was already, and had been long since, invisible in the moral sense. It was not only appropriate to bring his physical state into conformity with the rule; it was probably required were he to take himself seriously from this moment on.

So then and there, he started to become invisible. The process took a while to be completed. His face and hands, unadorned flesh, went quickly, but the clothing needed more time: he had not anticipated this delay, for as it happened he had always been nude when disappearing in the bedroom mirror. However, he went utterly unnoticed now, even though for perhaps as long as twenty–thirty seconds parts of his attire could have been seen by anyone who took the trouble to look.

He wore a pair of good wool trousers: they went with dispatch, as did his leather shoes. But the socks had a high synthetic content, and they stayed visible awhile. His shirt, though wash-and-wear, for some reason disappeared more quickly than his necktie. He wore no undershirt. His jacket, or anyway that which he could see of it — he had no way of knowing whether it might have faded away in patches — could be seen the longest. Thus if anyone *had* looked at him, what would have been visible for as long as half a minute were: mid-calf navy-blue socks, a knitted green tie, and a jacket of brown-and-tan tweed in a herringbone weave.

Now what? He had become invisible from a motive of sheer resentment. Remarkably enough, he had had no practical end in mind. He had not known whether the trick would work — he still thought of it as a trick at this point, certainly not something on which to build a mystique, a career! *I was a failure until I learned how to make myself invisible.* That was an advertising slogan for a correspondence course of the sleazier sort.

As Wagner stood there in the supposition that he would momentarily return to a state of visibility, for all the difference that would make, the postal employee wearing the gun, the dirty T-shirt, and now, across his forehead, a red sweatband made from a rolled bandanna, emerged from the civil-service sanctuary through the door-gate at the end of the line of windows and sauntered at a disaffected pace towards some cross-lobby destination.

The narrow door, paneled below, barred above, perhaps restricted by some mechanism that ordinarily would have closed and locked it promptly, stayed ajar. Wagner was appalled at the negligence of a federal employee, an armed one at that: anybody now could walk right in and steal stamps. He himself certainly had no such aim as he pushed the gate open just enough to slip through — a maneuver that would not have attracted much attention even if anyone had been watching — and entered the area behind the closed service windows.

He went to the nearest station and weighed his envelope on the postal scale there. This device was of course the official balance and not the cheap little springed gadget one could buy in stationery departments and which was sometimes off by as much as half an ounce. Wagner was the sort of man who could lose face by the return of a letter with postage-due charges: he feared the implied accusation that he had tried to swindle his government and been stopped cold.

Forefingering the brass weight on the balance arm, he now determined conclusively that the letter did not, after all, exceed the full ounce for which one first-class stamp was legally adequate. Therefore this entire expedition had been pointless! For an instant of annoyance — he had squandered much of his lunch hour on a pursuit without profit — he actually disregarded his precedent-making invisibility, which anyway must have been only the product of wish-fulfillment self-hypnosis, for here came a great burly postal worker, glowering, to punish him savagely for his trespass.

Fortunately he stepped aside at the last moment, else the big man would have run him down unwittingly. The latter plodded on. Wagner began to suspect he should come to terms with the fact that he could not be seen by his fellow man, but first he had to procure a stamp for his letter.

The drawer below the window, that from which a clerk would have sold stamps had one been in attendance, was locked — as were all the similar drawers in the sequence, when he tried them, until he reached the only operational window. This man's drawer, loaded with first-class stamps and both folding and metal money, each denomination in its own compartment, was fully extended. The clerk stood on the far side of it from Wagner's position, so that the latter could have had easy access to all compartments if he were to reach within at a moment when the clerk's hands were elsewhere.

Wagner was nevertheless not quick to take advantage of his situation. He had taken out his change, a big fistful of accumulated coins, and was searching amongst them for a quarter. Invisibility had transformed this task from the most routine of exercises into an effort that might be simple to a blind man but was most demanding of Wagner, whose fingers were not that sensitive when gauging diameters. It seemed almost more remarkable to him that he could not see the money in his palm than that he and everything else he wore or carried were invisible to all.

Finally he remembered that a quarter has a serrated edge as opposed to the smooth one of the nickel, and he had just identified the very coin he sought when the large postal worker whom he had earlier eluded returned along what, again, would have been a collision course had Wagner not detected his approach at the last moment and jumped aside, dropping the handful of change.

Though all the human beings in the vicinity of this event had been blind to Wagner's transformation into invisibility, they were universally alerted by the sound of money striking the floor, and all the necks bent simultaneously, all eyes were directed downwards.

The postal clerk obviously assumed that the sound of fallen coins had been made by money from his own cash drawer, as unlikely or even impossible as that would have been unless the drawer had got upset or at least jostled.

It was ironic that the accidental dropping of the coins proved to be just the distraction that was needed. While the clerk was scanning the floor, Wagner tore one stamp from a big sheet of fifty or more, then bent to collect his scattered pocket money, which he could not see.

. . . But suddenly the coins became visible. From his squat Wagner stared up at the clerk, who rubbed his eyes, then himself came down to floor level.

It had been Wagner's intent to drop a quarter in the cash drawer to pay for the stamp he had taken, but now that the coins could be seen he did not dare touch any. Not to mention that the clerk was now appropriating much more than enough to pay for the stamp. Wagner had probably lost a dollar in change. So much for invisibility!

He rose and left the post office, though not before mailing the stamped letter, which of course was invisible when he held it, but no doubt changed its state once dropped through the out-of-town slot. Not until he was back at the office (having eaten no lunch at all) did it occur to him that he could have taken more than one stamp while the postal clerk's attention was diverted. Nothing would have been more justified in view of all the coins he had dropped, which the clerk retrieved, no doubt to return to the drawer, so that only the wretched postal system would profit, and mysteriously at that: another confirmation that God looks after the interests of institutions.

But apart from stamps there had been money in that drawer: not simply a supply of coins, from which he could have replaced what he had scattered on the floor, but folding money, dollar bills and more. Invisibly, he could have taken some without incurring any risk whatever.

Wagner felt as though he were sweating heavily, but when he touched his brow it was utterly dry. He had thrown a scare into himself. What a foolish turn his thoughts had taken. He resolved not to become invisible again except for private amusement. Not only had it cost him all his change today, but he had had a very unpleasant experience coming up on the elevator.

He had just missed one car and therefore entered the next alone, but in another moment Morton Wilton and Jackie Grinzing stepped on board. Wilton had recently joined the firm in some managerial role Wagner could not quite identify, but Mrs. Grinzing was head of his own department. Their employer produced catalogues for firms which sold by mail order. Wagner and a half-dozen colleagues wrote the original copy; then it was edited by Jackie and usually returned for revisions before being shown to the clients, who could be counted on to ask for still more rewriting, seldom for reasons that seem justifiable to those who were obliged to do it. The art department also often proved a pain to the writers, as well: with most catalogues the illustrations and layouts were given precedence.

Jackie had never been celebrated for her manners, but she had never before been so rude as not to look at him when he was near. In this case he was so close that had he not stepped aside she would have bumped against him. Nor would Wilton spare him even a glance. Wagner could not refrain from making a bitter grimace that, so far as he was concerned, they could share. Not that it was noticed. People in power tend to become ever more overbearing.

At last he loudly cleared his throat, causing both passengers to assume startled expressions.

"This old contraption sounds almost human," said Wilton.

Jackie raised her heavy eyebrows. "I get worried by its grunts and groans. I know elevators have got devices on them to catch them if they fall, but still."

"In an emergency," said Wilton, who was all sandy mustache above the moist red of the mouth he exposed when speaking, "just hold on to me." He took Jackie's hand and put it into his crotch.

Wagner had actually forgotten he was still invisible! He felt his face grow warm. Unseen, he was blushing, not so much because of the indecency (which perhaps could not even be called that: so far as these people were aware, they traveled upwards in absolute privacy), but rather by reason of his own throat-clearing faux pas. How embarrassing it would have been for these two people in particular to discover his secret! It might be sufficient cause to get him fired. Who could tolerate an employee with the capacity to become invisible at will?

For it *was* pure will. Wagner simply decided to become invisible, and it happened.

Remarkable, and in fact pretty ugly, was the muscular way in which Jackie was caressing Wilton's groin, if that was the word for what looked more like punishment. There was no apparent tenderness on the part of either, and odder yet, not a hint of passion. Jackie was in her ash-blond mid-forties. In one way she looked her age. But coming at the matter from another angle, one might say her appearance was better than could rightly be expected. Wilton was shorter than she and may have been younger, but it was hard to tell with his strawlike hair, head and facial. He was leaning back against the wall of the elevator. He had not touched Jackie since putting her hand on him. His expression was inscrutable. Her own, owing to the shape of her closed mouth, looked almost angry.

It was Wagner, and not either of them, who suffered anxiety at the approach of the floor at which they all were to deboard. Suppose someone was waiting for the elevator directly in front of the door? Wagner was so sensitive to humiliation as to feel it vicariously when he himself was but an observer of an experience in which it was no more than an impending possibility. Thus he was quailing, invisibly, in the far corner when the car stopped and the door slid open.

In fact a little crowd *was* waiting just outside. Some of them greeted Wagner's fellow passengers. Others stepped quickly into the car, barring Wagner's own exit. None acted as if they had seen Jackie abrading Wilton, for surely she had simply stopped when the elevator had. It took no great sleight of hand. Wagner realized he was a nervous wreck. Penned in now by the new passengers, he was forced to ride back down to the lobby.

When finally he reached his floor he hastened to the men's room, locked himself into one of the booths, and returned to visibility. Again the flesh was first to be transformed, and had there been an observer he would have seen a stark-naked man some seconds before the clothes were phased in. However, the entire process was carried out in much less time than had been needed at the post office.

Someone did see Wagner emerge from the booth and in consequence turned away with flared nostrils, obviously supposing, in distaste, that he had produced a stink. An erroneous impression of this sort was very difficult to correct without being silly, unless of course the man had been a friend, but he was rather some half-recognized person from the art department. For that matter Wagner had no real friends at the office — nor, in truth, out of it with the exception of his old roommate Cal Cavanaugh, with whom he had continued to be close for a while after college, but by now seldom saw, Cavanaugh having since moved to the suburbs and fathered two children in quick succession.

After his wife left, Wagner had dreaded being seen in the elevators and corridors of the apartment house in which he lived, for there were fellow tenants who were inclined to strike up a conversation when in proximity to another human being of local residence. Wagner had himself been of this taste. He had mildly enjoyed the small-talk about sports with Marvin Benderville, who lived somewhere around the bend of the hall in circumstances of which Wagner was not aware and in fact had no interest in learning, and exchanging complaints with a cadaverous-looking man named Todvik about the absentee management of the building, unreachably remote except when the rent was due, and the all-too-evident though practically useless super, not the sullen, cynical type so often to be found in such employment but rather a young man whose habitual high spirits were encouraging, till one began to suspect, from his failure to accomplish any task he undertook, they were either chemically induced or the symptom of mental impairment. Whichever, after the ritualistic reference to this functionary's latest stunt ("Know what Glen did today? Threw a lot of old paint cans down the incinerator. Firemen put it out before the walls got too hot to touch, but the building's been cited for the black smoke that covered the neighborhood. We'll pay for that with the next hike in rents"), Todvik often added, "I certainly keep my daughter out of the basement." Though in Wagner's judgment Miss Todvik, who looking thirty-five was seventeen only if you had been so informed, was more than a match for Glen, physically or in force of character. She had the foulest mouth Wagner had ever encountered in a female; reeked, in the close quarters of an elevator, of hops and smoke; and once, perhaps drunk or worse, had intimated to him that she was available for sexual purposes though not for free.

There were more attractive females in the building, and he knew some of them well enough to exchange bromides en route through hallways or lobby. Two were roommates and shared an apartment with still a third young lady whom Wagner had never actually seen owing to her demanding schedule of college plus job. The two he knew, Ellen Mackintosh and Debbie Fong, worked for the same bank. They were both genteel and well dressed. The latter was presumably Chinese but pretty obviously native-born, speaking Standard American. Though both women were attractive, Wagner had never desired either — or, more's the pity, anyone else except Babe, whom, to his knowledge, they had never met, for their hours would have been different from hers: she worked in an art gallery that didn't open till late morning, and never used the basement laundry room. Yet since his wife had left him, he found meeting Ellen and Debbie unbearable. Perhaps it would have been easier with either alone, but together they represented the kind of team to which he himself no longer belonged.

The other woman with whom he was slightly acquainted was named Sandra Elg. She had red hair, ivory skin, a large bosom, and formerly a handsome, sinewy-necked husband who sold expensive imported cars and was thought to have been a racing driver in his prime, which obviously had been not long before. Wagner was no authority in this area, being licensed to drive only those cars with an automatic transmission. As it happened, Elg had died suddenly, out of town, only a few days earlier, as Mrs. Elg had informed him when, despite his efforts to slip down the hall to the incinerator at a time when he was unlikely to encounter any of the other tenants, namely, one o'clock in the morning, the elevator door opened just as he was passing it and she emerged, overdressed as always, with the usual décolletage and heavy scent. She was not in mourning attire but spoke in a melancholy tone when she told Wagner of her loss.

Such is the ruthless nature of the human heart, the news made him feel better, though certainly he hoped that this truth remained well hidden behind his remarks of condolence. But he could not expect to run into only Mrs. Elg from now on, and anyway he doubted that her sense of bereavement would endure as long as his own, which was perhaps unfair of him, but he was simply unable to believe that a female of her endowments could have his depth of feeling. After Babe left, Wagner honestly never expected to attract another woman his life long. Perhaps that, more than any other reason, was why he decided to try to become invisible — though it would be a misrepresentation to say that one ever makes an altogether conscious resolve in such a matter.

He had happened to be standing, naked, before the full-length mirror on the inside of the bedroom door, when it began. He had only just got out of bed on a Saturday morning, to face the rest of the day, indeed the weekend, alone. With no one to see him, he found he was unable to assume a good posture: he could throw his shoulders back but he could not keep them there. Though actually underweight, he was developing a small paunch: this was due not to an accumulation of fat but rather to the relaxation of abdominal muscles that comes naturally with the years but can be arrested simply enough by regular isometric tensing of the stomach, you don't even have to work up a sweat. But at this moment Wagner couldn't do that, either.

He had assumed, without putting himself to a possibly humiliating test, that he was impotent at this period, but to have lost the command of his body in other respects was too much to endure. He sank, in articulated segments, to

16

the floor, where he reassembled himself into what was supposed to be a rigid unit, and in one supreme effort tried to do one genuine pushup, as opposed to the weak-kneed kind, and failed.

The only force strong enough to raise Wagner to his feet was the thought that drinking a cup of coffee might give him strength: this would have been the suggestion of his mother had she still been alive and not gone to an early death to which years of caffeine overloading had probably contributed: *You'll feel better after a cup of coffee.*

But only a quarter-teaspoonful of powdered coffee remained in the jar. Babe had been responsible for maintaining the kitchen supplies; Wagner handled the liquor, the garbage, the laundromat run. Babe had done most of the cooking, that is, defrosting, except when he opened the necessary containers and did the stovework for spaghetti, franks & beans, or baked chicken with a coating acquired when shaken in a plastic bag. Babe had suggested the movies; he subscribed to the magazines. Babe had selected many of his ties. After four years all the duties and privileges had been allocated efficiently, at least in the well-managed marriage such as theirs. Babe certainly had not left because of disorder.

Still naked, Wagner had returned to the bedroom and was once again staring at his body. He wasn't built all that badly. He was a bit underweight, especially since Babe's departure. He could have used some sun. His legs looked almost blue behind the dark hair, but they were well shaped and straighter than those of any number of the parenthesis-limbed movie stars so often depicted in bathing trunks and underpants. If only he were able to assume a respectable posture, he could pass, at a distance, for the old Wagner, but alas this was still too extravagant a hope: his most ardent efforts could not correct or compensate for the degenerate slump that began at the bridge of the nose and continued in a broken line to his insteps.

He must now get himself together and go out for a jar of coffee. Suddenly he wished he could do so invisibly! He startled himself, he who had never been given to the fanciful. That was his father's way. If a sailboat was hauled by trailer down their street, Dad, seeing only the top of the mast from his dinner-table chair, might say, "What if we lived on a canal, Fred? Go everyplace by water, not blacktop. This very home might be a houseboat. How about that?" Not even as a child had Wagner found such fantasies especially entertaining. If he went along with them it was only for the sake of his father, in whom an infantile streak was prominent. Looking out the window into a thick fog, Dad might say, "Like we're suspended from a balloon! Scary: what if the cables break and we plunge earthwards at an ever-increasing speed? Can you imagine that, Fred?" Wagner couldn't, but he usually pretended otherwise, at least until a natural feeling of charity towards his father was exhausted in the middle years of teenhood when most human males surrender to meaner tendencies.

Dad, no longer living, would have been proud of him now. "What if I were invisible, Dad, and could go everywhere unseen? Wouldn't *that* be something?" *Play tricks on family members, fool friends & policemen*, as the mail-order copy of yore said in touting the instructional manual on ventriloquism.

How could India-Indian fakirs walk on red-hot rocks? By telling themselves they can. I wish I were invisible, said one Wagner to the other in the looking glass, who was not exactly himself, for the parting of the hair was on the wrong side, as was the scar on the knee, the arched eyebrow, and the longer half of the scrotum. His real feet were quite different one from the other, but that fact was not evident at the moment, for his right foot, the left one in the mirror, could not be seen. He was standing on air on that side, his leg ending at the ankle . . . no, at about mid-shank . . . but soon the entire calf was gone, as was most of the other leg, which suddenly had caught up and passed its twin.

Wagner was inexorably disappearing before his own eyes. However, as soon as he recognized that fact and reacted to it with an access of emotion in which fear was predominant, the process was promptly arrested and he stayed visible from waist to head. As yet he had looked at himself only in the mirror: it might well be (and he was praying for that state of affairs) that what he saw, or rather did not see, was some trick of or flaw in the silvered glass: this effect was surely of the fun-house kind, though how and why the mirror had been altered was inexplicable.

He bent now and stared at his actual feet, that is, where they had been, where indeed they certainly must still be planted, else he would not be standing. Despite that truth of physical law, when he could not see his feet or legs he immediately lost his balance and fell to the bedroom floor.

He lay there for a while, breathing as though he had been doing heavy labor, then, ingeniously, this half a man pulled himself by clawed hands and digging elbows near enough to the bedroom door to swing it open to the point at which the mirror went back into its own dark corner against the wall.

With his reflection no longer before him, Wagner had no trouble in rising to his feet. Yet he would not look down for a while. First he went to the liquor cabinet, in the living room, and took a draught of the only bottle left therein: a half pint of kirsch, which Babe had purchased as long as nine or ten months before in response to a newspaper food-page suggestion as to how to transform a mélange of frozen fruit into a *grand luxe* dessert. Kirsch taken neat was sufficiently revolting to make him feel less unworldly. He drank some more, grimaced not as violently as the first time, for his tolerance was already building, found the courage to look towards the floor, and saw both his old familiar feet. Even the persistent corn on the left little toe was now a friend.

Wagner refused to believe he had been hallucinating, though that would have been the obvious assumption of many a man. He simply wasn't that sort. Reality might be unsatisfying, but he had yet to find an acceptable alternative. Half his body had been invisible for a while — yes, it was back now, as he had finally had the courage to ascertain without taking a third drink of kirsch — but it had been gone for a few moments anyway.

He had not been in a condition to go out for coffee until almost noon.

2

BEFORE HIS NEXT EXPERIMENT WAGNER DRANK THE remaining quarter-inch of kirsch, with a purpose to settle his nerves before facing the full-length mirror. It was amazing how quickly, as a nondrinker, he could feel the alcohol. He stripped, went before the glass, told himself to become invisible, and did so. He had forgotten he was holding the little bottle from which he had drunk, but the vessel vanished along with his person. The implications of this event were interesting.

He returned to visibility, put on clothes, and easily disappeared again. One problem with fictional invisible men had always been the clothing or lack thereof: they had to remove it to be unseen, which is to say, could vanish only when naked. This was an inconvenient state of affairs in wintertime, and when rained or snowed on, the man's corporeal outline could be seen. Wagner also believed he could remember from one of the movies on the theme that the police caught an invisible malefactor by spraying empty space with opaque liquid or fine powder. He now dusted his head with talcum but could not see it, then shook his hair clean and next inundated his crown with water. He and his clothes were soaked, but all remained unseen.

Anything, any substance or object that came in contact with the invisible Wagner, was perforce itself put into a state in which it was undetectable to the eye.

Anyway, to his own eye. At this point the process had yet to be tried on anyone else. And for a while it seemed as though this might never happen. Suppose it was only an illusion of his own organs of sight? He could easily make a fool of himself, thus aggravating the very situation from which he wanted to escape through invisibility. Therefore some days passed before his gift was even exercised elsewhere in the apartment. Despite many complaints, Glen the super maintained a practice of making only the most perfunctory, almost inaudible knock and then letting himself into one's apartment with a passkey. Glen was one of the last people Wagner would have liked to catch him in a failure of invisibility. So it took a while before he went even as far as the bathroom.

When he at last did so he discovered some effects he had not anticipated: e.g., urinating when invisible is somewhat like doing it in the dark: you cannot watch the stream falling. However, he could see the disturbance in the water in the bowl, and thus oriented, did not pee on his feet.

Brushing the teeth was better done with the eyes closed, as was shaving electrically according to the gauge of the fingertips, but one of Wagner's weekend pleasures, a gracious old-fashioned shave with warm water from a mug and an antique cutthroat razor — presents from Babe at a bygone Xmas; she had a genius for giftgiving — had to be forgone if he couldn't see his face.

In the kitchen, when at last he felt comfortable enough to go there invisibly, there were other problems. If he lifted a boiling teakettle it could no longer be seen, and though the operation was the most common of those he performed

in that room, he had the greatest difficulty in pouring unseen hot water onto the instant powder in the visible cup.
Scalding fingers or even his wrist was routine. Of course,
slicing tomatoes or a loaf of bread would have been peril-
ous, so it was just as well that fresh tomatoes or a genuine
loaf had not been in his possession since Babe's leaving,
though it was true enough that there was no law compel-
ling him to become invisible. At any time he could have
said the hell with it and simply never done it again. Aside
from giving him a hobby with which to squander his eve-
nings, his ability to assume a state in which he could not see
himself had brought him no profit whatever.

And then came the episode in the post office, his first
public performance, at which he had actually lost money,
followed by the inadvertent voyeurism in the elevator,
which made him feel filthy and distracted him from his
work all afternoon. For hours he tried without success to
write new copy for an item that had been listed in a particular catalogue for several seasons but had never, according to the client, sold as well as it should have: a combination
ball-point pen and flashlight, the light mounted so that it
illuminated what was written by the pen. Obviously it
would be of use in a darkened room, perhaps to be kept on
the bedside table for jotting down those nighttime inspira-
tions that cannot otherwise be remembered next morning.
God knew Wagner had had many of them. When he sat
down with the manuscript of the novel he had been working on — seventeen pages, accumulated over, could it have
been?, six and a half years, but he had been a late begin-
ner — his imagination immediately packed its valise and
left on a tropical cruise. But just let him retire for the night!
His brain would proceed to furnish, unasked, far too much
for one sleepy man to handle, sufficient dramatic events,

vivid characterizations, and complex moralities for a multi-volumed *Comèdie Humaine de notre temps*.

Of course, little of this could be brought to mind as late as next morning. By the time he had the courage to confront his manuscript again, which might not be for weeks, it was as if he had never thought about it once during the interim. This certainly would not be the case were one equipped with the Write-Light Combo. So anyway he believed when he first saw the item (sometimes the client would provide samples of inexpensive products; less often these could be kept). He took it home (to do this openly one had to get Jackie Grinzing's OK), put it on the bedside table, and for the next five nights went quickly to sleep as soon as his head touched the pillow. But on the sixth and seventh came a succession of incandescent ideas like glowing pearls in long strands. The light-pen proved its worth, and in an *ad hoc* shorthand, a literal translation of the idiom in which his mind was dictating so rapidly, he recorded the lot.

Both mornings after, he woke to notepaper covered with nonsensical hentracks such as: "G dcs N w/ mplsmcz. Lake. 12–13. mem flg d. Larry Rdwqnq, & P. Etc. etc. H.O." Not even the two comprehensible entries served any purpose: there was neither a lake nor a Larry in the fragment of narrative he had accumulated over the years.

This experience had its effect on his efforts to write the new catalogue copy. People were probably not buying the Write-Light because, wiser than he, they correctly assumed that the idea that does not assert itself at an appropriate time comes not from the brain but the lower parts of the nervous system, the same that are responsible, especially in adolescence, for erections for which there is no apparent stimulus.

A hand cupped his shouldercap.

"I see the Muse isn't spreading her legs this afternoon." It was the unwelcome voice of Roy Pascal, a colleague who had the mistaken conviction that because they worked in the same office they were friends. Pascal had an instinct for arriving at moments when his presence was just enough to provide a negative solidification for a situation that until then had still retained a potential for movement.

Wagner tore the paper from the typewriter, which produced that near-scream of a platen spun too rapidly.

"Jesus," said Pascal, "there go the cogs. But maybe that's the only way to get new equipment. Come on, Ferdinand, let's get that cuppa Joe." He also used such terms as "head" for "toilet," and "glad to have you aboard" when greeting newcomers, though it was not he but rather his father who had served in the Navy. This was but one of his many affectations.

"I've had all the coffee I can swallow for one day," Wagner said.

Pascal agreed. "Me too. We'll get Cokes."

"No," said Wagner. "I've got to break the back of this copy. I just haven't been able to concentrate." He had continued to stare at his empty typewriter. Pascal was the only person in the office who would engage in nonbusiness talk to one's back. No doubt he would have preferred Wagner to turn in the chair but would settle for this. He seemed immune to feelings of rejection.

Wagner doggedly returned the paper to the typewriter. He would have liked to crumple it and bounce its ball against the partition, but management had been very strict about wastage in recent months, going so far as to ask that for original drafts the backs of used sheets be employed. Such measures had been instituted not long after Wilton's joining the firm. Perhaps that is what he did when not being dry-masturbated in the elevator by Wagner's immediate superior: dreamed up new economies to be imposed on the serfs.

"It's four thirty-five," Pascal, still there, said behind him. Wagner had assumed the bastard was gone! "It's too late now to find the words."

This was surely an accidental echoing of the very statement Babe had made on leaving — with reference to his novel — but it was no less cruel for that, and he was unmanned all over again, to the degree that he actually left his cubicle and accompanied Pascal to the soda-dispensing machine in the corridor on the route to the restrooms.

Over their cans of what proved to be grape soda — this late in the day everything else was gone — Pascal tried to gossip, but as he never had the real goods on anybody, he spoke in fantasy.

"I tell you Mary Alice is a lez if ever I saw one. Anybody looks like that and never dates." He was referring to their youngest colleague, a deep-breasted sallow-skinned brunette newly out of college. Wagner was helping her to learn to write catalogue copy but had identified in Mary Alice very little potential for this sort of work. Some of her efforts were memorably inept. He had started her on certain novelty items whose appeal would be only to a limited market so far as buyers went, but which might well amuse those who scanned catalogues, inducing them to linger here and there throughout the pages and maybe eventually come across a gadget they would wish to order.

There was a breast-pocket handkerchief for the jacket of a business suit, which when removed and shaken out of its folds appeared to be rather a pair of lace-trimmed underpants. There was a miniature version of a loving cup, inscribed with a mildly insulting title, e.g., "World's Champion Bullshooter." There was one of the classics in this tradition, the nutcrackers in the shape of a woman's legs. Mary Alice actually seemed not to get the feeble jokes of these infantile amusements. In her copy the fake panties were simply an "elegant lace-trimmed handkerchief" and the little loving cup was a "thoughtful award for prowess in some area which might ordinarily go unrecognized." The nutcracker was called simply that, and the text pointed out that it was also functional with lobster- and crab-shells.

Mary Alice Phillips had off-white skin and small dark eyes. She was not the type of female to whom Wagner was erotically attracted, despite her prominent breasts or perhaps because of them as well as her tender age. He was never altogether at ease with unseasoned women. Mary Alice still lived with her parents. He doubted that Pascal had any evidence she was lesbian. The man was usually wrong.

"How's Carla?" Pascal now asked, with an intimate intonation, as if he were a close friend of the family. He had encountered Babe but once, two years before, and that was certainly an accident. In those days the Wagners were on the town once or twice a week, prowling to obscure restaurants not yet assessed by food critics, then on to postprandial entertainments: penny arcades (Babe was good at machine games; Wagner excelled at the electronic-eye gun which if aimed accurately would reverse the little moving bear) or the movies: Babe liked narratives of contemporary life, the give and take between persons of opposing sexes, whereas Wagner's favorites were the cinematic nightmares in which the routine is hideously transformed, owing usually to excessive radiation: Uncle Ralph suddenly becomes an eater of human flesh or a common mosquito grows to the size of a dirigible. As ill luck would have it, on the evening in question they were emerging from a restaurant when who should be the only passerby but Pascal. For the instant before taking note of Wagner, he wore quite a different expression from that of the office. There, his nervous eyes were quick to focus on whatever they were directed towards. Among his tiresome traits was an insistence on noticing all petty phenomena in his vicinity — "there goes Irene for more coffee," "that pigeon almost landed on the sill but thought better of it, went to the steeple over there," "are you getting a pimple on your ear? . . . sorry, it was the way the light was falling" — but as encountered here, Wagner's colleague walked with a lowered head, and when he raised it his eyes were heavy-lidded and lusterless.

In the next instant, recognizing Wagner, he altered his state dramatically.

"Fred!" he cried, failing to say "Ferd" or some variant no doubt because they were not alone. Wagner would not have credited him with such delicacy. "What are you doing in another part of the forest?"

Wagner's response was a lugubrious "Hi." He might have had the nerve to proceed onward without introducing his wife had Babe not claimed the initiative.

"I'm Carla," said she, going so far as to extend her hand to a person who had no greater recommendation than that he knew her husband's given name. (Wagner chided her later: "He could have been a criminal." "Oh, come on, is that likely?")

Of course Pascal was thrilled for once to have acceptance thrust upon him. "I've certainly heard a lot about you," he eagerly lied, shaking her hand too long.

No doubt Babe would have stayed and talked to the man

had her husband not insisted they were late for the movie, a misrepresentation that was exposed when they reached the theater, twenty-five minutes early.

If Pascal had seen Babe only once and by chance, he had certainly not been apprised of her flying the coop.

"She's fine," Wagner said now, through his teeth. He brandished the soda can. "This is awful!" He disposed of it in the nearby container, baffled as to why he had drunk so much of it as he had.

"Ferdie old boy, we need stronger stuff. Close up your desk and I'll meet you at the elevators and we'll stop off at Swan's." Pascal referred to the nearest watering place, or anyway the closest that was acceptable to the office gang. He quickly walked away, before Wagner could say no. Which meant he would stand guard at the elevator and be all that much tougher to reject.

Wagner had never been one of Swan's crowd. Now that Babe was gone, he returned home as promptly as ever, so that he would not be asked embarrassing questions if found lingering.

Despite the vow he had made after the unsatisfactory experience at noon, he now returned to his desk, which was so situated that no one routinely could see all of it on passing, pressed himself into the least conspicuous corner, and became invisible. It seemed to him that the process took less time than it had in any of the trials or in the post office. In any event he could not be seen only a few moments later when Mary Alice Phillips' quizzical expression appeared at the entrance to the cubicle.

A moment afterwards he heard her ask Delphine Root, the woman whose space was separated from his by their respective fiberglass partitions and a water cooler, "Fred's still here, isn't he?"

29

"Darned if I know," said Delphine, no doubt amidst escaping smoke, for a lighted cigarette was her constant companion.

Invisibly and quietly, Wagner covered his typewriter and dropped the papers into the deepest drawer, wincing in revulsion at the thought of the flashlight-pen. Hardly was this completed when back came Mary Alice, who peeped in again, almost impaling the unseen Wagner on a nose sharp with chagrin.

Again she stopped at Delphine's lair. She complained, "He must have walked right past me. His stuff's all put away for the day."

"He'll be back tomorrow," Delphine said indifferently. She added, "Death and taxes." She was beginning to sound malicious, though he had never quarreled with her.

"Well, it *is* closing time," said Mary Alice. "I came around too late."

"Sticking up for him, I see," Delphine said drily.

Mary Alice's voice was soft. "He's just been nice to me, is all."

Wagner had stepped out of his niche and come forward as far as the water cooler. He wanted to observe Mary Alice's expression at close hand. She was scarcely the glamour girl of Pascal's fantasies, but she was comely enough. Her skin though slightly sallow was finely textured. Her eyes could easily be enlarged with cosmetics.

He could see Delphine as well, or much of her. She extended her naturally apelike upper lip and took such a deep draft of her cigarette that the glowing ash traveled a third of the length of the paper tube.

She winked at Mary Alice and said, significantly, "OK."

The girl reddened and went back to her own desk. Wagner followed, lurked nearby until she put her things in order for leaving and donned a trench coat in which, when it was belted, she cut another and more lively figure than that afforded by the dun cardigan worn in the office.

At the elevators, he and she, she not knowing of him of course, came upon the wretched Pascal, waiting for Wagner, who in fact had forgotten about him.

"Hi there," Pascal said to Mary Alice. "Say." This word had no immediate successors. It was Pascal's means of holding on to someone encountered by chance until he could think of a reason for such detention.

It failed to ensnare Mary Alice. While she completed her nod a car arrived. She boarded it briskly. Pascal would have been on her heels, but Wagner caught the back of his topcoat and, using both hands, restrained him for a moment. Meanwhile, a number of other people stepped into the car, solipsistically preoccupied, and thus no one seemed to notice the man's preposterous struggle against his own coat, which was stretched tautly from his shoulders to a point in sheer air.

Wagner thought he had done enough once Mary Alice was insulated by a double layer of people, and he permitted Pascal to pull away. He was even a bit too quick to open his fingers, and the suddenly liberated Pascal plunged recklessly, clawing, into the front rank of those on board, which earned him abuse from at least one small woman.

Wagner realized he could not himself board a crowded car without probably bringing about some consternation that would serve no one's purpose: invisibility would be ineffective when tactile matters were uppermost. Some people, himself included, knew desperation when enclosed in a crowd: suppose they were pressed against a body they could not see, and the *unreasonable* were added to the existing claustral stresses?

Nevertheless, Wagner wanted to continue to follow Mary Alice Phillips and thus he dashed to the heavy metal door at the end of the corridor, hurled it open (regardless of consequences, and there were some: two young women from the art department, en route to the elevators, raised their eyebrows and pursed their lips, and one said, "Ghosts"), and plunged down the stairs. If the car stopped at other floors, and it always did, his ETA at the lobby might be competitive, and so it proved, though he fell once, luckily sustaining only a bruised knee, and avoided doing so subsequently by not looking at where his feet were or should have been.

He burst out onto the ground floor (again providing some spectators with the mystery of a door, in this case a stainless-steel one, that opened violently as if of its own volition (but such phenomena are soon dismissed amidst the distractions of the city), just as the elevator car arrived.

Naturally, for he had been nearer the front, it was Pascal who was seen first — but a truth soon became apparent to Wagner as the car rapidly was emptied of its passengers. Mary Alice was not amongst them. How could that be possible? Wagner demanded of himself, as if it were an absolutely unanswerable question, whereas the explanation could scarcely be exotic: there were eight whole floors between where he stood now and where he had seen her last. She had stopped off on one of them: yes, even though it had obviously been necessary for half the car to deboard so as to permit her own exit. That Wagner wouldn't have had the nerve to ask this for himself, had no necessary bearing on what Mary Alice was capable of.

Did she really have the special interest in him that was suggested by the interchange between her and Delphine

Root? This matter had intrigued him when he eaves-dropped, but it would have been degrading now to search half the building for her, or boring to wait till she reached the lobby, perhaps with a companion, and then be forced to judge whether that companion was indeed in some sex-ual association with her.

Pascal lingered just beyond the bank of elevators. It would have been simple for Wagner to evade the man, but had he done so he would have acquired the obligation to explain next day in a credible fashion how their trails had failed to cross despite a surveillance that would have done credit to an undercover police officer. It was easier to clear the air, and the deck, forthwith.

Wagner slipped back behind the door to the stairway and made himself visible, then boldly strode out and confronted his colleague.

"Why in the world would you have come down by stair-way?" he was asked. "Claustrophobia?"

"You know my secret."

Pascal grimaced, an expression that briefly improved the appearance of his weak chin. "*I'm* sorry. I was kidding."

"So was I," said Wagner. "Look, uh, Roy, I really don't have time for a drink."

To his surprise, the other gave him no argument, instead said, "Sure, Ferdie, I understand. I'd rush home too if I had someone like Carla waiting for me." His right eye looked as if he wished he had the nerve to wink.

This was one of those times when Wagner, fundamen-tally a peaceable sort, felt on the point of smashing Pascal in the face. Instead he nodded abruptly.

"See you tomorrow."

"Or maybe in front of the Mexican Standoff."

"What?"

Pascal said, "Remember last year when I ran into you two lovebirds coming out of the restaurant?"

"That wasn't Mexican," Wagner explained with asperity. "That was A Guy from Calabria." And taking advantage of Pascal's deflation, he grunted a farewell and vanished — not literally this time but so rapidly and deftly that it would have required a greater effort to pursue him than even Pascal could exert while retaining any pride whatever.

After a block he slowed down, being in no hurry to reach the apartment, to which he intended to walk all the way instead of taking either of the two buses required to reach home on wheels. The fact was that he had to do something about food, having had none for lunch. He had lost some pounds since Babe left, he who even in good times verged on the underweight and thus was envied by his wife as he had been by so many of his associates his life long.

The restaurant he had been forced to identify for Pascal had been a favorite of his and Babe's. The Guy's name was Jimmy and though he himself had not come from Calabria he was descended from several persons who had and whose recipes were presumably on the menu, which, thank God so far as Wagner was concerned, offered no surprises, he being an old-school man who ate spaghetti sluiced down with the harsh house red that came in the thick glass decanter. Naturally, since Babe's departure he had dined anyplace but there. Indeed, he had not eaten out at all except for workday lunches. At home he had hardly eaten, period. Dinner for six days in a row, until the carton was exhausted, might well be scrambled eggs.

But now, having been forced boldly to pronounce the name of A Guy from Calabria, he felt as though the taboo had been lifted thereby. All at once he was hungry for the first time in weeks: that thick, acidulous tomato sauce in which all of Jimmy's dishes were inundated might be just the balm he sought. He turned west. The fall evening, with its new darkness, the clock having only lately been changed, was clement and just cool enough, when taken at a measured pace, for his raincoat without its zippered lining.

For the briefest moment, as he passed from the tiny vestibule through the inner door and was flooded by the heated air of the restaurant, so aromatic as at first to be overwhelming to nostrils still pinched from the atmosphere of the sidewalk, Wagner felt a twinge of horror, but in the next instant, being gripped by Jimmy at his hand and then elbow and shouldercap, he knew nothing but kind emotions.

"Mr. Wagner," Jimmy was saying, working his entire arm, "my gosh I thought maybe you got sick or something, or mad at me, it's been so long. So tell me —" He was interrupted here by the man who tended the short bar.

"Jimmy, phone. Want to take it here?" He brandished the instrument.

"Hey," said Jimmy, and went to lean over the bar. His office was in back, between kitchen and the restrooms.

Though a habitué, with, whenever convenient, his own table (which by the way was empty now; it was earlier than most cityites dined, unless they were as unrepresentative as Wagner now found himself, and he was the only customer except for a middle-aged couple on the far right), he never seated himself but rather waited quietly to be led, another of his habits Babe saw as passive. But to him it seemed no more than good taste, and it made sense, as he had always heard, to keep on the good side of restaurateurs and maîtres d'hôtels, who had both privileges and punishments at their disposal, could seat you in the preferred section or in front of a toilet door, could steer you to rareties unlisted on the menu or staunchly reject legitimate complaints about corked wine or gristly meat.

Jimmy seemed to have settled down to a long conversation, for he had now perched himself on a bar stool. Why should Wagner need permission, in a room full of empty tables, none of them, so far as he could see, bearing "reserved" signs? He started into the dining area. But a waiter suddenly emerged from the swinging doors at the rear and advanced to block him before he got far.

"Seating by management only," said this functionary. He was new since Wagner had been there last. He had dead eyes and a downturned mouth.

"It's just that Jimmy —"

"You wait at the bar," the waiter said, spun around, and rapidly marched through the kitchen doors. He had made a special trip to perform this one bleak function. This was a new tone for Jimmy's establishment, where the service had always been informal, to say the least, but genial. The soup might get sloshed onto the tablecloth, but not without a compensatory grin. Forgotten side dishes were routine, but when they did finally get delivered, there would be a quip enjoyed by all: before the chef could deep-fry the zucchini he had to slaughter one and butcher it, or some such.

Wagner now honored the proscription against self-seating, but had no intention of ordering a drink before being assigned a table at which to sip it. But the bartender, a young, sandy-haired man whom he did not know because he never drank at the bar, now shouted at him, so loudly that one would have thought Jimmy, on the phone nearby, might have objected, but the restaurant owner was immersed in his conversation to the exclusion of all the rest of life.

"What's your pleasure?" cried the bartender.

"I'll wait till I get to the table," Wagner answered, purposely using a voice that though quite audible was at a relatively low volume.

"I'll make it now," bellowed the man. "Get a head start before the gang arrives."

That made sense, or would have if he had wanted a precise kind of martini for which the vermouth was to be measured by the droplet.

"I won't give you a problem," Wagner said. "I always drink the house wine with dinner."

"Coming up!" screamed the bartender, and quickly brought up into view a gallon jug that had apparently been kept in ice water, for it was dripping. He used it to fill a stemmed glass to the very brim with white wine.

"No, red," said Wagner, "and I don't want it yet."

The bartender's next speech was somewhere between a plea and a threat. "It's already poured."

Despite hearing a private voice, very like Babe's, that told him, fiercely, that he *didn't have to take this*, Wagner went to the bar and stoically lifted the glass by the stem, which was the wrong way to address its natural top-heaviness. Some white wine flowed across the back of his hand. The bartender was ignoring him now: he had to ask twice for a rag. The one with which he was at last grudgingly furnished was slimy. He got no help in cleaning the top of the bar. Would Jimmy never get off that phone?

But when the restaurateur finally hung up, he spoke only to the bartender. "Hey, I got to go around the corner for a minute." He left without a glance at Wagner.

After a moment Wagner shrugged and asked, "What should I do about my table?"

"Go sit down at one," the bartender said with an impatient gesture of his trunk. "But pay me first."

"You can't put it on my bill?"

The sandy-haired young man gave him a steady look. "I'm asking nicely, sir."

"So am I," Wagner said, seeking to placate him with a smile, but of course paying for the glass of wine he had not ordered. Jimmy's prices seemed to have doubled since his last visit. He felt it politic, in view of the bartender's manner, to add more of a tip than the standard. "Oh, I might as well order a glass of red as long as I'm here."

"You'll pay for it before you go to the table," said the bartender, who had for no reason at all turned into his nemesis.

"I'll take a raincheck," Wagner said. Quickly, before anyone could run out again and oppose him, he went to a table, nowhere near the one favored by himself and Babe, and put up a fence of lifted menu, even though he always ordered the same meal at Jimmy's.

He sat there, untended, for ever so long. By the time the waiter appeared, three more tables were occupied by people who had seated themselves without opposition. The waiter took all these orders before finally coming to Wagner.

"No more osso buco," he gloatingly announced. "The other special's haddock Parmigian'."

"Spaghetti and sausages," said Wagner. "Salad. Glass of red. Have you got any breadsticks? There always used to be a glassful on the table."

The waiter was scribbling on his pad. "That all?"

"Breadsticks? You don't have them any more?"

"Look, I only work here, uh . . ." He stared and added with hatred, "*Sir.*"

"That's why I'm asking you."

The man continued to stare. "OK, *be* sarcastic. I'm the one's doing the work."

"I'm sorry," said Wagner. "I wasn't trying to hurt your feelings."

"Apology received," the waiter said sardonically.

He went breezily through the swinging doors and, as if in a cartoon, came back almost immediately with Wagner's order, on a cold plate that was growing tepid by the heat it extracted from the spaghetti, which was perforce losing it. At first it seemed that the sausages had been replaced by meatballs, undersized examples, but in fact further investigation established that the sausages had been cooked so long as to fall apart, which if unfortunate was so only aesthetically, for the flavor had not been lost but rather incorporated into the sauce, now sufficiently assertive to deny to the tongue any other taste till next morning. But that, the classic aftereffect of Jimmy's cuisine, was for Wagner all to the good. And the harsh red wine had the taste of old. The waiter had forgotten the salad: *he* in turn must remember not to pay for it. Otherwise he went untouched by the omission, for truth was, he believed greenery belonged in a landscape and not on a plate. It had been Babe who pushed salads on him, along with citrus fruits, which he swore, to her derision, gave him chapped lips.

In time the waiter asked him whether he wanted "expresso" or regular, and though Wagner ordered the former, he was brought the latter, along with a check on which his fears were exceeded: he was charged, at one of the new hefty prices, not simply for salad but rather for that mix named for some Caesar not the author of *De Bello Gallico*.

His anticipation assured him that the waiter — whose own name seemed to be, remarkably, "Gonzo," or such anyway he had scrawled in the space provided on the check for "Your Servitor" — would give him an argument, perhaps even a nasty one, if the subject of the missing salad were broached, and he was weighing his dislike for a quarrel, especially one that had the capability of tainting what had been, on balance, a pleasant experience, against his memory of Babe's contempt for his habitual failure to claim justice from the petty tyrants of quotidian life.

While he was so occupied Babe herself, accompanied by a short, thickset, very hairy man, entered the restaurant and in fact went to "their" old table. She took no notice of Wagner, and sat down with her back to him.

The hirsuteness of her companion was only a matter of his head, Wagner could see now: the face, though pitted, was clean, but his wiry scalp began just above his shaggy eyebrows, then fell on both sides to conceal his ears under muffs of thick black wool. He looked in a triumphant mood, his dark eyes glittering all over Wagner's estranged wife.

If he reaches across and takes her hand, Wagner swore to himself, *I'll take this knife and go over there and stab him in the heart.* But in the next instant the man enacted to the letter his part in the fantasy, yet Wagner could not begin to bring off his own. For one thing, the knife at his disposal was blunt as a tongue-depressor. For another, though he lived in a world in which some human beings casually killed others to gain possession of a piece of costume jewelry, he could not murder an unarmed man merely for ruining his life.

Instead he left enough cash to pay the check plus tip, slipped back to the men's room through the now crowded tables, and, in a toilet cubicle, became invisible.

3

INVISIBLY, WAGNER LEFT THE TINY MEN'S ROOM, squeezing past a stocky man who had entered after him and who while standing at the lone urinal was airily whistling a tune without melody.

Wagner almost found himself saying, "Excuse me."

Out in the dining room, he steered towards the table Babe shared with her ugly escort. To keep to the direct route was not easy: people kept coming and going in a space which, unless they saw someone else in the way, they assumed was theirs to occupy exclusively. Of course, if three or more persons were in a cluster, Wagner found he could push past them or even be involved in mild collisions with impunity; no one looked for a man who wasn't there but rather blamed those at hand. Invisibility could be used to cause a lot of mischief, but at the moment he had a grimmer purpose.

Who was this man Babe had got hold of? Or vice versa: the skunk was still clutching her hand.

The answer came shortly, for just as Wagner reached their table, so did the waiter named Gonzo.

"Hiya, Mr. Zirko," the servitor crooned sycophantically.

"Yeah, Tommy," said Babe's hairy escort. "Hop to it."

"Tommy," who couldn't even write his name legibly, scuttled obsequiously into the kitchen. Speaking of names, who would have one like "Zirko"?

Wagner couldn't bear to look too closely at Babe. Luckily the nearest table was still vacant, and he therefore had some choice of standing room.

"This poor slob," Zirko said to Babe, "loves me. And not just because of the tips. It's because I give him distinction, make him feel important. That's it. He won't let anybody else come near!" He had a raspy voice that went with his pitted skin. He wore a dark suit, a gray shirt, and a black necktie. He was some kind of thug, for God's sake. What could Babe be thinking of?

Wagner tried to keep from looking at her. She had a new sideswept hairstyle that gave her a cheaper aura, but she was still a far cry from the kind of woman whom Zirko should frequent.

"You're not going to let me order a drink?" Wagner was startled to hear Babe's new voice. Or perhaps it was rather the tone that was new. She was not chiding Zirko; she was submitting to him.

"That's right," said Zirko, who left off fondling her hand to erect an index finger. "Trust me."

"Oh, I do, I do."

How awful this was for Wagner to hear; yet he stayed. Right now nothing was more important than trying to understand what she saw in this hoodlum, painful as it might be. Until this moment, if asked what kind of man might appeal to Babe, Wagner would have put Zirko's type at the bottom of the list.

And he had pondered a good deal on the matter of whom she would eventually take up with — if anyone, for she seemed off men entirely at the time she left him. Not that she was unnatural: he was no Pascal, to call inverse those women who spurned him. But in truth, he had half expected her to be attracted to one of the effeminate male artists who exhibited at the gallery where she was employed. Wagner had attended only one opening and had soon despised all the persons he encountered there, men or women: something seemed to be wrong with all of them. Of course he said nothing derogatory to Babe about the people or that which was exhibited — a series of sculptured forms that resembled coned coils of dog stool, which were even colored dung-brown. But she must have intuited his lack of approval, for never again was he pressed to come. Which was quite OK with him. That's how smoothly things had always gone with them. It had been a no-fault marriage, and yet she had left him after four years. For the likes of Zirko?

Tommy returned, bringing filled plates, though no audible order had been placed with him.

"Uh-*huh*," Babe breathed, considering her portion with every evidence of delight. "Prosciutto and, um, figs? Fresh *figs*?"

Zirko's index finger, bearing a large brute of a vulgar ring, was raised again. "Parma ham," said he. "Not the 'prozoot' that is slapped on a cheap hero. And *black* figs only and always."

Tommy lingered to grin slavishly. "Mr. Zirko, you know your gourmet foods."

The object of his worship ignored him to pick up a fig in short thick fingers and split it open to show Babe the indecent red vulva of its flesh.

"Look like somebody you know?" he asked.

This seemed humorous to Babe, who simpered as she cut a fragment of ham.

43

Wagner was too shocked at first to feel anger. During her years with him Babe had been famous for her modesty. She rarely made a sexual reference of any kind, and never used foul language. Wagner in fact would have been embarrassed to repeat to her, even in derision, some of Pascal's comments and jokes. Yet she now watched in delight as Zirko obscenely tongued the interior of the split fruit.

"Did I ever tell you —" Zirko then asked, lowering the fig.

"By the way, this is delicious," Babe told him, tapping her fork on the plate.

Zirko frowned at the interruption, even though its purpose had been to praise his taste. *"Did I ever tell you,"* he doggedly repeated, "I was dirt-poor in my earlier life. I was a street kid. I used to press my face against the windows of places like this, watching everybody stuff their gut while my own belly was empty, and I used to think, by God I'll get me a gun and then I'll eat regular and get respect besides!" He actually gritted his teeth.

Babe continued to enjoy the first course. This too was new; in the past she had eaten merely to live. "A perfect combination, and you're right, the Parma —"

Zirko's voice rose shrilly to drown hers out. "I tell you I came *this* far from doin' just that." He showed two fingertips. "I was raised by my dear mother, God bless 'er, to hate violence above all things. But I could be capable of taking life in one or two circumstances, like racial injustice, you know, or old people. So I come close but never robbed anybody, actually. What I did was use my head, see. Me and my friend Petey, we'd go to a restaurant and eat a big meal and when it was time to pay Petey would pull out a bratwurst he brought along for the purpose, and he'd slide down under the table, and I'd hold it between my legs and he would suck on it."

Babe was now listening intently.

"So they'd see that, and we'd get thrown out as degenerates, see, and never had to pay."

Babe asked, "Are you serious?"

"So after we done that a few times, my friend Petey says, 'Hey, how about letting me hold the sausage for a change while *you* suck it?'" Zirko grinned extravagantly: he seemed to have more teeth than a normal man. "So I asked him, 'What sausage?'"

After an instant, Babe squealed with laughter, and when she could breathe again, said, "Oh, Siv. I took you seriously. How can I ever tell?"

Zirko was the kind who would not laugh at his own jokes. He shrugged, then squinted at his ham and fruit and began to eat.

Siv? His name was Siv? As if "Zirko" wasn't enough. Irrespective of his name, he was a hyena. Couldn't Babe see that?

The waiter showed up with a bottle of wine, displayed it, label up, to Zirko. "Hit me," Zirko said. Tommy extracted the cork, handed it over, and Zirko elaborately smelled the discolored end, then scratched it with a thumbnail. "Vino," he said to Babe and rolled his eyes. "If I was ever starving again I'd take wine before food."

When Tommy poured a sample, it was no surprise to Wagner that Zirko sucked and slurped and sniffed and closed his eyes and worked his tongue behind his closed lips and finally, eyelids lowered again, made a majestic nod.

Wagner could endure no more of this. Why should he? He was invisible.

He waited till Tommy had filled Babe's glass and brought the bottle to Zirko's; then, stepping to the waiter's side, using two hands he forced Tommy to pour wine into the lap of the pretentious little thug.

For a few moments nothing else happened. A stream of red fluid was falling into Zirko's lap. Tommy was struggling but not too vigorously, for he knew not what he was struggling against. As to Babe, she was serenely tasting the contents of her own glass.

Then Zirko began to shout obscenities. But still he made no move to elude the falling stream. Wagner now used both hands to maintain the bottle in the offending position and while he might not have been stronger than Tommy in a fair match, he was for the first time experiencing a noteworthy concomitant of invisibility: greater physical strength, or perhaps merely the illusion thereof. At any rate the waiter was unable to alter the situation, or the attitude, of the bottle.

Babe had now begun to observe all of this — well, scarcely "all," for she couldn't see the man who pulled the strings! — but thus far had remained noncommittal. Not that much could be done except by Zirko himself, who could simply have moved away from the table. No one was stopping him. But some kind of vanity kept him in place: he intended to triumph over this inexplicable adversary. So, though shouting vile language, he stayed. Moreover, he stared into his wine-soaked lap and not even at Tommy.

The waiter was sniveling piteously. "I don't know — I can't seem — oh God, I'm *sawry*. Oh Christ. Oh shit."

Wagner released him only after the last drop had fallen. Tommy's response to freedom was to drop the empty bottle and sprint through the kitchen doors.

Still Zirko stayed in place. At last he raised his eyes from his lap to say, through his teeth, "I'm going to carry this off, you'll see. I don't want anybody to think they got ahead of Zirko. I know I do crazy things, but they're always *my* idea. If I'm a clown, then I'm my *own* kinda clown. Not some fuckin' waiter's."

Wagner had not had time to note the reaction of the many other diners to Zirko's cries. He was interested only in Babe.

Who said, "I can't think he did it on purpose, Siv. It must have been a nervous fit of some kind. He didn't look well. Here, can you use my napkin?"

"I'll fucking sue 'em," Zirko said, rubbing his nose, ignoring the extended napkin. "Let's get the fuck out of here."

Suddenly Wagner's satisfaction turned flat. Not until now did it occur to him that Babe's dinner would be ruined. True, she might be said to deserve it for going out with such a man, but Wagner found it difficult to bear her ill will. His basic approach to the matter of Babe was that she was confused. Her specialties were things of the spirit. What she lacked was good judgment when it came to humanity. While they were together Wagner had been able to help her in that regard. But now look at whom she was dating.

"Gee," Babe said regretfully, "I was really looking forward to the meal."

Though Zirko had only lately been shouting at the top of his voice, he leaned discreetly towards her and spoke in a malign murmur. "Fuck what *you* want. *I* been humiliated."

Her sympathetic expression vanished. "Do you have to speak like that to me? I'm not your enemy."

"Shit on you. I saw you smirkin'. You're *still* doing it."

That was due to a peculiarity of Babe's upper lip. Wagner had always found it attractive, but until you caught on, it did look as if she were in a sardonic state of mind when she might not be. For example, she probably was not amused by what happened to her escort.

She certainly was not amused by his sudden verbal assault on her. She pushed her chair back and marched out of the restaurant.

Wagner followed her invisibly. Near the door to the street, a small man left the bar and, stepping into him, bounced off, almost falling down, recovering to tell the bartender the drinks were having a weird effect tonight.

Out on the pavement Wagner's first intention was to shadow Babe until she caught a cab, but no taxis came along for a while, and he wanted her gone by the time Zirko left the restaurant. So he ran down to the end of the block, materialized, and came walking back.

"Babe," he said before she saw him.

She was startled. "Oh, hi, Freddy."

"If you're looking for a taxi, you'll never catch one here. Come on, we'll walk to the corner."

She hesitated.

"Come on."

"You're not going to —"

He lifted his hands. "I swear." She was referring to his practice, during the earliest weeks of their separation, of using any pretext to discuss why she had left him. "Not a word."

"Uh-huh." She was walking more rapidly than she used to, but no doubt was still agitated by the incident with Zirko.

"So what brings you to this part of town?" Wagner

asked. Seeing her familiar profile so near had an effect on him. Babe was just about his own height.

"Oh, business," said she. "Do you really think there'll be a cab at this corner?"

"Business at this time of the day?"

Babe frowned. "I might ask you the same." With him she used her old voice, had abandoned the dulcet tones of the early part of her conversation with Zirko.

"I'm supposed to meet a date at Jimmy's."

She turned quickly. "Jimmy's?"

"What a coincidence," said he. "Didn't you just come out of there?"

"All right, now that you mention it."

"I'll be going back to my date as soon as we find you a cab," said Wagner.

They had reached the corner. Babe said, "Thanks, Freddy. You go back now. Don't keep her waiting." She put out her hand. "Listen, I couldn't be more pleased. Is she anyone I know?"

Wagner could not suppose she was jealous, so he disparaged his fictional companion. "A co-worker. Someone from the office. Listen, Babe —"

"Don't, Freddy, please."

"I just wanted to ask how things are going for you."

"They're fine. They haven't changed since your last call. Another thing that hasn't changed is you are still using that name."

She meant "Babe." Her claim was that she had never liked the name, had put up with it for four years simply to be nice.

"I'm sorry," Wagner pleaded. "I just can't remember to think of you as Carla."

"Oh, there's one." She was about to wave at the taxi when Wagner caught her arm.

"Fact is, I was at the bar when that altercation broke out at your table. What was that all about?"

She sighingly gave up on the cab. "God." She sighed again. "You *would* see that. I honestly don't know what happened."

"Who was that guy you were with?" He cleared his throat. "Sorry, I didn't mean it to sound like an interrogation." He decided to lie again. "It's just that he looked kinda familiar, somehow."

Her eyebrow arched. "Since when have you been interested in art?"

"He's a collector?"

"He's a sculptor," said Babe. "Siv Zirko. He's very well known. He's getting raves for his new show, which was sold out before it opened. We've got it. That's what I mean by business, having dinner with him. I don't have to explain it to you, but I'm doing it anyway. He wasn't a date. Cleve could have eaten with him instead of me."

"But he's not Cleve's type, I gather, or Cleve would not only have eaten with him: he would have eaten him." Wagner realized his bitterness had got out of hand.

Babe glared at him under the streetlight, but said nothing: that was her way when she was really angry.

"I'm sorry," said he. "It's not my business. I shouldn't have said that. Uh, Siv Zirko. What kind of sculpture does he do?"

"It's good enough for museums all over this country and Europe, but you wouldn't like it." Ironically enough, Babe was now showing the same expression that Zirko had called a smirk: maybe he had been right, after all.

"I just wondered."

"You wouldn't like it."

Which probably meant it was more piles of dog shit.

"What did he do to make you walk out? Get fresh?"

"I'm taking this cab, Fred. We were supposed to live separate lives, remember?" She shook his hand again, while waving at the taxi with the other. "Thanks for walking with me." The vehicle pulled up to the curb. She opened the door and climbed in.

Wagner considered making some desperate statement before the cab pulled away, but could think of none. He had conflicting emotions with regard to Babe. He thought he admired what could be called either her independence or her courage, but it was a kind of ritualistic admiration. He assumed he loved her to some degree, and he knew he hated her for leaving him.

Another thing he knew was that artists whose work sold as well as Zirko's were rich as movie stars or big business-men. There really ought to be money in invisibility, perhaps working as a magician. But how did one get started?

"You need an agent," Pascal said at lunch next day. "You need eight-by-ten glossies. You need a personal manager. You need a publicist. Finally, I'm told you need a business manager, the complicated world of finance being what it is. Now, all these people cost money, but I am led to understand that they'll bring in and/or save you more than they cost. Or so I've heard."

Wagner had as if idly pretended he knew someone gifted at parlor sleight of hand who was wondering whether to go professional. It was one way to get some use out of Pascal, who kept *au courant* with show biz through the gossip columns and chatter programs. He had trailed Wagner to a luncheonette, where the latter had hoped to be alone.

"Why?" said Pascal. "Who is this person? Do I know them?"

"Friend of the family," Wagner said, trying to masticate thoroughly the cold roast beef he had found to be a thin but resistant layer between the lettuce and the tomatoes. It was his first food of the day. Breakfast was always just black coffee. And when he had got home from the experience with Babe and Zirko, he had thrown up his dinner.

Denied access to the identity of the amateur magician, Pascal turned his notice on Wagner's lunch.

"That going to hold you till dinnertime? You've been losing weight lately, haven't you? How long's it been since your last checkup? Might look into it." He was shaking his head. "Wouldn't hurt." In between sections of his commentary he had managed himself to stow away a big plate of, wouldn't you know, spaghetti, and he was impatient now with Wagner for taking so long to consume about half the sandwich: he wanted his dessert.

"Go ahead and get your pie or whatever," said Wagner. "This is all I'm eating today." He was sorry he hadn't asked that the white bread be toasted; as it was, it acted like a sponge and exuded previously concealed mayonnaise when bitten into.

"Should get some meat on your bones. It's that zany, action-packed lovelife of yours."

If he mentions Babe by name, I really will hit him, Wagner swore, but whether or not that was likely Pascal failed to pursue the subject. Instead he spoke of the "widely known linkage between sudden weight loss and, well, do I have to say?"

"It has not been sudden," said Wagner. "And I don't have cancer. Fact is, despite what you think, I needed to lose a few pounds, because my clothes were getting too tight. Now as for this magician friend of mine —"

"He's a close friend?" Pascal asked jealously. "I see. I thought you were speaking of just somebody who was a friend of someone else in the family."

"What difference does that make? I was wondering where an agent could be found. The yellow pages?"

Pascal maneuvered a red strand of spaghetti around his plate with a fork. Presumably he had preserved it just for this function, to give him an activity while Wagner finished the main portion of his own lunch. He refused to order dessert until the time Wagner himself would have done so, had Wagner intended to order dessert, even though the latter had told Pascal he had no intention of so doing. Funny, whenever Babe had asked him why he considered Pascal such a creep, he could never think of this good an example. Even if he had, however, he suspected she would have said, Look, the man's just trying to be friendly. What's wrong with that? But did a divine law enjoin one from rejecting unwanted friendship?

Pascal raised one eyebrow. "You've really got to *know* somebody in the business. I just can't see an unknown come waltzing in off the street and getting some top agent to represent him."

"But what about not quite top but good enough? You have to start somewhere."

Pascal made a tough-guy grin. "You haven't a prayer unless he *is* top. Beware of these fakes who want a fee. The genuine article takes a percentage of the money he gets you, and nothing beyond."

This supposedly inside dope was known to everybody. Wagner hadn't really expected to learn anything from Pascal. He pushed the remains of his sandwich away from him: a vulgar but necessary gesture in this place if one wanted the counterman to appear. He then waited until Pascal had ordered, and been delivered, dessert — the man actually ate rice pudding at a lunch counter — and then, treacherously, got off the stool saying, "I've got some errands," left a tip in change for the service, and departed from his astonished and discomfited colleague.

The move succeeded perfectly, but he soon knew his own dismay, for a grope of the inside breast pocket reminded him that his wallet had been left behind in the middle drawer of his office desk, the one that could be, and was, locked. He wasn't known in this place. He would have had not only to return to Pascal but also, by asking for a loan, to affiliate himself with a man who would exploit any association, however slight.

He would have had to do just that, had he not, while pretending to fumble within an overloaded coatrack, disappeared.

He left without paying the check. This was his first piece of dishonesty as an invisible personage. However, he intended the delinquency to be only temporary. He would drop by with the money after work, or at the latest, next noontime. Invisibility was still, except perhaps for the incident with Zirko, a device to avoid inconvenience or embarrassment, not a means for the shirking of responsibility.

He reached the lobby of the building at which he worked (still invisible, for he believed it not impossible that Pascal might bolt the rice pudding and launch a hot pursuit) and was heading for the door to the stairs, back of which he could materialize, when who should come in from the street but Mary Alice Phillips. More hastily than he would have moved could he have been seen, he followed her into an empty car. He believed it unfortunate that two other persons boarded before the door slid shut, yet the car was of generous proportions, and so long as Mary Alice moved no farther towards the corner, where he was as it were espaliered, his purpose was not defeated.

Mary Alice was a good deal more attractive than he had formerly believed and profited by a close-quarters assessment. What might seem like sallowness at a polite distance was, in tight focus, a delicate tint. Her nose was all but poreless. That part of her right ear that could be seen beneath her hair was exquisite, tightly whorled and the color of the inside of a baby's nostril. Again it occurred to him that her hair would profit by a rearrangement of some sort, or perhaps merely a fluffing: at the moment it was lank to a fault. And the preponderance of breast (which the likes of Pascal might find exhilarating, but Wagner saw as slightly disproportionate according to the classic rules of female architectonics) might be corrected by better posture, a stiffer spine, a lifted chin. Mary Alice when in repose tended to droop — rather like Wagner himself on that occasion, which had now proved historic, when he inspected himself in the bedroom mirror just prior to becoming invisible for the first time. A girl so young and so comely should have a heartier morale. He was tempted to whisper something encouraging into the ear that was so close to him, but the chances that she would believe not that the voice was that of a divine adviser but rather a symptom of madness were too great. Mary Alice did not suggest self-possession. She might well panic at an unexpected occurrence. She was hardly cut from Babe's fabric. (Once while Wagner searched ineptly for a weapon, Babe got out of bed and boldly went unarmed to investigate the odd sounds coming from the living room. An unscreened window had been left open on that balmy night, and a starling had got in.)

A strange thing happened now. The other passengers deboarded on a lower floor, and Wagner and Mary Alice rode alone for a while, yet the girl did not avail herself of the space newly at her disposal. She remained just before his corner, keeping him a cozy prisoner. Perhaps the explanation was to be found in her natural stolidity. Despite his ability to make himself invisible, Wagner placed little credence in things like extrasensory perception, auras, psychic emanations, and other related intangibles.

On reaching their floor, he let Mary Alice go to her cubicle without escort. He decided to proceed directly to his own before materializing, rather than go by way of the men's room. Seated at his desk he had sufficient privacy in which to resume visibility, which along with the dematerialization, recent experiences had proved, had been getting nearer to the instantaneous. In this as in life's more humdrum exercises, practice did make a difference.

He had assumed Delphine Root would still be absent from her desk, she being the kind who took 110 percent of a lunch hour — as it was typical of Mary Alice to take as little as 85 — but even before he was opposite her niche he saw the smoke rising, like that signal which announced, on the horizon of a western movie, imminent Indian troubles. On closer approach she proved to be not only smoking: simultaneously she was eating at a sandwich of which the bread was exceedingly limp and the filling of some substance the self-cohesion of which was not reliable, like egg-, chicken-, or ham-salad, concoctions scrupulously avoided by Wagner, who had a horror of finding small hard dark foreign objects within. A dollop of this stuff separated itself from the edge of the mass and fell as he watched, just clipping the rim of the desktop, so that a cluster of yellow (it was egg) adhered there, though most of the nasty little bomb plopped on the floor and would have exploded had it not been stickily restricted by the constituent mayonnaise.

Delphine herself was ignorant of this event, for she was not only eating; she was reading as well and, for God's sake, smoking.

Wagner was suddenly furious, and when she anchored the open volume with an elbow, so as to bring the burning cigarette to her mouth from the nearby ashtray, her other hand occupied with the collapsing sandwich, he leaned in and snatched the butt from her.

In her reaction she dropped the entire sandwich on the floor; indeed, half of it fell onto his foot and thereby was invisible until he jiggled it free. The cigarette too was invisible but still burning. He stepped to the water cooler and extinguished it. Delphine might have heard this but owing to her immediate catastrophe was distracted.

She shouted, "Kee-*ryst!*"

Wagner went into his cubicle and discarded the wet cigarette butt in his wastecan. He was regretting his impulsive act. He hadn't expected to ruin Delphine's lunch.

She cried, "Oh, shit."

Wagner guiltily materialized and went around to her. She was stooping to her fallen sandwich.

"Drop something?"

"I must be going nuts," said she, grunting in the cleanup effort. She brought her face up. It was of a higher color than usual. Wagner hoped he hadn't brought on a heart attack. "For no reason at all, I dropped my lunch," she said, grinning in a vulnerable way that was, at least with him, unprecedented. "I'm losing my grip."

But she made no mention whatever of her cigarette, so he asked, looking around, "Anything else?"

"Naw." She pointed. "Tea's OK." A light-gray mug, tagged string hanging over one side, stood just beyond her book, which of course had sprung shut as soon as she had taken her weight off it. He had never before seen Delphine with any reading material. This was no doubt a romance. Surprising as it might seem, he had read that confirmed spinsters were among the habitual readers of such.

"Sorry about your sandwich," Wagner said. "There's time: I'll run out and get you a replacement."

Delphine peered at him in what seemed to be astonishment. "It's hardly your fault," said she. "No thanks, but aren't you nice." The strong lines of her face softened. "Thanks, Fred. You really are awfully nice." Of all things, she now winked. "Unless you're just after my money."

Wagner felt himself blush. To get away from the moment he made the banal observation, "You stayed in today."

"I do most of the time. You don't notice because you go out."

"You like to read?"

She nodded at the book. "This is an assignment."

"You're taking a course?" Asking these wooden questions had not, however, yet relieved his embarrassment.

"Intermediate Spanish." She wiped her hand on a paper napkin and picked up the book. "*La Pata de Zorro*, by Hugo Wast, if that means anything to you."

"Funny name for a Hispanic personage," he said, intentionally being parody-pompous.

"I believe it's supposed to be a pseudonym."

"You must be good: you don't even have a dictionary."

"Not really. I just forgot it today. But this is a textbook edition, with a vocabulary in back." She smiled at him. This could be called the only conversation they had had in five and a half years of working in neighboring stalls. "I went to Mexico a couple of years ago." He had not even been aware of that. "I swore I wouldn't go again till I learned some of the language. Why not? I've certainly got the time."

Wagner shrugged. "I made the same resolution as far back as when my high-school senior class went on a trip to Quebec. I took a lot of French in college, but by now I'd be lucky to be able to ask the time of day." He saw a smear of egg salad on his shoe and said hastily, "Let me get you a wet Kleenex."

"Let *me*," said Delphine, pulling out the bottom drawer of her desk, exposing a box of tissues. "Gee, that sandwich flew everyplace." She pointed at his shoe. Luckily she was not so careful an observer as to ask how the *top* of the shoe had been befouled by walking to her cubicle after the accident.

Wagner cleaned the smear from his upper and again was claimed by an access of guilt as he watched Delphine squat and swab the floor. But this feeling was soon canceled by her returning to the chair and, without even looking for the one he had confiscated, lighting up another cigarette. He had however been impressed with her ambitious and commendable effort to learn another language. She was not simply a hard-smoking old maid who wrote mail-order-catalogue copy. Ever striving, she would be more tomorrow than she was today.

Nowadays he had plenty of time at his disposal in which to study French, not to mention work on his novel. Babe's departure could be seen, in the long run, as precisely what brought about his personal renaissance. He admitted there were great gaps in his culture, and there they had remained year after year. He had always told himself that writing

59

catalogue copy was beneath him, but was it? Perhaps he had found his place. The incident with Delphine had had this unfortunate effect on his morale. Even judged by its positive results, snatching away her cigarette had been an utter failure if she only lighted another in the next moment. If invisibility was to be used for policing other people, it was obvious he'd have to become much more deft in its employment, else it would resemble those efforts which with the best will in the world exacerbate the very problems they were created to solve.

That morning he had finally finished the copy for the flashlight-pen. The text was much like the one it replaced, though he did invent a few more uses for the device: following and making notes on a musical score in a darkened concert hall; recording the figures from a utilities meter in a dark corner of a basement; scribbling reminders in a parked car at night. While he was away at lunch the copy had vanished from his Out box, presumably the work of the office boy, who in this firm was called officially a messenger, and that was more reasonable a name, for the young man who held the job was at least twenty-five years of age, and he gave the position even more substance by always wearing a full suit, sometimes even three-piece. In between his rounds he was permitted rather than encouraged to try his own hand at writing copy, and was much better at it than Mary Alice Phillips. In time he would probably be promoted, if he persisted and if someone left or died.

This fellow, whose name was Gordon, appeared now, just as Wagner was about to start on the copy for salt and pepper shakers with magnetic strips on their backs, enabling them to be stuck to the front of the doors of refrigerators and stoves and cabinets made of metal. Once again, like the flashlight-pen combo, these could be said to be somewhere between utility and novelty. They would certainly not be appropriate to the catalogues of highbrow *batterie de cuisine.* On the other hand, the condiment shakers were in a different, category from the outsized towel, made of inferior-grade terrycloth, imprinted: I DON'T SWIM IN YOUR TOILET / PLEASE DON'T PEE IN MY POOL.

"Fred," Gordon said, for first names were the approved idiom in this office, even *de bas en haute,* "Jackie wants to see you."

"Oh sure," said Wagner, happy to be relieved from coming to immediate terms with the magnetic shakers, for which he had no examples but rather a sheet of specifications and two colored photographs, one of which would be chosen, by the art department, to accompany the printed text. "How's it going, Gordon?"

"You mean personally?" Gordon was a clean-featured young man, perhaps even handsome, with his fine thin nose, and therefore looked as if he might breeze through life, but apparently he was more careful, for the question was typical. He added, "Or professionally?"

"Neither," said Wagner. "Under the aspect of eternity."

Gordon was not humorless. He made a smile, in which expression his features were not as regular, for some reason, as when his face was in repose. Wagner recorded such phenomena from time to time for use in his novel.

"I'm trying not to offend the Holy Ghost," said Gordon.

"What does that mean?"

"To despair," Gordon explained. "In the Augustinian sense."

"I didn't realize you were that religious," said Wagner.

"I'm not."

Gordon was getting pretentious. Wagner still didn't

really understand the comment, but if Gordon said it, it could scarcely be too abstruse. This place attracted would-be writers and intellectuals. He would not have believed that Delphine was one of them, but there she was, studying Spanish. It occurred to him that perhaps Gordon was a seminary dropout.

Jackie Grinzing never displayed intellectual pretensions. No doubt that was why she was head of the department, with an office that had real walls that went all the way to the ceiling.

She was wearing her outsized eyeglasses as he entered. When he had first seen the spectacles he had assumed they were a joke item from one of the catalogues, but apparently the lenses were prescription. Jackie wore them when reading, but now she was staring at the building across the street: either they were bifocals or she wasn't actually looking at anything.

Wagner said hi to her back.

Jackie turned ever so slowly. She wore more costume jewelry than usual with the familiar gray suit. "Fred," she said simply, and went to sit down back of her desk. She gestured at him. "Fred, we've known each other a long time. . . . Is that some kind of moral pressure you're applying, standing there like that?"

"I wasn't asked to sit."

"After all this time we're being *ceremonious?*" Jackie asked incredulously. He took one of the straight chairs and brought it before the desk. Jackie resumed. "You know me. This isn't a finishing school, and I certainly don't care about anybody's private life. But there's a point where some things extend from the private sphere."

She plucked an unsharpened pencil from a leather cup of writing implements that sat next to one of those decommissioned blue-glass high-tension-line insulators that are sold as paperweights. She put the eraser end near her mouth but had not yet bitten it.

"Jesus," she said. "This is a hell of a thing to have to deal with but I don't see how I can dodge it and keep my self-respect and maybe yours too. Morton wanted to do it, but I said, No sir, he's not only under me, he's my friend since I joined the firm."

"Morton?"

"Morton Wilton," Jackie said with special feeling. "He's been here for months. You know that."

"I'm not sure exactly what he does," said Wagner. Aside from being indecently fondled by her, of course.

She laughed at the bright blue blotter on her desk. "Well, you don't keep up with things, I must say. He's executive vice-president. He's our boss. Well, there's technically still the president, Mr. Grayling, but as you know he's not very active any more."

"I'm just one of the troops, Jackie," said Wagner. "I just write my copy and go home."

She lowered her chin. "Are you still working on that novel?"

He was startled. "You know about that?"

"You told me. How else would I know?"

Obviously she was telling the truth. "I'm sorry. I forgot. I always intended to keep it a secret until I had finished it at least, but it's taking so long I guess I ran out of patience."

"My lips are sealed," Jackie said. She seemed to be taking pains to be considerate, which care was not characteristic, irrespective of their old office "friendship," which was scarcely that: they had simply found themselves in the same place for some years.

Suddenly Jackie colored. "Damn! It's being even tougher

than I anticipated." She took off her glasses. She cleared her throat. "Your, uh, lunchtime, uh, visits . . ."

This absolutely could have nothing to do with invisibility: he was sure of that. But still . . .

"Yes. I do go out to eat lunch. Delphine however stays in the office and studies Spanish. Did you know that?"

"It's not like you to use levity," Jackie said. "I'll admit there's something ridiculous about it, but it just can't be tolerated, Fred, and you know it. Aren't there more discreet places than the men's room? Can't you wait until after work?"

"Jackie," Wagner began soberly, "I won't joke if you stop being mysterious. I don't begin to get your allusions. They may be well intentioned but they're simply not intelligible."

He received what was a level look if there ever was one: the several furrows of her brow were firm and parallel.

"All right, then. OK. I understand the stalls in the men's room are being used at lunchtime for homosexual activities. I have been informed that you have been recognized as one of the participants. Speaking for myself, I never condemn anybody for any sexual tastes, barring those for children, animals, and the feebleminded." Which meant that her condemned list was actually extensive. Wagner was seeking distracting thoughts at this moment. Jackie went on: "But some things are out of order in an office, and I don't think we're being unreasonable in saying this one very much is."

Wagner at last asked, "And just who said I was doing this?"

She shook her head. Jackie's hair today was that kind of brown that looks red around the edges when the light comes from behind. "Let's not get into names. Someone told Morton, Mr. Wilton, and Mr. Wilton told me."

"It isn't true, you know," Wagner said.

"Oh, it isn't?"

He cried, "Of course it isn't, for God's sake."

"Don't shout at me!"

"I'll throw this chair through your window," Wagner said, "unless you stop nodding in that smug way." He was surprised by his own fury.

Jackie was not frightened. "Any more of that talk and I call the police. You want to get tough, mister, you got the wrong lady."

"I'm just trying to get your attention," Wagner said, imposing control on himself. "It's not personal. Somebody is slandering me, and I just wonder who and why."

"No," Jackie said firmly. "I don't think it's that at all." She raised a hand to stifle his protest. "I'm not saying I believe them, Fred, but I don't think it's malicious."

"*Them?* Then there are more than Wilton?"

"I told you someone informed Mr. Wilton. It isn't Mr. Wilton's accusation. Obviously he has his own private washroom." She swiveled rapidly from side to side in the chair. "Look at the problem I'm facing. It's hard to believe the whole story is a total invention. If what you say is true" — he bristled, and she was quick to say again that she was not necessarily indicting him — "still someone must be doing something in there. Why else would it have been reported?"

"Who's out to get me, Jackie?"

"No," said she. "That's the wrong tack to take, Fred. The question that interests me is: If not you, then who?"

He glared at her. "I submit my resignation."

She sniffed disdainfully. "Don't be asinine. No, the

problem remains. What's going on in there? Obviously I can't investigate personally."

"I'll tell you this," said Wagner, seething. "I have never, in all my years here, seen the least suspicious thing in the men's room. True, I don't linger there when my own business is done, nor do I squat down and count the number of legs in any one booth at any one time."

Jackie widened her eyes. "One of them sits with crossed legs on the toilet seat."

"You seem to be an authority on the subject."

"I am anyway in authority in this department." Her respect for him was not increasing.

"Look," Wagner said. "If the report came by way of your friend Wilton —"

"What do you mean by saying 'friend'?"

He paused for a moment and then resumed. "Wilton should investigate for himself, stay in some lunchtime and catch the culprits redhanded, if that's the appropriate figure of speech in this case."

Jackie said, "You're going to answer my question."

"Aren't all bosses friends?" It was not brave, but it wasn't bad.

"I don't know how far you can get on sarcasm, Fred," Jackie said. "I really don't."

"All right then," said he. "I'll be straightforward. I neither give nor receive homosexual favors in the men's room, and if I find out who says I do, I'll kick him in the teeth and then sue him. But I won't serve as your spy in the toilets."

He rose and marched out. This was the first time he could ever remember having finally held his own with Jackie Grinzing. It was ironic that this kind of success would have come in response to a defamatory accusation.

4

℘ WAGNER'S FACE STAYED WARM FROM ANGER FOR SO
long that it began to itch. He did little work for the next
hour, so distracted was he by the outrageous charge against
him. Could it be a case of mistaken identity or did he have
a secret enemy somewhere in the office?

As if more wretchedness were needed, he soon was sitting in discomfort: he needed to take a pee but had a horror
now of being seen, by secret eyes, crossing the threshold of
what had formerly been one kind of sanctuary. However,
at last he was sufficiently uncomfortable to resort to invisibility. He did not like to do it, being altogether in the right
as he was, and he was also concerned as to whether van-
ishing so often might take its toll on his system — perhaps
one had a quota that could be exceeded — but he had no
other option at this moment.

But before he could dematerialize Mary Alice Phillips
appeared in her usual importunate condition. She handed
him a piece of copy.

"Do you mind? I know there's something wrong, but I
just can't put my finger on it."

He suppressed a sigh and quickly read what she had
written about a self-draining soap dish. There was an

accompanying photograph of a little vessel of acrylic, slightly higher at one end than at the other, where a tiny downspout-shaped place of egress had been provided for accumulated water. To the brief description of this device Mary Alice had added: "No more snotty soap!"

Wagner winced. He explained. "This is vivid, but not in good taste."

"Yet it's what I always think of when I want to use a bar that's been sitting in the wetness," said she.

"That may be true," said Wagner, his distended bladder throbbing, "but terms like that give the product an unpleasant connotation to some people, and they wouldn't buy it. Our copy is supposed to sell the goods, after all, not claim attention for the pungency of its style."

Mary Alice grinned. Owing to the faint freckles that appeared at such a moment, this was her most advantageous expression. Had she grinned more often, she might have been thought of as cute. "Then 'toejams' and 'boogers' are ruled out?"

"I should hope so," said Wagner, suggesting by his attitude that he wished to rise and therefore she would be kind to step back from the entrance to the cubicle.

But Mary Alice either did not get his message or callously defied it, staying in place. "But the rest of it's OK if I killed the snot?"

Wagner peered closely at her, hoping she spoke in conscious irony, but unhappily decided she did not. "I guess so."

"How about 'slimy'?"

He shook his head. "You don't need any elaboration. Everybody knows how a soap dish gets when a bar of wet soap sits in it."

"Of course you're right," said Mary Alice. "You always

get straight to the heart of the matter. That's what good writing is, isn't it?"

He shrugged. "I guess so, but we're not talking about Flaubert. This is only commercial-catalogue copy. There are only two considerations: not much space and it should help sell the product."

"You could say that about serious literature too," Mary Alice offered brightly.

"No doubt. Gus Flaubert would probably do a great job on the soap dish, only it would take him all month."

While Mary Alice was temporarily off balance with his cheekiness towards the great master, Wagner managed to get to his feet in the available space and step out of the cubicle. For a moment, then, he was out and she was yet inside.

"Of course," she now said, still stuck on "literature," "there are those who were pretty wordy. Take James Joyce."

So he was to be saved by a *mot juste*. "A case in point," he said. " 'The snot-green sea.' " He feinted towards the water cooler and got past Delphine's lair and around the corner without losing a step. He could be seen from the cubicles he passed as well as, at one point, through the glass door of Jackie Grinzing's office. There was no suitable way in which he could become invisible at any point along the route to the men's room. However, his wits were fertile, and the answer was soon forthcoming: there was another men's room, away over beyond the reception area, at the other end of the floor, convenient to the accounting department to which he had gone some years earlier, at Babe's instigation, to question the amount of deductions from his paycheck, and on emerging from this undignified and fruitless pursuit, he had paused to use the paymasters' toilet.

By now Wagner had reached a remote back hallway devoid of other people, and he therefore vanished, for it would seem impolitic in this era, damnably, for him to be seen even in the accountants' facility.

However, no sooner had he got there without incident and positioned himself before the nearest urinal than in burst a large man so bluff-mannered as to have begun to unzip his fly before he pushed open the door, and had Wagner not leaped away he would have been soaked, for this person performed as though extinguishing a brush fire otherwise soon to go out of control. Nor could Wagner have used the remaining urinal without apprehension, for it was mounted too near the other if one's neighbor were as hearty as this guy, whose akimboed left arm not only intruded into the next space but also fanned the air as if it were an element of a pump that was emptying his reservoir.

Wagner fled into one of the toilet stalls and at last found relief. The sound he made was of little concern, for the other man could not have heard it over his own Niagara, but there came a moment when the latter had finished and Wagner couldn't stop.

"Artie?" The man was obviously directing his question, somewhere between a loud whisper and an undertone, towards Wagner's stall.

Since he had to keep going for another moment and if he remained vocally silent his questioner might stoop in search of a pair of feet beyond the stall-door, Wagner without hesitation, and assuming a gravel voice, said, "Al. From maintenance."

"Oh, sorry," said the other and was soon heard rinsing his hands and departing.

Wagner hoped he would not have to go to these extremes every time nature called, but until the air cleared and the real culprits were identified, he should probably do well to drink less coffee during working hours.

Back at his desk, visible again, he found in his Out box a new sheaf of assignments. Under the rule of Jackie's predecessor each copywriter or, in the case of an exceptionally large book, two writers might be assigned to do all the text for the same catalogue. If there were two, they could divide the task as they wished, each taking the items individually preferred. Jackie changed the old system, which in her theory had produced uninspired copy. By the end of a catalogue a writer's energy had flagged. Obviously the tendency was to deal first with all those products that were easy to write about and leave the tougher ones to the end, when of course the deadline was near. Thus it was often true that the very items the client wanted to push, because of the novelty that made writing about them an unusual effort, got either short shrift or what was perhaps worse, a description that was the issue of laboriousness and desperation. Anyway that was Jackie's opinion. She offered it with a self-righteousness based on (1) her own experience as a copywriter, which was hardly unique, and (2) her current power, which was.

Next she had given each practitioner an area of focus: the copy for all products falling in or near any such, in all the catalogues prepared by the firm, would be written by her or him whose specialty it was. Wagner for example had bathrooms. Were this policy still in effect he would have had the self-draining soap dish with which Mary Alice was now struggling. Delphine, raised as a city girl, could not drive; she was assigned to automotive products. Pascal was obliged to supply the texts for eyebrow tweezers, depilatories, dress shields, etc. Athletic equipment, jump ropes, medicine balls, and so on, went to two-ton Meg Mulhare, who brought a daily bagful of midmorning snacks and waddled out to an enormous lunch.

The incongruity was not by accident. Jackie's theory was that that person to whom a given product was foreign would write about it with exceptional care and clarity.

The policy was not successful. Meg was profoundly hostile to barbells, and at one point Delphine made the rare application to Wagner for assistance. "Maybe I don't get the point of this: a pump you attach to an electric drill, with a hose that goes down into the motor and pumps out all the oil. Wouldn't all the gas get pumped out too, and if so how would the car run?"

As to coupling Wagner with bathrooms, he had never been a lingering habitué of either water closet or bathtub and thus had little sympathy with the cylindrical transistor radio that fitted inside a toilet-paper roll, enabling the owner to tap his toes to the beat while at stool, or the likes of bubble-bath dispensers, neck-pillows, heated towel racks, loofah mitts. What had the merchants made of the place to void wastes and wash one's hide!

The current system had been in effect for three weeks now. Its conditions were "simplicity itself," as Jackie was wont to say: everybody did anything. Each item for all the catalogues currently being compiled was given a special code number that identified the catalogue to which it belonged, and the manila envelope in which the information about it was contained was collected by Gordon the messenger and placed to join the scores of others in a big bin at his work station. In compliance with the rule by which all occupations, pursuits, have each its own jargon, the coding was called "tagging"; Gordon's pickup, "catching," and his delivery, "dropping." The specifications of the products, the photos, etc., in the manila envelopes were "re-search."

Periodically Gordon went about the cubicles wheeling a wire cart, similar to the supermarket kind, and from the bin that rode thereon he would take at random sufficient "research" envelopes to bring the number to five in any copywriter's In box.

While Wagner was at the men's room near the accounting department, Gordon had "dropped" two new envelopes. Wagner opened each and peeked inside, hoping to find more attractive products to deal with than the three he had had at hand, which happened to be: a set of hand puppets; a calendar with a pseudoreligious one-liner for every day of the year (e.g., "Though you have no shoes, thank Him who has left you with feet"); a collapsible luggage cart that when folded up fitted into a briefcase. He had been working on the copy for the last-named before he went to the toilet. Distracted by his other cares, he had not got far. It seemed to be a useful device until you thought about it: you wheeled your valise to the baggage pickup, then collapsed the carrier and put it into your briefcase. Or in any event you might so try. But even when folded for stowing, the cart was a bundle $2' \times 2' \times 7''$ and had a mailing weight, anyway, of 11 pounds. However it was transported, such a burden would be meticulously examined by the inspectors of carry-on luggage: a lot of mischief could be concealed in its hollow tubes and amidst its network of articulations. It wasn't Wagner's job to make judgments on a product's merit, but lately the utility of some gadgets had begun to seem questionable.

The first of the two latest envelopes concerned a hassock in the form of a giant cheeseburger; and the second, a kitchen machine, capable, by means of its multitudinous accessories, of every process from grating ice to making sausages and priced accordingly.

His skepticism with regard to the folding luggage cart was inhibiting, so he returned the "research" to the In box and instead wrote two sentences for the calendar.

> 365 different pearls of spiritual wisdom, one for every day of the year. Perpetual faith calendar, nondenominational.

This text would appear below a colored illustration of the page for May 17, for which, printed in red type, the day's slogan was:

> A mighty fortress is our God.
> — Noted Hymn

Which would seem not to be altogether "nondenominational," even though Martin Luther was denied his proper credit. However, from the descriptive notes provided by the manufacturer, Geist Printing, it appeared that the inspirational messages for other days were provided by several popes as well as Moses, Mohammed, and even Buddha, not to mention several show-business personalities who were conspicuous believers of one or another persuasion (for example, the standup comic Joey Spang, to whom was attributed the sentiment with respect to shoelessness). "Multidenominational" should rather be the word, but Wagner knew by experience that Jackie would rule it out as having a prefix sufficiently different from the routine as to alienate the average man. So more imprecision was given currency. The vulgarity was expected, though perhaps this calendar went too far in identifying holidays that had no credentials but those supplied by trade associations: below the quotation from Luther's hymn the seventeenth of May was called National Scalp Care Day.

Wagner was capable — as who on the staff was not, excepting Mary Alice Phillips? — of producing such a piece of copy at least once an hour without a hint of strain, but it had taken him no time at all, on first joining the firm, to develop a measured pace, for he had been trained by a laconic man named Ray Olenberg, since retired; indeed, deceased. Olenberg's most urgently imparted piece of wisdom was that Wagner must not write more than four pieces of copy a day, or else he'd be "goddamn unpopular with the others."

The threat was not one which Wagner would disregard. He had a natural sense of professional fraternity even though he was something of a loner. Anyway, he had a moral or perhaps an aesthetic queasiness about distinguishing himself from his fellows as a Stakhanovite, though he dreamed of doing so one day as a literary celebrity. So he did not violate the common quota, good soldier that he was, but of course when Jackie Grinzing was hired and, as her trainer, he passed along the traditional word, she proceeded to ignore it and persistently turn out more copy than any two of the other staffers, and when the former department head had been hired away by another firm, she naturally assumed his post.

Olenberg was still there at the time. When Wagner brought up the matter, though without reproach, the older man asked, savagely, "But who would want the fucking job?" The truth was that Olenberg was one of those people Wagner's father, a World War II soldier, had characterized as being by nature "enlisted men," while fewer were "officer material." Needless to say, Dad himself was a confirmed member of the former group.

Wagner agreed with Olenberg that he wouldn't have wanted Jackie's position, but neither could he place himself with the common soldiery, except insofar as the work quota went.

In the remaining hour now he at last wrote the copy for the collapsible luggage carrier, naturally failing to mention any of his reservations.

> *Portable Porter:* Lightweight but strong aluminum luggage cart supports 70 lbs., then folds to fit in legal-size attache or briefcase. Rubber padded steel spring shock cords, heavy duty wheels. A real boon to the frequent traveler.

Then, his luck holding for a change, he managed to dispose of everything for the night and to have become invisible only a second or two before Pascal arrived at the cubicle.

"Damn!" the latter said aloud, even though there was ostensibly no one there to audit him, not even Delphine, who had been heard to leave a moment or two earlier.

Pascal started away — and the invisible Wagner was not far behind him, his rubber-soled tread not audible above Pascal's foot-slapping plod — but abruptly spun around and started back. Wagner only just was able to dodge him by stepping into Delphine's vacant niche.

Pascal continued back to Wagner's cubicle, where he stopped and peered in. Since the three-sided cell was only large enough to contain a desk, the accompanying chair, a wastecan, and a hat-tree, no one could be hiding there except if invisible, and for a moment Wagner wondered whether Pascal had any suspicions with respect to his whereabouts.

But the other man proceeded to demonstrate that he had

an interest which would not have been served by Wagner's presence: he stepped into the cubicle and began to try the desk drawers.

Wagner had lately become aware that someone was regularly pilfering from his supply of office supplies — pencils still innocent of the sharpener, shiny paper clips in three sizes, creamy new file folders, and not so much of the cheap yellow paper on which the original rough writing was done as the expensive sheets (two sheets of white bond, one pink, one onionskin, with carbons between each pair, all glued together at the top) on which the final version of each piece of copy was typed for submission, minus the onionskin sheet, to Jackie Grinzing, who kept the pink layer and forwarded one of the whites to the client, reserving the other for the printer.

Nowadays each copywriter had to sign a voucher every time he went to the stockroom for supplies. This was another of the measures put into being by Morton Wilton. Thus the more materials pinched from Wagner, the oftener he had had to apply to the sulky young man who presided over the stockroom. Unfortunately, only the middle drawer could be locked: he kept personal possessions therein, including, for security, his wallet, which he feared might be swiped if he left it in the inside breast pocket of the suit jacket that he hung on the hat-tree while at work.

He noticed now that after retrieving the billfold he had failed decisively to shut that drawer: it missed closure by no more than an eighth of an inch, but Pascal, with the sharp sight of the stealthy, went straightway to the appropriate knob.

There was nothing of value to others in the accumulation of the drawer. There was a little gold-framed picture of Babe that had formerly stood on the desktop. There was a letter or two from his sister, for he usually answered the latest at the office, and a couple of postcards sent from foreign places by vacationing colleagues. The odd stick of gum might be found therein, generally hard and brittle, for Wagner's dentist had discouraged him from exercising this habit, and though he had never smoked since college days, several matchbooks of the kind provided by restaurants and bars. A thorough search might also uncover a petrified example of the peanut-butter cheese-cracker sandwiches which were already stale as they came from the machine.

It wasn't much, and as Pascal was fingering through it now, Wagner was humiliated that the man would not encounter anything valuable enough to steal, if that was his purpose, or even some item that might be associated with a secret predilection or condition: a studded condom, a concealable weapon, even a vial of nitroglycerine pills for an unpredictable heart. It took him a moment or two to decide that Pascal, and not himself, was at fault here.

So as the man was bending to root in the farthermost recesses of the drawer, Wagner gave him a furious kick in the hindquarters. In quest of his lost balance Pascal kicked the wastecan, bumped his head against the fiberglass partition, and jostled the empty hat-tree so violently as to knock it over had it been top-heavy with garments.

Wagner used the stairs again this evening, though he made himself visible before his feet touched the first tread: it was too precarious to descend on unseen feet. Only the invisible could know such a problem; it was quite another situation than that of the blind, whose remaining senses were compensatorily supersensitive.

He was spurning the elevator because he wanted to reflect in the absence of other human beings, and perhaps there was no better venue for that exercise than the deserted staircase of a commercial building, with its unyielding metal stairs, undecorated walls, and relatively dim light, a shaft of nullity at the core of the humming beehive. Choosing a place and a time for such deliberation was new for Wagner, whose habitual means of dealing with unpleasantness had been to postpone thinking about it until it either went away — as eventually did the neighbors with the deafening stereo — or by becoming so routine it was seen as normal a part of life as bad weather. Only by viewing certain phenomena in such a light was it possible to endure in the city.

But lately things had happened that were unacceptable. Merely showing indignation was not an adequate response to the charges made by Jackie Grinzing, and pouring wine into Siv Zirko's lap had brought only the most transitory of satisfactions, long gone by the time Wagner had accompanied Babe to the cab. Until he saw her in Zirko's company he had actually been able to suppose that she left him to pursue a career unencumbered by any association with a male that was warmer than her friendship with the homosexual who owned the gallery at which she worked. Wagner had simply refused to entertain even the possibility that Babe was going to bed with anybody. But Zirko was obviously not the type to settle for being just a pal to any woman: if that had been his first dinner date with Babe, he was counting on his pound of flesh; if his second, he had already tasted it at least once.

Wagner had to try to get habituated to such an ugly way of thinking if he ever hoped to survive. And to win Babe back he would have to discredit Zirko in some more profound fashion than merely bringing about some brief embarrassment or inconvenience. After the incident in the restaurant he realized he had the means to work the ruin of not only Zirko but anybody else he chose to use it on. However, in Babe's case the greatest delicacy was called for. Knowing her, he would say that, odd as it might seem, she would not be unduly impressed by his ability to become invisible. To Babe that would be a trick, not a talent; an ingenious trick, to be sure, but if *he* could have learned how to do it, so could others. Whereas talent was unique. Oh, there were lots of people who had talent, but the issue or product of each was one of a kind. No one made the same music or played a role as did any other artist — nor could they even repeat their own performances to the letter. As to the primary arts, nobody painted exactly like another, and obviously each poet, each composer and sculptor had a voice or hand peculiar to himself alone irrespective of quality judgments.

But there was only one way in which to be invisible; if it were done partially, or badly, leaving anything that could be seen, then it couldn't be called by the name.

He could expect no admiration from Babe for the process or the resulting state, even though, so far as he knew, it was, except in make-believe, unprecedented, many would have said impossible. No, he must use invisibility to achieve something more than merely bringing mischief. But that was a problem, for how being unseen would help to write a line of his novel, let alone complete it, was beyond his powers of projection at the moment, and until he worked out a strategy towards positive achievement, he would do better to bring some grief to his enemy than to sit home brooding. To that end he decided now to visit Babe's place of business, the Guillaume Gallery, with its current show of Zirko's sculpture. And of course the only state in which this could be done without Babe's displeasure at seeing him — for he had agreed never to go there — was to make the visit invisibly.

While he was formulating this as yet simple plan — tonight the gallery would be open till eight o'clock, and until that time Babe wouldn't be dining anywhere, with or without Zirko — he heard footfalls on the metal stairway a floor above him, sharp step-sounds of the kind made only by high heels. For an instant, not wishing to be bothered to react to the astonishment and probably the fright of a woman encountering a man in such a confined and relatively remote place, he thought he would vanish.

But as it happened he waited a second too long. In his distraction she had moved closer than he expected and now came around the landing just above and saw him, and not with the least surprise or apprehension.

"Oh, hi, Fred," said Mary Alice Phillips. "I thought I recognized you, looking down, and that's why I put on speed. Do you do this often?"

The exertion had produced a desirable color in her cheeks. She wore a tight-belted trench coat, which certainly gave her a kind of dash, but she would have done better to brush her hair.

"You mean take the stairs? Only when I want privacy to think in." Her face fell. "No," he said quickly, "it's OK now. I've done enough pondering at the moment. What about you: do you often walk down?" Last evening she had rather mysteriously not reached the lobby in the car he had seen her board.

"Sometimes," said she. "When I think there are too many people on the elevator."

They had resumed the descent. "Oh," Wagner said, "I don't really think there's any danger. There are several safety features on the modern elevator. I understand that when it's really overloaded, a device locks the car where it is and won't let the motor start."

"I don't mean that. What I don't like is someone pressing up against me."

Did she mean a *frotteur*? Or was she confessing to a mix of generalized misanthropy with claustrophobia? It was probably more tasteful not to ask. Hardly had he made his decision when she told him.

"Men."

"Uh-huh."

As they were rounding the next landing, Mary Alice glanced at him. "I hope I haven't offended you."

"Since I don't do that sort of thing, you haven't."

Her brown eyes were dismayed. "Oh, I didn't —"

"I know you didn't," Wagner said, with a quick sober sort of smile.

"I don't have a very good sense of humor, I guess."

Wagner frowned. "I don't think that's got much to do with not liking a stranger to take liberties with you."

"They're not always strangers." Mary Alice's tone was plaintive.

Of course, Pascal! "I understand how you might not want to create a public disturbance," he told her now. "But you really ought to get him aside and tell him privately, in no uncertain terms, it's got to stop, or else."

"Or what?"

"You'll take measures."

"What measures?"

Mary Alice was beginning to show her irritating way of asking foolish questions: she did that quite a lot with regard to catalogue copy. How could he know what she should do next? Women were expected, somewhere along the line but at a much younger age than Mary Alice's, to

82

acquire a technique to repel at least this kind of man, who after all was not a rapist.

But Wagner found himself constitutionally unable to appear to her as less than an authority on any matter at hand.

"Tell him next time you *will* make a public disturbance."

"You mean scream and yell? I couldn't do that."

"But the idea is to make him *think* you would," Wagner said. They were moving smartly, and had only one more floor to go, according to the number stenciled alongside the latest fire door. "You could have him arrested."

"My God, I couldn't do that."

"Well, once again it would be the threat that would probably do the trick."

They were descending the last flight of stairs. "Listen, I've got it," said Wagner. "Here's something you can do." He suppressed the impulse to say *even you.* "Tell him privately, quietly, that unless he doesn't quit, you'll spread it around the office. Now that should do it, and without any commotion. Nobody could stand that kind of embarrassment."

She said nothing for the few steps remaining, but stopped before the door to the lobby. "Thanks, Fred." She put out her hand. After a moment he gave her his, and she shook it. Hers was larger and stronger than he expected. "As usual," said she, "you're the one with the answers."

Ordinarily he would have uttered some self-effacing sentiment, but he sensed that here it might be taken as a failure of responsibility. "I'm pleased to have been able to help, Mary Alice. I'm sure it will work. Let me know." He was still shaking the hand with which she held him. He had never before touched her in any way, not even in the slight contact of brushing by at close quarters. He was not the kind of fellow who was given to that practice, and if he had

83

been, she would not have been the kind of woman to whom he would have done it. That Pascal was rubbing his groin against her behind — which was undoubtedly what she meant — was peculiarly outrageous, but it was probably no worse than searching the personal drawer of a colleague. Wagner regretted only not having kicked him more savagely.

Finally he got his hand free and opened the door, ushering her out. The roar of the lobby at rush hour, after the quiet of the stairs, was startling. He had intended to escape from Mary Alice at this point, but he now knew a need to be protective. Actually, as a team they posed a certain menace to others, for they both walked quickly and collided with slowpokes several times before reaching the sidewalk.

As a result of this shared experience, which became richer by their stepping amongst the even more alien throng on the pavement, people who didn't even work in the same building — competitors, even potential enemies abound in the city — Wagner again acquired an interest in Mary Alice. It was however too slight to affect his immediate behavior.

Therefore at the corner, where they were detained by both a red light and the heavy traffic, he said, "I'm taking a left turn here. I'll see you tomorrow, Mary Alice. Have a good evening."

A strain in her eye suggested she might insist on accompanying him anyway, but she did not. Instead she shook hands again, and thereby delayed him long enough for the light to turn red in the direction in which he was heading, notwithstanding which he dashed across the street, only just managing to elude the surge of front bumpers. From the other side he looked back, so as to make a kind of shrug to let Mary Alice know his escape had not been intentionally that desperate, but already she could not be seen.

As usual, the most likely way to proceed where he was going was to walk, even though the Guillaume Gallery was quite a hike. As he passed the lunch counter from which he had slunk invisibly without paying the check at noontime, he remembered his earlier intention to drop off the money at the next opportunity, but did not so much as slow his pace at this moment. It would have been a different matter had he been on conversational terms with the owner or even one of the countermen. Then he could have stepped inside and made a joke of it. As things stood it would have been too embarrassing. Anyway, their food, which was often stale and always overcooked, was outlandishly overpriced as well, and the service was at best indifferent. Wagner had been present once when the owner, a stout swarthy man with an unkempt mustache, had actually threatened bodily to throw out a customer who had begun by complaining about the tepid coffee and gone on justifiably to several other delinquencies, such as fork tines webbed with dried food and the sweaty T-shirt on the short-order cook.

A block before reaching the gallery, Wagner took the precaution of stepping into an unlighted areaway full of garbage cans and becoming invisible. He wanted Babe to remain ignorant of his visit from start to finish, and for all he knew she might be out in the neighborhood someplace, fetching coffee for Cleve Guillaume, for she did that sort of flunky work from time to time, and Guillaume was too "fastidious," her word, to keep a coffee-making device of any kind in the office of the gallery: after all, that's where he took clients to write out checks. Babe was supposedly working as his assistant only until she learned enough about the profession to open a gallery of her own. She believed she had sufficient capital to get started, having got a bequest when her father died, which was the immediate pretext for leaving Wagner. She had actually tried to make him see his advantage in the new arrangement: he would not need to contribute a penny to her support. It was this sort of thing that made him suspect that in four years of marriage he had never penetrated to the core of Babe's being.

Invisibly he now approached the big show window. When he was near enough to see what was on display therein, he recoiled. Siv Zirko, in the flesh, was sitting on a high stool, just behind the glass, staring, even glaring in his direction. Since Wagner could not be seen, this meant that Zirko's expression was intended for anybody who looked at him. At the moment, despite the plentiful pedestrians abroad, he had no visible audience. It interested Wagner for a time to witness how long the egomaniacal artist could maintain his features in the same fix, without so much as the faintest tremor of eye.

It was ever so long before he first began to suspect that the figure under his surveillance was not the living Zirko but rather an extraordinarily accurate replica of the man. His certainty was still not absolute on leaving the window to use the door; he would not have been startled had the figure at last stopped holding its breath.

No one could be seen inside the gallery as he entered, but opening the door sounded an alarm somewhere, and from a room at the left emerged Cleve Guillaume, whom Wagner had met that time he attended an opening. It was difficult to think of Guillaume as sexually deviant when he was silent, for he was a thickset young man who would not have been questioned if seen in the uniform of a contact sport. And even when he spoke, he was not noticeably effeminate.

But now he *was* piqued, and petulance gave his voice a girlish rhythm.

"Will you look at that? Either the wind managed to open that door, or, more likely, someone had concealed himself and then, when the coast was cleared, *seized* one of the pieces and ran out." He was silent for a moment before lifting his thick chin to the ceiling and shouting, "Carla! Where *are* you!"

Babe came through a door in the rear, a door that was almost concealed, flush-fitting as it was and of the same off-white as the walls.

She was wearing a dirty blue smock. "What's the trouble?"

"I could wish you would stay on the *qui vive*," said Guillaume. "If you don't mind."

"I was just crating the —"

"I know very well what you were doing," Guillaume said. "But all the same I wish you had been keeping an eye on who comes and goes out here. Now somebody has gotten in and swiped something."

She was dismayed. "My God, what?"

Guillaume turned away, his chin still held high. "How do *I* know? Take inventory. Let's hope it was just the wind."

"What wind?"

"Honestly, Carla." Guillaume turned back with a reproachful lower lip. "You don't listen to anything I say. The buzzer sounded, I came out, and no one was here. *Ergo*, it was either the wind or a sneak thief, wouldn't you say?"

Babe glanced around the exhibition space, which consisted at this moment of one large room, though by means of movable partitions it was sometimes made into two or even three enclosures.

"Must have been the wind then," said Babe. "I don't see anything's missing."

Guillaume's hands rose to his hips, a gesture that given his build did not suggest the maidenly: he might have reacted that way to a penalty call at the ten yardline. "That's your idea of an inventory?"

Babe sighed, groaned, and then said heavily, *"All right, Cleve,"* and in a dramatic plod went methodically around past each of the exhibits, which in most cases were mounted atop white, shoulder-high columns and seemed to be human organs molded from the same material, wax or plastic and amazingly lifelike, of which the show-window Zirko had been fashioned. The nearest to where Wagner stood consisted of a familiar complex of five fingers joined to a palm. This had such verisimilitude as to cause him queasily to look for the bloody stump: it was as though the hand had been cleanly severed at the wrist and mounted upright on the column. The label below read: ARTIST'S LEFT HAND. Wagner had to admit it was a remarkable piece of work: in addition to the lines which palmists trace there was a scar of a healing cut at the base of the thumb, and on the reverse were prominent blue veins and even two dirty fingernails.

A more disquieting piece was just beyond. At the ends of thin vertical rods were two little spheres. The accompanying card read: ARTIST'S EYES. They were brown-irised and bloodshot. Detached as they were, they could have been anybody's, but on a pillar just beyond was a nose that, deeply pitted above each flange and with sprouts of hair from each nostril, really was a dead ringer for Zirko's.

Next was a right foot, with what looked very like an incipient ingrown nail on the big toe.

Babe meanwhile had made a brisk inspection tour. "Nothing's gone," she announced. "How could it be? Somebody making a quick grab would have to take the stand and all: Siv's got everything tightly anchored."

Guillaume was still in place. *"Hmmm."* His murmur was rich. He was jowlier than when Wagner had seen him last. Finally he said, "Frankly, I don't understand this at *all.*" His voice had almost returned to normal. Suddenly he showed a radiant grin. "But then who does?" He did have a boyish charm. He returned to the office.

Apart from the soiled smock, Babe was perfectly groomed as always. Indeed the smock was unprecedented to Wagner. It was also too large: the cuffs were rolled at the wrists. Surely it was a borrowed garment. Since he was invisible, Wagner could inspect her at close range and in a better light than on the sidewalk the evening before, and he moved to do so, but she now went, even more quickly, into the back room, the door to which she closed in his face.

He was reluctant to open it immediately. Curiosity might be provoked by too many consecutive inexplicable events.

Anyway, he had come here really to do something about Zirko, not Babe. On the wall near the door to the street was a plaque under the clear-plastic lamination of which was a dark-gray surface imprinted in white type. Wagner returned to it now.

ALL OF SIV ZIRKO was the headline, below which appeared the following text.

> "Like most people," Zirko says, "I never before actually ever looked at myself. I mean *really* looked. Or

maybe I looked without seeing. And what is art anyway but a way of seeing? And if you think about it,
where should an artist begin if not with himself? This
is especially true with a sculptor, to which is added
the truth that can be learned through tactility. So I
have dissected myself. I have let you in on my secrets.
Use them well. Touch me, stroke me, fondle me,
caress me. Let's exchange love!"

This statement was followed by encomia from critics
whose publications — major papers, newsweeklies, art
journals — were eminent.

Zirko has no peer as a plastic rhetorician. His is the
language of conclusive conjecture.

"Cruel," "imperious," "paranoid" are some of the
terms that have been applied to Zirko's work, and
perhaps justifiably so, but it has as appropriately been
called "genial," even "tender," and so it certainly is
as well. What all agree on is that it is unquestionably
eloquent.

Zirko is free-swinging, true enough: that much must
be admitted, and as such he has been seen as irresponsible. Well, okay, but I maintain that thoughtful examination of any of the pieces in question cannot help
but reveal that the irresponsibility is superficial. Sig-
nificance is there, but it must be sought after. Zirko
makes one demand: that the viewer become a criminal
accomplice. This is not unprecedented, but for once it
is serious.

Wagner chewed on his invisible lower lip. Grammatical
barbarism could be expected from Zirko, but for a national
magazine to print a solecism like "not help but" was dis-
gusting. The matter of these critical statements was another
thing: they read as so much contemptible nonsense, but, as

Babe had been wont to remind him, he had no true sympathy with art whose language was nonverbal.

He was, however, as familiar with male anatomy as Zirko, having lived with his own for more than three decades, and what he now recognized, on one of the stands halfway along the western wall of the gallery, just beyond a red fire extinguisher in a glass-enclosed recess, was a set of masculine genitalia: hair-fringed phallus with dependent bag.

Wagner approached this exhibit, but before he got there he encountered a work of another sort than the others, not a standing sculpture but rather a wall-fastened white panel from which five large glass or clear-plastic bubbles protruded. Each container displayed a substance, two of which were colorless. On the near side was posted a card of identification which dealt with the lot: ARTIST'S SHIT, PISS, SWEAT, SPIT, AND COME.

At no point in his rage did Wagner consider molesting this frieze of filth and thus perhaps effecting the release of some vile material, should any of it be genuine. Instead he moved on to the genitals, which he now noticed had a companion piece of which the principal element loomed so massive he had assumed, from a distance, it was a forearm. These works were labeled, respectively, ARTIST'S LIMP COCK AND BALLS and ARTIST'S HARD-ON. The detailing of these imitation organs — swollen, tortuous purple veining, etc. — was extraordinarily precise. As to the erection, Zirko had been outlandishly generous to himself: if this were even half true he had made physiological history.

The man was a pestilence. Wagner opened the glass door to the niche and withdrew the fire extinguisher, which was not as large or as heavy as he would have liked, and with it he struck the rampant sculpture as violently as he could

. . . establishing that the material of which it was fashioned was not wax but a remarkably resistant, nonbrittle plastic, but doing little harm to it beyond a slight smudge of red paint, and not only was the counterfeit phallus invulnerable but, as Babe had said, the works were snugly fastened to the stands. The stands were screwed to the floor on all four sides with L-shaped metal straps. Wrestling with force, Wagner got nowhere in a frenzied effort to topple this one.

He did however succeed in making sounds that elicited a distant gibe from Guillaume — "Carla, you're getting clumsy in your old age," followed by a watery chuckle — but the gallery owner was not sufficiently interested to emerge from his office when no response was forthcoming.

It was clear that Zirko, even in absentia, was winning this round thus far, the inertia of his plastic prick in exultant contrast to Wagner's impotent attempts to deflate it. On the other hand, none of this was being seen by anybody, and his humiliation therefore was known only to Wagner himself — even if it could properly be called humiliation in these circumstances. How could one be truly embarrassed in the absence of an audience? Invisibility continued to disclose new advantages. He was in one of Zirko's strongholds: he could not expect, even when unseen, to glide right in and have his way, first time out. On his next visit he would bring the proper demolition equipment.

. . . Just a moment, he was not the kind of man who could destroy works of art in cold blood, even when the "art" was such as this. Premeditation would make any such action reprehensible according to the same code by which he despised Zirko's work: the shit encased in plastic was not art, but shit. And so would be any studied effort to destroy it.

Wagner was morally invigorated by this insight. He left the gallery without making any further invisible overtures to Babe. He understood it was time to put invisibility to better uses than the service of jealousy, spite, and convenience.

It really was a remarkable gift. He who possessed it should be rich, and not loveless. His life long, Wagner had never taken anything that did not belong to him, and now he was thinking of robbing a bank!

But having the ability to vanish does, sooner or later, work a change in a person.

5

ΦΦ WAGNER'S MAIDEN EFFORT AS BANK ROBBER TOOK place at lunchtime on the following day. Fortune favored him at the outset: Pascal had a dental appointment late in the morning and therefore would not be in a condition to eat lunch, even if, as he boasted, nothing more was done to his teeth than the semiannual prophylaxis. Naturally he make no reference to the kick Wagner had given him the night before, but apparently it had done its job, for nothing was missing from the desk. Presumably something of this sort could be used to correct unpleasant or even dangerous addictions. If every time a heavy smoker lighted up, he received, from thin air, a boot in the behind, he might well be able to overcome the habit. Whether this would be a powerful enough deterrent to the use of addictive drugs, however, was another matter. And of course to have any significant social effect such measures would have to be enacted by an army of invisible men.

Wagner couldn't kid himself: invisibility must be used to further his own interests, and as soon as he began to take money that was not his, those were antisocial, which was to say, criminal, in the same area as embezzlement and forgery. He had a choice: he might have walked into a bank with a real or fake gun, stuck up a teller, then escaped by becoming invisible. But for a man with no experience of action, this plan had little allure. Pointing a genuine, loaded firearm at another person would be difficult for him, and even with a toy pistol he would not have adequate confidence to hold it steady. With either, he might well be shot down by bank guards or a fortuitous police officer. . . . He chose the other option.

And another bank than the one at which he maintained a checking account, for though his was a large branch with many tellers, all of whom were incessantly being exchanged for newcomers, and none of whom gave him so much as a glance as he stood before the window, not to mention that while committing the crime he would be invisible from start to finish, Wagner intended to err only on the side of caution. Should the invisibility fail — and it seemed to him it might; it had yet to be tried under conditions of extreme stress — he still would have a chance to escape unrecognized. Most of his colleagues took their paychecks to the same institution used by him, whereas he was certain to be utterly unknown to all mortals found on the premises of a bank say four blocks north and two west. Which was the way of the city: that not in one's immediate neighborhood was Mars.

However, having found such a bank and entered in the most unobtrusive manner an invisible person could enjoy, *viz.*, occupying the slot of a swinging door being moved by a visible man in the compartment ahead, Wagner got quite a shock, for who were the first people he saw as the door came around but Jackie Grinzing and Morton Wilton! The latter was handing a sheaf of small documents to a teller at the nearest window.

Discouraged, Wagner stayed right in the door and let

himself be turned on around to where he had come from. On the sidewalk he was roughly jostled as a remarkably robust man stepped with energy into what seemed an empty space. Encountering the unseen but palpable Wagner, he was confused but even more determined to make headway than at the outset. The result was a short but violent episode in which Wagner got punched in the nose by a flailing arm, perhaps even his own. Witnesses of the event were not quick to believe the other man was even eccentric. One passerby addressed a companion: "Must be a bee or wasp in there." "Or maybe," said the other, "just a stink."

"Damn," said Wagner, aloud, having finally realized his escape: he felt a wetness on his upper lip. "Do I have a nosebleed?"

"I don't see any blood," said one of the latest people on the scene, walking on Wagner's invisible right foot, addressing her companion. "It's just your imagination."

Wagner had to find somewhere out of traffic to plot his next move, else he would continue to sustain damage, for the to-and-fro parade was growing. He stepped to the side of the door just as Jackie and Wilton emerged.

On the sidewalk Wilton grinned at her and asked, "E.F.?"

"No, F.F.," said Jackie, with an expression that looked at first like pain but was apparently a form of desire.

They went west, undoubtedly en route to a hotel. Invisibility would be a boon to the blackmailer. The technique certainly should be kept out of the hands of a real criminal.

It was unlikely that Wagner would encounter anyone else he recognized, but this bank seemed jinxed for him. There was another at the catercorner. He headed for it, and immediately had another unpleasant experience. Being invisible had, despite the punishment he had only just received in the swinging door, made him feel immaterial, and as he started to cross the street in defiance of the heavy traffic moving on it, he was almost struck by a lurching van.

Leaping back to the curb, he was pretty close to giving up the project for this day. Yes, his nose *was* bleeding. In his current condition he could not see the liquid on his exploratory fingers, but blood it had to be. Perhaps it was dripping on his tie and shirt. He put a handkerchief to his face. When he returned to visibility what a mess he would be! He must clean himself up in one public toilet or another, and to do that he would have to be visible. He was really botching what had seemed simple enough in projection, at least for the preliminary phases. If he had such trouble merely entering a bank, what could he expect when helping himself to money?

But in fact the last-named turned out to be the most easily accomplished achievement of the day. He crossed the street with the light, went into the other bank, lingered near the electrically latched door-gate between the executives' desks and the tellers' area until it was opened — which took no time at all, for persons came and went frequently in the incessant transaction between the two — moved along the counter as he had in the post office, and, when one of the tellers (who were all female), took a step to the side, he scooped a handful of hundred-dollar bills from her open cash drawer. As the designers of this bank had shrewdly placed these drawers below the line of vision of anyone not abnormally tall, given the width of the fake-marble counter as it extended towards the customer, plus the plate-glass barrier above it, the eyeglassed, balding man on the other side did not observe the theft — though no doubt if he had so done he would have assumed the fault lay in his own vision. That was the beauty of being invisible: in questionable circumstances people tend *not* to believe their own eyes.

Wagner's leaving the scene of the crime was as neat as had been his arrival. He now applied himself to the problem of the blood on his clothing. Ironically enough, this proved insuperable to the successful bank robber, the man who could vanish at will. He could not clean himself unless he could see what he was doing. If he materialized before the mirror in a public toilet, he could be seen by others. Now, there was nothing to link someone suffering from a nosebleed with a bank robbery, especially when the thief had been invisible, and the money might not be missed until the tallies at the end of the day, so Wagner had no serious reason for worry. He was nevertheless averse to showing his bloodstains; they could be interpreted as having been received while committing a crime of violence, and under the subsequent interrogation by the police, he might crack. He was after all a bona fide lawbreaker now, for the first time in his life. Stiffing the lunch counter had been in the guise of taking a loan. There could be no alternative characterization of the means by which he had filled the pocket of his jacket with hundred-dollar bills.

On the way back to the office he stopped off at a five-and-dime and stole a little pocket mirror. At his building he had to share the elevator with a sudden crowd of lunchtime returnees. His presence was unknown to the others, and with innocent brutality they crushed him into a corner. The man just ahead turned to see what could be the baffling obstruction, and flooded him, at the range of four inches, with foul breath. He was not released until the car climbed to three floors above his own and the throng departed as one.

Finally arriving at his own offices, he went to the men's room and into a booth. He became visible there and inspected himself in the pocket mirror. There was some blood on him, but less than he had supposed: a few drops, now dried brown, on his left lapel, none on his tie. He was able to make himself presentable with a saliva-moistened handkerchief.

He brought the beautiful new bills from his pocket. They were so fresh and crisp as to have cohered as if they were yet in the teller's drawer. He felt the emanations of their power. He would not have been astonished had the stack emitted an audible hum of generatorlike might. He counted them. He had taken twenty-two bills. That was two thousand, two hundred dollars, a long ton of money to obtain during a lunch hour with very little work.

Pascal was standing before the mirror when Wagner emerged. Even in his discomfort the former never missed so slight an event as another man's leaving a toilet stall. He was angled over a washbasin, face all but touching the glass, palpating his upper lip.

His reflection spoke. "It feels all puffed up." He pulled his face back. "How's it look to you? Swollen?"

"No," said Wagner. "Why? Were you punched?"

Pascal winced in reproach. "Didn't I say I was going to the dentist's? He gave me not one shot but two. Then drilled for what seemed like an hour, but said it was only a minor cavity." Now he poked out a cheek-swelling with his tongue, deflated it to add, "Hope never to see a major one." He moved quickly so as to accompany Wagner out the door.

But Wagner certainly did not want to be seen leaving the

men's room in such company, in view of the vile charges that had been anonymously placed against him.

He snapped his fingers. "Damn." He showed the sick smile with which one sometimes confessed to a weakness and said, knowingly, "Go ahead. I've got to finish what I came here for."

Pascal would have argued — that's the kind of guy he was — but Wagner grimaced, put a hand to his belt buckle, and returned quickly to the booth. He heard Pascal reluctantly leave, but would wait awhile anyhow, for the other, keen on sharing the banalities of routine dental work, was capable of lingering in the hallway. Or even, for the door now was reopened, of returning for more facial examination, anything to keep Wagner captive. Goddamn the man.

Wagner therefore decided, rashly, to become invisible: let Pascal cope with the mystery of where he had gone. . . . But might it not be more likely that in Pascal's quest to understand he would prove more intrusive than ever?

While Wagner was pondering on the matter someone went into the booth just next his. That did it; he must leave before the new arrival began to strain.

Invisibly, he stepped from the stall and went towards the door, but before he got there it opened to admit the sallow-faced clerk whose sullen manner made visits to the stockroom so unpleasant. It was no surprise that this young man moved more quickly now than when filling an order, but what did seize Wagner's interest, just as he caught the door on its way back to the jamb, was what the stockroom clerk, whose name was Terry something-or-other, now said aloud, for it was identical to what he had heard the day before, from the large, bluff man in the men's room of the accounting department.

"Artie?"

The difference now was that Artie answered, saying, "Yeah," from the booth next to the one Wagner had vacated.

Terry proceeded to join Artie.

Wagner was not tempted to remain and replicate Marcel's celebrated eavesdropping on the transaction between Charlus and Jupien. By accident he had successfully carried out the assignment that he had rejected when Jackie Grinzing tried to impose it upon him. There was something chagrining in the experience. He had to remind himself that he was also the man who had marched into a bank and taken, with impunity, $2,200: simply plucked it up from a cash drawer, with nobody the wiser. This was the perfect crime, achieved without so much as the threat of violence . . . though it could hardly be called victimless. No bank would be likely to write off two thousand dollars or believe that the person nearest the source of the loss was without guilt. Of course the teller would be blamed, that pretty and pleasant-mannered young woman. Losing her job would be nothing beside the certainty that she would be prosecuted for grand theft. He had simply destroyed a life, which had proved an easier accomplishment than he could have imagined. The fact was that taking the money at gunpoint would have been preferable, furnishing an obvious villain.

So much for his initial and, as it now seemed, infantile sense of earning a profit without depleting anyone else's account. It could not be said that he was making good use of invisibility. Thus far he had collected shameful information on several persons by means of inadvertent surveillance, bilked a greasy spoon of several bucks, stolen a sum of money for which an innocent young woman would be blamed, lost some change in a post office, ruined Babe's dinner date, and run afoul of a plastic model of Siv Zirko's penis. There could be no satisfaction in the perusal of a record of that sort.

He really must make such amends as he could. He visibly returned to his desk, where after a good deal of sober reflection, he determined to deal by anonymous letter with all the correctable matters except the twenty-two hundred-dollar bills. He would have to return the money in person, invisibly. The mails could hardly be trusted, and even if the parcel reached the bank, the teller would get it only after it had passed through a number of other hands, some of which might be unscrupulous. The unfortunate young woman from whose drawer he had taken the bills might never see them again. No, he must revisit the bank before closing time, before she had done her sums for the day. That could be managed; it was only 1:10 at the moment. Think of that. He had made a frustrated attempt on one bank and successfully robbed another, returned to the office and accidentally caught at least two of the people who used the men's room for sexual activities — all in scarcely more than an hour. There was an efficiency in being invisible.

As to Terry-from-the-stockroom, a note would surely suffice. Wagner was fluent in epistolary composition. It took him no time at all to type, on the same kind of paper used for copy, the following.

> Terry:
> Your restroom activities have become known. What you do is certainly your own affair, but there has been criticism of your doing it at the office. I gather I'm the only one so far who can identify you, and having no wish to do you harm, I thought I'd give you this warning without saying anything to anyone

else. But if you don't heed it, and the executives discover your identity, you might lose your job. You might pass the warning along to "Artie" as well, and to anyone else you know who uses his services.

That seemed to say it all. There was no need to add a phony name such as "A Friend," because he wasn't one.

The time was now 1:30. Wagner next wrote to Jackie Grinzing.

You have been observed, quite by accident, in a compromising situation with Morton Wilton. The person who saw you is not a moral policeman and neither approves nor disapproves of your liaison. But it has occurred to this person that if you could be observed by one, you might well be seen by others who would not be so tolerant of human foibles. Both you and Wilton, if his ring can be believed, are currently married. It would be easy for some malicious person to make trouble for you. Discretion is advised.

His wristwatch now read 2:05. This note had taken him a bit longer to compose than the one to stockroom Terry, for it was slightly elevated in literary style. For example, he would not have used "liaison" when writing to Terry, nor "foibles," which, though one could hear its occasional use by a certain whimsical, avuncular kind of TV newsman, had Jamesian connotations: someone in "The Liar" calls the eponymous hero a "fetching dog, but has a monstrous foible." Or approximately: he hadn't read it since college.

It was time for him to start for the bank, if he hoped to get there before closing, which might be as early as 2:30. Being invisible had no effect on the speed at which one could move. He enclosed the letters in the manila envelopes used for interoffice mail, and because these were not equipped for sealing, had no closure but the string-and-spindle, he scotch-taped the flaps, which of course would disqualify the envelopes from further use once they were mutilated by the removal of the tape. This was why such employment of tape was forbidden under the rules for office economy newly imposed by Morton Wilton, the adulterous executive.

But were Wagner not to apply some obstacle against the accidental examination of his letters by unauthorized parties, he would once again be responsible for bringing needless discomfort, perhaps even pain, to others. However, since Gordon the messenger had been directed to remain on the alert for the illicit use of scotch tape, dropping them off at his station would probably call Jackie's unwelcome attention to the envelopes — unwelcome even in the case of the one addressed to her, for if he knew the woman, she would first react to the infraction of the rules and only read the enclosure as an afterthought. She might also even confiscate and read the message to Terry.

Therefore Wagner now entered her office invisibly — she was still out, perhaps by now even finally eating lunch — and, after borrowing the desk-set pen to inscribe "Personal" on the flap, just above the tape, deposited her envelope in the In box. He then delivered Terry's to the stockroom.

Unless filling an order, the man was never in evidence at or near the counter. If you wanted him, you struck the button of the old-fashioned bellhop's bell and proceeded to wait interminably. It occurred to Wagner to wonder why Terry did not invite "Artie" into the fastness of his lair, into which no one else, not even Jackie, ever penetrated and which was surely more private than the men's washroom — unless of course it was the very violation of social modesty, with the concomitant risks, that attracted the stockroom clerk, whose habitual sullenness might well be the symptom of a profound grievance against the way things were. Such persons abounded in the city: their statements, made in the vocabulary of vandalism, could be seen anew each day, on buildings and public conveyances and in parks. No doubt it could be expressed sexually as well.

Wagner rang the bell and placed the envelope upon the counter that obstructed the doorway at waist level. As soon as it touched wood it became visible.

His time in which to reach the bank had somehow dwindled to but eleven minutes, he now saw on the clock mounted above the elevators. Perhaps his watch had been slow; he could not check it now, for, like the rest of him and his, it was invisible.

All cars were on the ground floor. Therefore he took the now familiar staircase. Running down the steps was still a dangerous exercise, but he reached the bottom without tripping, crossed the lobby at so smart a pace he could not alter it or dodge when, at the doors to the street, he met the entering Wilton, of all people, who was two steps ahead of Jackie Grinzing. Wagner did have the advantage, though a captive of his own momentum, of being able to see Wilton, who of course was blind to him and therefore got the worst of the collision; indeed, was knocked out the door and, being palpably of slighter substance than he looked, finally lost his balance and when last seen was likely to fall to the pavement.

As to what either Wilton or Jackie made of this surely puzzling event, Wagner did not have time to pause and observe, but he did reflect that had her escort been more gallant, it would have been she with whom he might have collided.

En route to the bank, he only narrowly averted running into a series of other people, then was himself almost trampled by a husky youth who could have had no idea that a human being occupied what looked like a clear field of play.

The bank's clock was at 2:21½ when he arrived. Good luck now ruled the swinging door: three of its compartments were filled with persons on their way to the street, and no one but him awaited entrance. Inside, however, he had to linger overlong for someone to pass through the electric gate to the back-of-counter area, and when finally a plump young woman did so, she was detained by a man playing the role of the traditional banker, i.e., middle-aged, gray-suited and -sideburned; and these people effectively blocked all access to the gate . . . until, after an eternity, another officer begged their pardon and dislodged them, but he went swiftly through the gate and, instead of letting it look after itself, paused to see the latch close — for all the world as if he knew Wagner stood invisibly by, waiting to pounce.

But at last the young woman, uttering a series of OKs, turned from the man in gray and moved her plump person, dressed in bright green, through the barrier, the switch that controlled which was operated by an employee just inside and to the left. Paperwork was the latter's main job, but she reserved the corner of an eye for whoever might appear on either side of the gate. Wagner followed quickly in the fat girl's wake, but, studying the document in her hand, she moved at a deliberate pace, and the gate, in its automatic, prompt return, struck him before he could clear it. It had no significant force, and he was not hurt, but the gate was detained for an instant in its travel. Wagner noticed that and wondered whether anyone else did, but he was inside now and had work to do.

He went swiftly to the station of the teller from whom he had taken the hundred-dollar bills. She was currently occupied with a man buying traveler's checks. To get the blanks for this purpose she moved far enough from her cash drawer for Wagner to return the notes, though he could not manage to do the job as neatly as he would have liked. The bills had been crisply new when taken; by now, what with his counting them several times, they were not quite as they had been: even a nonprofessional could have seen that at a distance.

But the bank teller was back in place before he could smooth down even the topmost bills. He sprang away, but then, in an effort to reach the drawer from a position just behind her, leaning at too extreme an angle, he was obliged suddenly to alter his center of gravity. He moved one foot and clutched out instinctively with his left, free hand: the latter found itself just below the seat of the teller's skirt, performing a grasp that partook of both jokey "goose" and grim indecency.

The young woman emitted a steam-whistle shriek, more hurled away than dropped her burden of documents, whirled around, her features gargoyled with indignation . . . and of course saw no one near enough to have made free with her and got away clean. She clasped her face.

She was being stared at or towards by every human being in the bank, as was he who had brought this mess about, though naturally no one could see *him*. And now the guard arrived at the window, his revolver trained on the poor devil who had ordered the traveler's checks.

"Freeze! . . . *Put the case on the floor, back up two paces, lean forward, placing hands on counter, and spread 'em.*" The guard, a seamy-faced man with a head that was probably bald under his cap, gingerly toed the black attaché case away from where the customer had placed it. He shouted in at the teller, "Jane! He say he got a bomb?"

The young woman, still breathing heavily, turned. "Oh, God, no."

"A pistol, huh?" cried the guard, and then deafeningly addressed the man who was bridging his spread-eagled body, at an extreme angle, between the counter and the patch of floor, four feet out, where his feet were. "Awright, you sack of filth, I'm going to take your piece. If you go for it meantime, say goodbye to your head." He put the muzzle of the pistol into his captive's nape. His jargon might be TV-synthetic, but he was surely a genuine menace.

Jane finally rose above her own distress to say, "Joe, he didn't *do* anything!"

The prisoner himself found the strength to second her. "I didn't do *anything!*"

But Joe kept the gun where it was, telling Jane, "They'll *say* anything. Call the boys in blue."

"Please, Joe," said Jane. "I had a muscular spasm, is all. It had nothing to do with this man. He's all right. Please let him go."

Joe did not relish hearing this plea, and it took much more persuasion to induce him to holster the weapon and permit his victim to stand erect. The latter in a voice of fury assured everyone in the bank that he would not only never again do business with this institution but furthermore intended to hold it legally responsible for his public shaming.

Fortunately for Joe, the distraction of closing time was at hand, and he hastened to go lock the front door against newcomers. No less self-righteous, he stayed there to let people out.

Having made full restitution, Wagner was certainly eager

to leave. This episode had been no more successful than his encounter with the so-called artwork that had been modeled on Zirko's private part. He simply didn't think these projects through before embarking on them. They were products of his nerves and not his faculty of reason — perhaps because there was nothing reasonable in being invisible.

The electrically operated gate was stuck tight, he learned as he approached the little group of persons on his side of it. A like party stood on the other side.

The woman whose job it was to press the switch was saying, "Didn't close all the way, so I pushed it shut, and that did it."

A scowling officer looked through the plate-glass panel that formed the upper half of the gate. "You *forced* it, Sherry: that tells the mechanism to freeze. It also sounds the silent alarm, for God's sake. The police will be on their way."

By striking Wagner, the gate had got itself warped.

"Shit," said a female voice. "That's all we need to end a crazy day. Everything's going wrong all of a sudden."

Wagner silently agreed. He wished he could, without compromising himself, explain to these decent human beings why such phenomena were taking place. They looked to be much the same kind of people with whom he worked: though culturally superior to them, he was in the same moral boat, like them at the mercy of a city that was heedless of the individual.

A maintenance man was sent for, but, before he arrived, the police appeared as predicted. Fortunately, they were not in an overreactive mood but rather brusque and blasé, a relief after the performance of Joe the guard. They soon left. But when the technician came, it was ever so long before he disengaged the gate so as to permit Wagner's exit into the lobby, and then there was the matter of the front door, to pass promptly through which one would have had to apply, visibly of course, to Joe.

It was almost 4:30 when Wagner reappeared at his desk. He thought it politic not to make typing noises but rather to edit, by pen, some rough copy he had written that morning, and furthermore to pretend, if need be, he had been doing so all afternoon.

But hardly was he seated when Gordon came along and asked, "Where have you *been*, Fred? Jackie's really burned."

Obviously the plan to maintain that he had been in place for hours could not stand up. "I haven't been feeling well," he said instead.

"Well, you weren't in the men's room," said Gordon. "If you mean you went to the doctor, you should have told somebody."

Wagner rose. "I was over in the accounting-department washroom. It's more private."

"It is? I never knew they had toilets of their own."

Wagner said, "I'll go explain to Jackie. Then I'll be right back and type this up for you. I'm still not behind schedule." He regretted sounding as if he had to justify himself to Gordon, who was technically his only inferior in the department.

"She's left," Gordon said. "There's some meeting of the department heads, and then the day's over." He had a very slight edge of girlishness to him. However, it had not been he whom Wagner had seen with "Artie," but rather Terry, whose manner might be called virilely disaffected. And the guy from accounting, apparently another of Artie's habitués, was as far from swishy as could be. Undoubtedly there was a dimension of sexual inversion that Wagner could not as yet, with his fragmentary information, delineate.

He now gestured towards his typewriter. "I'll type this up, then."

"The Robot Carver copy had to be rewitten," said Gordon. "Maybe you remember? That's the electric knife, with the cut-out that automatically stops it when reaching bone."

"Of course I remember. I did that the day before yesterday."

"Jackie gave it to me to rewrite," Gordon said. "I thought you should know that, Fred. . . . So you wouldn't think I was going behind your back."

Wagner was annoyed with the young man's sanctimoniousness. "Why should I possibly think that, Gordon? You only do what you're told."

Gordon shrugged. "I guess that could be said of us all."

Wagner couldn't let him get away with the implication that they were professional equals. "When you've been around as long as I," said he, with a wry twitch of the mouth, "you'll find it possible to rise above office rivalry. We're all just earning a living. None of us, except maybe Jackie, would otherwise be working *here*, that's certain."

Gordon blinked his very pale blue eyes. "Oh, I don't think it's so bad. The people are a lot brighter than I arrogantly assumed at first, and better educated. Just about everybody has a BA, anyway, and Judy Rumbaugh taught social studies at the college level for a while. And look at you, the budding novelist."

Wagner made a polite sneer. "I hadn't realized I let the cat out of the bag. Can you call someone 'budding' after five or six years?" He honestly could not recall having ever mentioned his literary aspirations, but obviously he had: first Jackie, now Gordon had made an easy reference to what he thought he considered intimate information, yet he had apparently imparted it to at least two office acquaintances. On the other hand, he could go too far in self-deprecation, especially with someone as young as Gordon, who furthermore had been assigned to rewrite copy of his that had been perfectly all right as it stood.

"My trouble is that, unlike a lot of my contemporaries, I am as severe with myself as I am when reading others. I discard at least one word for every half-dozen I write. Wish that could be said for hacks like Wulsin and Musgrave, not to mention the tedious Miss R. Kelsinger."

"Well, they're all pretty much out of fashion by now anyway," Gordon said, a little smile twitching at each side of his mouth. "Lesbian satire is pathetic."

Wagner was taken by surprise. "I didn't know she was a lesbian," he foolishly observed.

"She's not," Gordon said, clucking twice. "Her last book was a vicious attack on them."

Wagner groaned," Of course. That was —"

"*Girl's Girls,*" Gordon said impatiently. "Trash."

"You keep up with things," said Wagner, with the slightest edge of derision: after the day he had had, he did not intend to sustain a defeat at the hands of this junior. "I admit I don't. Call me self-concerned, but —"

"*Vous avez bien ici autre chose à faire?*" Gordon was tightening the screws. "I do some reviewing," he went on to say. "*The Critical Edge* — ?" He shrugged. "Poetry." He bent and spoke *sotto voce.* "In fact, just between you and me, OK?, I've been offered a job there. Doesn't pay what this one does, naturally, and if their grants stop at any time, they'll have to close shop, but it would be a good place to be, don't you think?"

To maintain any pride at all, Wagner promptly agreed. The publication in reference was a literary monthly, unreadably pretentious, financed by either some cultural foundation or a university: he had seen only one copy, brought home by Babe, and had not read more than a few pompous lines of the text, certainly none of the poetry reviews. Nevertheless he told Gordon, "I must have seen some of your criticism there, just didn't realize you were the same person."

At last he had said the right thing. Gordon looked pleased. "Yes, *I* am G. S. Calhoun. 'Gordon' just doesn't sound like a poet to me."

"You're a poet as well?" This was a mistake.

"The collection's not out yet," Gordon said. "But most of the poems *have* been published in periodicals, so I think I can use the name."

"You've got a book coming out?"

"Next spring," said Gordon. "Burbage."

"You couldn't do better than that."

"They're never going to make me rich," Gordon said, "but they really do have a fine tradition of publishing verse. Almost nobody else does nowadays."

Wagner said dolefully, "They can afford it, with what they make from Wulsin's novels. By the way, I apologize for taking a crack at him before."

Gordon smilingly raised his hands. "I'm not to be held responsible for all the other books published by Burbage. As it happens, I agree with you about Teddy's work. But he's an awfully nice old guy."

Wagner was under the impression that Theodore Wulsin was only a year or so older than himself. He clasped his hands together. "On another subject, Gordon: you haven't, have you, noticed anything odd in the men's room lately?"

Gordon had a steep and smooth brow. Faint furrows were rippling its surface now.

"What kind of odd things?"

Wagner saw the chance to make a minor point. "Well, if they're 'odd,' then I guess they don't belong to a kind."

A tremor of eye indicated that Gordon had been anyway grazed, though you'd never know it from his speech.

"Uh, no, I can't say I spend any more time there than necessary. Why?"

Already suspecting that it was quite possible he would regret having brought up the subject, Wagner nevertheless said, "There have been complaints."

"About what?"

Wagner lowered his voice. "Deviate activity."

Suddenly Gordon flushed. He spoke in a high-pressured undertone. "You're saying this because I'm a poet? Shit on you, Fred." He spun on his toes and went swiftly away.

What did that signify? Was it a red-herring reflex, or had he really wounded Gordon? Anything could be called poetry, after all, and apparently everything *was* called sculpture. Wagner decided not to worry about Gordon's snit, he who had just returned two thousand two hundred dollars so as to save the job of a little teller whom he did not even know. That's the kind of man he was.

What he had to do at this point was design a means that would bring him a lot of money without hurting anybody. He did not understand how it was possible for him to become invisible, but he was convinced he should not let his gift be used for ignoble purposes.

6

එ WAGNER ARRIVED HOME INVISIBLY. THOUGH THIS meant he had to wait for another arrival on whose heels he could enter the building, it was worth the trouble to evade the evening doorman, an effusive type who the night before had commented quizzically on Wagner's return alone and after the dinner hour.

"Mrs. under the weather?"

The provocative question forced Wagner to produce an ungrammatical answer, something he detested doing, but he felt he had to respond quickly and decisively, and therefore could not afford to be impeccable with a man who habitually said "they was" and "he don't."

"We each have our own independent career." His shrug was false, but the internal shudder was genuine.

"Yeah," said Max the doorman, who seemed too young for what was most of the time a passive job, "but you always eat together." By means of such particular observations he hoped to ingratiate the tenants, with an eye to holiday tips, and perhaps it was not the worst strategy — except of course in the case of someone with something to hide.

This was another menace against which invisibility was

marvelously efficacious. But he should probably remember to show himself periodically. Tonight he slipped into the lobby unseen, just behind an elderly woman who was leashed to a small woolly white dog. The animal of course was aware of him, but luckily was so spoiled as to be aloof and, after a quick twitching of nostrils, dismissed him from further consideration.

Swinging back the door, Max asked, "Sugar's bowels get settled down?"

"Just as I think so, he'll let go, wherever he is," said the old lady. Sugar led her around the corner to the northern wing. Funny, while Babe was with him, Wagner would have liked to own a pet, but had no such urge now he was alone and could be expected to want company: his old idea of having a dog or cat was related to his concept of family.

He stopped off at the alcove in which the mailboxes were mounted, prepared to wait or go away if it was occupied. But nobody was there, and he slipped in and quickly unlocked and unloaded his box. One practice he had changed since Babe's departure: he had abandoned his old habit of discarding junk mail without opening the envelopes. Nowadays reading this stuff gave him something to do on entering the apartment.

The precedent, however, was to be broken this evening: the genuine first-class letters for once outnumbered the commercial importunities — which of course he could see only after he reached the apartment and became visible. (Using the elevator would have been too risky; anyway it was good exercise to climb the four flights of stairs.) Indeed, the only impersonal communication consisted of a pitch for a new dishwashing detergent, along with a discount coupon to be presented on the purchase of a box. Wagner opened this envelope first, prolonging the suspense evoked by a pink oblong unmarked except for his name, and postponing the displeasure he knew awaited him inside the letter bearing his sister's return address. It was too soon for Nan, across the country, to have received the communication he had sent but a day earlier — even though in some ways it seemed long, long ago, for he had first become publicly invisible on the occasion of that mailing, and had done so many things since in consequence.

To read a message from a Nan who would naturally assume that her sister-in-law was still in residence had to be a painful experience, for though his sibling always addressed him exclusively, her only acknowledgment of his existence was so to speak reflected off his wife: *tell me about Carla.* He could not remember when Nan had last inquired as to his own state of being.

Finally, on the simulated elevation of a deep breath, he opened her envelope. For the first nine handwritten pages, in a small but almost painfully clear script, the letter proved to be not so bad as he had anticipated, consisting of but a dogged list of the recent activities of each member of her five-person family, over which his eyes could soar without ever coming in for a landing. Then suddenly, there it was, on the last quarter-page: "Please pass along my love to Carla. How she can put up with you, I can't imagine. Must be charity, don't you think?"

In some families, no doubt such sentiments would be affectionate chaff, but not here. Nan candidly disapproved of her brother; she still clung stubbornly to her conviction that he should have entered a profession, preferably law, but even university-level teaching would have met her minimal requirements. The trouble was that being six years his senior and of a much more assertive temperament than

117

their male parent, Nan had taken over when their mother went into the lengthy illness from which she eventually died. It had to be admitted that Nan did everything well. At seventeen she was an excellent cook and a much more efficient housekeeper than Mother had ever been, and despite her new burden of work, remained the same honor student as before.

Though offered scholarships to glamorous campuses, she went on to attend the local university, so she could live at home and maintain care of her otherwise helpless menfolk, then in the interests of the same responsibility endured an overlong engagement to a successful young corporation lawyer. She married only after their father died and Wagner obtained his BA. She assured her brother she would have stayed on had he gone to graduate school. But he told her that such was his principal reason for not doing so. The one reward Nan could never earn from him was not gratitude, which he could allow, but rather forgiveness. The constant emotion he evoked in her appeared to be resentment. They rarely spoke together on the telephone, and had never met since she and the lawyer moved to the other coast and produced three children, in addition to which Nan sold real estate and was involved in the many other activities enumerated in the quarterly newsletters, which Wagner not even in palmier days did more than scan. As to the admired Babe, his wife had had no more interest in Nan than he had.

He now took Nan's pages to the bathroom, where he tore them into bits which he flushed down the toilet. Only by such means could he hope to withstand the impulse to reply spitefully and thus nullify the effect he had hoped to create with the almost serene message of his previous letter, in which with all his literary talent he had contrived to make Babe's departure seem to be the product of their collaborative and amicable best judgment and not really a separation so much as the establishing of alternative residences which they might well, according to the prevailing winds and their respective professional responsibilities, occupy together or severally. The point was not to let the world define the limits or for that matter the expanse of their association. That he knew before the fact that not only would such a picture immediately be seen by Nan as a false one, but also the style in which it was painted would infuriate her, went without saying. Whenever Wagner wrote to his sister, his real statement was a rejection of her values.

Now for the matter of the pink envelope, unstamped and still warped from having been folded into a form slender enough to be inserted into the slit of the mailbox. Wagner knew it was technically illegal to place anything that did not bear a stamp into any receptacle for which the Postal Service was responsible, even these personal boxes in the lobby of a private apartment building. In practice he had never even heard of an attempt to enforce this law, so it stayed a mere curiosity.

"Dear F. Wagner," began the pink note he took from the envelope,

> I have just learned, quite by accident I assure you, that like me tho for a quite different reason, you too are living alone and lonely at the present time. I've just got a bright idea: why don't we combine forces for dinner tonite? At my place. I'm buying, but I wouldn't be offended by a bottle of wine. It's now 4:10. I'll wait till 8 for your reply, phone or in person preferably.
>
> Your neighbor,
> SANDRA BARROWS (formerly Elg)

Wagner wondered whether it might not be bad taste for her so quickly to replace her husband's name with, presumably, that by which she had been known as a maiden. He thought about that so as to avoid reacting to the surprise of the invitation. He never liked being taken socially unawares; he usually tried to contrive a nonchalance on such occasions. For example, he had first seen Babe in a supermarket. He had been attracted by the sheen of her hair. But then when he saw the ivory ovoid of her face he was put off slightly, not by her features but rather her expression as she pondered on the oranges. However, having at last rejected this fruit in favor of Anjou pears — to Wagner a somewhat incongruous alternative, since the replacement was not in the citrus family — she rounded off her chin and retracted the nose which had been slightly extended, and Wagner's judgment too was altered. She was not pretty, but she might be beautiful. She was certainly beautiful to him: when he was so convinced, he cared little for the tastes of the world if they were at variance with his own, and he did not know that they were. But having made this assessment, he had selected his own three tangerines and moved on. It was three aisles later on, at the frozen-dinner case, that he was spoken to by someone who turned out to be the young woman he had noticed in the fruit department.

"Are those *really* nourishing?" The question referred to the cold, hard package he was at the moment extracting from a stack of same on the freezer shelves.

He was much taken with her voice. In those days Babe was in the habit of giving arbitrary, soprano emphasis to certain words. Formal analysis might deny any special meaning to the results of such a practice: for example, he should not have said his selecting the Down Home Meat

Loaf implied that he was authenticating the product as to its nutritive content. But the musical liquidity with which she pronounced "really" was irresistible.

"I never have thought about that," he answered. "I just buy it because it tastes better than the other dinners. And the little compartmentful of cherry pie isn't bad."

"I don't know," said she. "I really hate to let some company choose the *entire* menu for the dinner I'm going to eat alone."

"Oh," said Wagner, "but now you're no longer speaking about nourishment."

"I don't care," said she, presenting him with her full face, her candid brown eyes just below the forehead-fringe of precisely cut bangs. "I *just* wanted to say something."

This confession startled Wagner to the degree that, though it seemed as if it might well lead to the realization of the stillborn fantasy he had undergone at the fruit bins, he was now disconcerted.

"I'm glad you did then," said he. "It's nice to do something one wants to do and not be punished for it." It was a statement that had no intentional purpose: it represented mere nervous *gaucherie;* he had of course not been at all prepared to be spoken to by anybody on this occasion, let alone by her.

Yet her assessment of it was honorific. "Then I *was* right," she said, with a movement of mouth that he learned in time was her version of a grin. "You *have* a sense of humor."

Nevertheless he still had no self-command. "Thank you." He produced a niggardly smile. He closed the case, but then immediately opened it in courtesy, offering the door to her.

He was actually moving away when she asked, holding

the freezer door open, "What about the Sauerbraten with Red Cabbage and *Potato* Pancake?"

He turned back. "That comes with the apple strudel, which stays awfully soggy if you don't heat it longer than their directions say. If you do, the meat gets dried out."

"You never thought of *taking* the strudel out and heating it on its own?"

"It's not worth that much to me," said Wagner. "Fact is, I don't even like strudel when it *isn't* soggy."

Now the woman whom he eventually knew as Babe laughed outright. For a moment he worried about the kind of person who would even see that confession as humorous. But to his relief, she did not. Apparently she had laughed, the way people do, because she shared a particular prejudice.

"I hate *strudel*," she said with enthusiasm.

"A meeting of minds," Wagner lamely observed.

Carla shrugged. Without warning she turned all but indifferent. She showed him a slight frown, took from the freezer case not the Sauerbraten but rather the worst of all available frozen dinners, the Filet of Fish: if heated sufficiently to crisp the breading, the fish would be much overcooked, not to mention that the garnishes did not inspire respect: so-called Spanish rice, flecked with pimiento and something green, and a paste made of yam surmounted by several miniature marshmallows: dessert was butterscotch pudding, not that different in color from the mashed yam and not quite as sweet.

Wagner returned the shrug, though with her back towards him she would not have seen it. "Fair enough," said he, turned, and began to push his cart away. But then he remembered a detail that stopped him.

Carla had no cart nor even one of those hand-baskets. It

looked as though all she was buying was the fish dinner. She carried nothing else.

Wagner wheeled back to her. "Did you lose those pears I saw you take?" He had an impulse of panic: she wore a baggy coat, perhaps was shoplifting the fruit.

"Had second thoughts," she said. "I don't *like* pears. I'm awfully cranky about food. I used to drive my mother crazy: wouldn't eat most of what she put on the *table*."

"I usually ate it, or some anyway," Wagner eagerly admitted. "But I rarely liked it." This was not an appropriate place to say that the meals prepared by his sister had been an immense improvement.

"On the other hand," Carla said, "I can be a glutton if it's *something* I like."

Wagner asked what would fall into that select category. He was cautious about listing his own favorites first, afraid that she would shoot them down, diminishing the affinity that seemed to be in the air.

"They change from time to time," was however all she would say, and the statement was certainly borne out through the subsequent four years spent in her proximity.

. . . Sandra formerly Elg was well-upholstered, upstairs and down, though bisected by a conspicuously small waistline. He was not quite sure what she wanted of him. If it was sex, he might have a *mauvais quart d'heure*. He could not envision having any desire for her, and a man was not expected to be able gracefully to extricate himself from the grasp of a lustful woman: it would seem to go against nature's design. The only two possibilities were: professing to either inversion or intimate disease. Cal Cavanaugh, Wagner's old college friend, had claimed as an undergraduate to have been sexually importuned by his own stepmother; when he pretended to be attracted exclusively to his own kind, she threatened to inform his father unless Cal submitted to her cure, so he had no choice. Wagner might have believed this story had Cavanaugh not been an established Munchausen, with a ready tall tale on any theme, and had not their current assignment in French been *Phèdre*. However, like so many of Cal's imaginative constructions, it seemed sound in its approach to human character. It was Cavanaugh, with his sense of things that might even be called Balzacian, who should really have written novels. Yet Cal sold real estate, and insurance, in a little town too remote to be called suburban, and had a sizable family and no regrets. Unfortunately for Wagner's purposes, Cal had long since become a bore who no longer even told tall stories.

There was no lack of good reasons why Wagner should have refused the invitation of Sandra now Barrows, perhaps foremost amongst them his weariness owing to the taxing events of the day — becoming invisible certainly took some energy both physical and psychic, added to which expenditure must be the demands made on the nerves by the two episodes in the bank, the second of which had been unusually stressful. Then he had had abrasive moments with both Jackie Grinzing and Gordon the glorified office boy, who however was a published poet — and now, that his reaction to Wagner's remarks was examined in cold blood, pretty likely to be queer.

No doubt Wagner found himself dining with Sandra because on this evening she was the only person extant who knew of his domestic plight and still approved of him to the degree that she would ask him to her home; that she might have selfish designs on him did not alter the foregoing truth. Mutual back-scratching is no perversity in this world of ours.

It was understandable that Sandra began by talking about her own marriage, and what she said was instructive. Though hers had been terminated by chance, she revealed it to have been no more trouble-free than his own. As it turned out, her late husband had never been more than a fake, and to a degree not even she had suspected until he was dead. For example, he had never been a racing driver. Nor, despite a gaudy military decoration he had once shown her as that of an award for bravery under fire, had he ever been under arms. He had once been tried and found guilty in a court of law for his role in a confidence scheme and given a suspended sentence. This, with other depreciatory information, had been furnished Sandra by her spouse's elder brother, and it seemed true enough, for not only was it in accord with what Sandra knew as facts, but her brother-in-law, a modest high-school teacher, had nothing to gain by unjustly disparaging his dead kin. Indeed, he had, in an offer that must be called saintly, vowed to do what he could to help the widow meet some of the many unpaid bills left behind by the fraudulent one.

"Of course I refused," Sandra said over the main course, which throughout her monologue she never touched. "The poor man obviously needs every cent from his little salary. Turns out he's got three kids. You know Miles never *mentioned* a brother?"

"Miles Elg," said Wagner, who was eating with a better appetite than he had had even at A Guy from Calabria. If he dined away from home often enough, he might begin to recover the weight he had lost since Babe left. Funny: he recognized what he was chewing as none other than the Down Home Meat Loaf that had been a regular feature on the weekly menu since his bachelorhood and through the time of Babe, but nowadays he could hardly swallow two forkfuls of that which he thawed for himself. "Interesting name." He felt an obligation to say something favorable about the late Elg, whom he had known only as Sandra's companion on a handful of chance meetings in hallways or lobby, during the less than two years in which the Elgs had been fellow residents of his.

"The real one was Milton Alger," Sandra now told him, blinking her eyes as if to relieve the burden of the heavy makeup on the lids. Her scent had been used too lavishly, as well, and apparently not only on her person but sprayed throughout the living-dining room, obliterating any aroma that might have emanated from the food. Wagner was not displeased: the smell made the place seem homey — not with respect to the apartment he had shared with Babe, who eschewed the use of perfume for the reason that it gave her a headache, but with memories of his childhood home, for his mother, a feckless cook who often burned dinner, was wont lavishly to distribute sweet-smelling sprays throughout the house.

"Miles," Sandra went on, "couldn't leave anything as it was. Maybe he could have, had anything he was associated with been a genuine success, but that never happened."

She paused for a swallow, not a sip, of the red wine Wagner had brought. He himself had never honored the Down Home Meat Loaf with wine, but he realized he had been wrong: there was a nice wedding of tastes here, something his hostess had yet to experience, at least at this meal, for while she was on her second glass — after probably three vodka-rocks, anyway, the last in accompaniment of the first course, that shrimp cocktail that comes, already ketchup-sauced, in its own thick flutelike glass — she had not put a fork in the plate before her.

"He was trying to enhance his life," Wagner said, making something between a statement and a question.

"That's putting the best face on it," said Sandra, whose décolletage was not now as immodest as it had been while her spouse was alive. "He could just simply be called a goddamn phony."

Her basic emotion might be bitterness and not simply self-pity, and it caused Wagner to reflect on his own emotional response to Babe. No, he would have to stick with feeling sorry for himself: he could not selfishly disparage her motives to succeed professionally in the absence of the detrimental effect he had had on her self-determination even though (as she had admitted) wishing her well.

Sandra put her glass down for a change and, with extra feeling, looked across the table at him. "I don't enjoy talking ill of the deceased, Fred, but a lot of these things I never knew earlier, and the things I did know about I seldom mentioned just so as to keep the peace. So if I kept silent now, I wouldn't ever be able to have my say. It's just not fair."

"You've got the right, Sandra," said Wagner. "You say anything you want."

She took more wine. As yet she had shown no effect from the alcohol. "People think Miles died in a car crash. He didn't. He was in a hotbed hotel with a whore, and there was a toilet just over the room they were in, which some drunk put too much paper into, and it overflowed when he flushed it. This had happened once too often, and the ceiling collapsed, coming down on Miles. He was on top at the time, so cushioned her from the worst of it, but she got a broken leg and some bruises. And you know what? She got a shyster lawyer who's filed a suit against the

127

hotel and also the *estate of Miles Elg* — which means me, in effect."

Wagner now sipped some of his own wine. He had had but a quarter-glass thus far, and not even half a vodka martini. The warmth he felt could hardly be from brooze. Unexpectedly he was enjoying himself, in spite of Sandra's woe: but wasn't life like that?

"I seriously doubt," said he, "that the case will actually get into court. The law is often foolish, but there's a limit."

Sandra went on after taking more wine. "That's the least of my worries. The laugh's on the bitch: Miles doesn't have an estate. All he left was unpaid bills."

Wagner wondered whether she would eventually get around to putting the bite on him for a loan. The fact was he had more funds at this time than he had ever before possessed. Babe was self-sustaining, indeed she had refused his offers of money: had her inheritance and then the salary paid her by Guillaume. She assertedly lived in a modest apartment at an address she kept secret from him. He had the phone number, and he forwarded to the gallery any mail that came for her. He had no urge to follow her home from work: she claimed to live alone; he did not want to catch her in a lie.

"Uh," he said now, "I'm not rich, but if you could use a little something to tide you over . . ."

"Well, aren't you nice," said Sandra, "but you see, I'm no worse off now than when Miles was alive. In fact, I'm financially better off. I *supported* the fucker! Forgive me for using the vernacular, but I'm not just being foulmouthed for its own sake. That's the only word I can use for him, because that's all he could honestly do, but he was a genius at it. I'll grant him that. It was natural for him to die in the saddle."

Wagner was not disconcerted by this information. He certainly felt no rivalry with the late Miles Elg, perhaps because Babe had thought the man so vulgar, everything she detested: i.e., tall, tanned out of season, conspicuously fit. She liked ugly bad-skinned runts like Siv Zirko — this bitter reflection appeared from nowhere.

"Isn't it odd then that he would have gone to a prostitute?"

Sandra snorted. "I just call her whore. She's somebody's wife. Miles never paid for sex. He didn't have to, for God's sake. Everybody was after that schlong of his. I wouldn't have put it past *him* to have asked for pay from some." She breathed deeply and looked down at her plate, but still did not touch its contents. When she raised her head she was in another mood. "But I've been doing all the talking, Fred. Don't you want to tell me *your* troubles?"

"I've been trying to keep them secret around here," said Wagner. "Would you mind telling me who told you?"

"I ran into your ex," Sandra said. She wore large gold circlet earrings that bounced when she spoke on an ascending note. Wagner had never been a good judge of whether red hair was genuine or dyed. He was trying to divert his attention from Sandra's encounter with Babe. "She came in for tea where I work."

"A restaurant?"

"The Tally Ho English Lounge of the Hotel Pierce," said Sandra. "They serve sandwiches and drinks except from three to five daily, P.M., when we have our teatime, which is famous around town, with an assortment of little canopies and petty fours. The waitresses dress up like Elizabethan barmaids."

Wagner was just trying to picture Sandra in such a costume when she elucidated. "I play harp there."

He was impressed. "Golly. I'll have to drop in, but you say it closes at five?"

"Just teatime. I continue on till eight, throughout cocktails. Today's one of my days off, because I work weekends."

"You're a harpist."

"That's right. I keep the instrument at the Lounge. It's too bulky to bring back and forth. Else I'd give you a private recital."

He had postponed the question as long as he could. "I suppose Babe was not alone."

"Babe? Oh, your wife?"

"Sorry," said he. "Carla."

"That's all right," Sandra said. "I was Kiddo. But that wasn't really a nickname of my own. *Everybody* was Kiddo to Miles, male or female, or for that matter, a dog or cat." Her eyes quickly filled with tears. "Excuse me," she said, dabbing at her face with the paper napkin. "Worthless though he was, he was an awful lot of fun to be with, sometimes, and I miss the hell out of him."

Wagner's feelings of well-being were now in question. He did not belong here, at an end-of-table that was the rightful place of another man. He could never be a substitute for Miles Elg — not that he would necessarily want to be, though it was true enough that he found Elg's amorality not unattractive: it was not rare for such characters to have a concomitant verve of the kind to which Sandra had just referred. Whereas people with his own sense of responsibility tended to be sentimental, which in practice often meant melancholic. Were the situation reversed, with a living Elg's having usurped his own place at table, one could be sure that the charming scoundrel would not feel inadequate though Babe despised him. Wagner even had the advantage: he was liked by Sandra.

"Forgive me, Fred," she asked, lifting both hands with all their rings, the crumpled napkin in the left. "No more, I promise. It's not fair to you. Please go on. I'm interested, believe me."

Wagner swallowed the rest of the contents of his glass. Sandra immediately refilled it and topped off her own.

"The facts are simple enough," said he.

"By the way," Sandra said, "she came into the Lounge with a woman, not a man. Their table was nearest the harp; they had cinnamon tea and toast. I stopped by on my break, and she told me she didn't live here any more."

"Carla left supposedly so she could be on her own, whatever that means." Using her proper name transformed Babe into a stranger, whatever he meant by saying "whatever that means," for obviously her intent was clear enough: to escape from him. "She works at an art gallery. She knows a good deal about the subject, majored in art history. I guess she's always wanted a gallery of her own. Recently she inherited some money. Not a fortune, but apparently enough in her view to make a start. She's still at the old place, but is preparing the ground for the new enterprise. After all, she's got to find the right space. But most importantly, a gallery can't get going without art-works. Any artist already established naturally has a gallery. She needs a few people of that sort, so she can afford to launch the unknowns." Considered in this light, nothing could have been more reasonable than her eating dinner with Zirko. Wagner realized his explanation was meant more for himself than for Sandra, who in fact, with wandering eyes that were still retaining tears, gave evidence that his remarks had failed to distract her from her memories.

He decided to be dramatic, forgetting briefly that the account of his own role could hardly be literal. "Still, it was quite a shock to run across her having dinner in a restaurant with some guy I had never seen before. He turned out to be a famous artist, though, so it was not personal."

He had now caught Sandra's interest. She smiled. "Probably a fag."

Wagner was jealous of what he saw as his own peculiar right to speak ill of Zirko and therefore now defended his enemy. "Oh, no. He's world-famous."

"All the more reason, then," Sandra said smugly. "That's the normal thing, not the exception." She divided between their glasses what was left in the wine bottle.

"Not true in this case! In fact, this man, who's named Siv Zirko, is quite a, uh" — he at last found an inadequate term — "ladies' man."

"If that's so, then why weren't you more worried?" The question was affectionately derisive; she was gently baiting him.

He opened his hand. "All right. I *was* worried. I tell you I wasn't sorry when they had a fight and Babe left the restaurant in the middle of the meal."

"You were sitting there watching all of this?"

"I was quietly eating my own dinner. Am I to go away hungry just because my estranged wife comes to the same restaurant?"

"Know what Miles would have done?" Sandra asked.

Wagner said resentfully, "Oh, sure: beat up the other guy."

Sandra smirked, her earrings dancing. "Are you kidding? He was as yellow as they come. He backed down from guys half his size. Naw. He would have gotten hold of me later on in private and slapped me silly."

"You can't be serious."

"I told you he was a bastard. Not that I condone that, but it did serve to get it out of his system."

Obviously he and she were in different traditions. "Uh-huh. Well, that's not my style."

"Maybe it should have been? At least it shows you care."

"I'd like to think there are" — he had been about to say "better ways," but that would not have been considerate if Sandra, in her bereavement, missed the loving punches of yore — "there are other ways to show affection."

Sandra moved her chair back and rose. "Oh, affection," she said contemptuously. "I'm talking about passion." She went, in a not altogether straight line, to the secretary desk, the bookshelves of which served her as liquor cabinet. She opened the mullioned glass doors and considered the several bottles therein. In Wagner's boyhood home, such a repository held the twenty-five volumes of an encyclopedia his mother had purchased inexpensively, one book per week, at a supermarket; this reference work was never opened by anybody, for he trusted only the encyclopedias at school.

Sandra turned and spoke over her substantial right breast. "What is your pleasure?"

"Nothing, thanks. I've got enough wine to get to the end of the meal."

"I'm not much of a wine drinker. Not enough pizzazz, you know?" She reapplied herself to the cabinet, selected a bottle, and returned to the table. She half-filled her wine glass with an amber fluid. A whiff of the unpleasant odor, even without looking at the label, told Wagner it was Scotch.

She indicated the bottle. "Sure?"

"I'm no drinker," he said. He had cleaned his plate. He now saluted her with his glass and swallowed the remaining spoonful of wine.

He expected Sandra to gulp the whiskey, but he was wrong. She took only a modest sip. Holding the glass, she fixed him with a flushed eye. "No doubt you're aware I'm somewhat . . ." She fluttered her hand. "No." She waved off his ritualistic protest. "No, I *am.* That doesn't mean I talk through my hat, though. It does give me the nerve to say you may be too nice a guy for that woman you were married to."

"*Are,*" said Wagner.

"Are married to, OK. I see you still have hope of patching it up. But frankly that's never going to happen unless you change drastically." Sandra took another gingerly sip of the Scotch. Wagner disliked the smell, which seemed to him to be akin to the odor emitted by the transformer of an electric train, remembered over the years.

She gently shook the glass at him: the whiskey was un-iced. "I know I'm talking out of turn, but what good is booze if it doesn't come to that?" It sounded as though it might have been a bon mot of the late Miles. She grinned brilliantly. Perhaps her teeth were capped; entertainers after all had to meet a certain public standard. "She's a little cold-blooded snob. OK, so she's educated. Does that make her better than you? You're quite cultivated yourself, for gosh sake. That girl's just got a lot of bitch in her, Fred, and you've got to —"

"I can't listen to this," said Wagner, rising, catching the paper napkin before it slid to the carpet. "Thanks for dinner, Sandra. I really enjoyed it."

"Now, come on . . ."

"I'm sure you mean well, but I can't listen to such abuse. You wouldn't want me to attack your late husband."

Sandra smiled with an open mouth. "There's nothing you could say that would be too bad about that son of a bitch."

"You don't mean that. You loved him."

"What's that got to do with it? That doesn't alter the fact he was a shit."

"Well, Babe's not," said Wagner. "She has a right to live as she wishes. I have nothing to criticize her for."

"C'mon and sit down," said Sandra. "I'll give you some dessert in a minute, and coffee." She raised her right hand. "I won't say anything more on the subject. Promise."

He had nowhere else to go except home, where it would still be early enough to feel guilty about not getting out his manuscript and rereading it hopelessly. Therefore he sat down, and, as good as her word, in a moment his hostess had gone back to the kitchen and returned with a wedge of pecan pie.

"Water's on," said she. Then, having poured herself more Scotch, "OK, she had her reasons. You can tell me, Fred, you know that: were you having troubles?"

He shook his head, chewing a forkful of pecan pie; it had been frozen and even now was only partially thawed. Finally he said, "I'm not that crazy about my job, which is writing, but not the kind of writing I really want to do. I guess I talk about that a lot, but I just can't seem to sit down and write when I'm home. I'm always too exhausted, and the ideas that come to me easily at other times vanish completely when I actually have to put them down on paper."

Sandra made a glittering, dismissive gesture with her free hand, which was even more beringed than the right.

"Forget about that. What I meant was sex. Did you have trouble giving satisfaction?"

Wagner could not believe the question was as he heard it. Chewing, especially on some substance like the cold nuts of the pie, could alter sounds considerably. His response was therefore limited to a trace of a smile.

"Because," Sandra went on, after so short a pause that he would not anyway have had time to answer, "it wouldn't necessarily be your fault. I don't automatically blame the man, like some girls I've known."

Wagner made a movement with his head. Once warmed by the mouth's natural heat, the pie was intensely sweet and impeded him from speaking, which was no doubt just as well.

An anguished shriek was heard from the kitchen.

"That's the water," Sandra said and got up. As she passed her guest she touched his shoulder, whether in friendship or merely to catch her balance, he could not have said.

When she returned with the cup of coffee and the cream-and-sugar tray and saw that he had finished the pie, she took away the dish and the Scotch bottle, then asked him to move slightly back. Reaching under the top of the table, she did something that made its legs slowly collapse and seize rigidly again only when it had reached the height of a coffee table.

"It's convertible," Sandra said. "You've got to have things like that to eke out the room in such a tiny apartment. Else you'd have to eat at the kitchen counter."

"Yes," said Wagner, "that's what we've always done." He had thought it nice and cozy, but he realized that if he confessed as much to Sandra she might think him soft.

"We can sit here now," said Sandra, indicating the adjacent sofa.

Wagner would have preferred to keep his chair, which was still in reach of the now stunted table, but he did not wish to offend. He sat down on the sofa.

Sandra retrieved the Scotch bottle from the floor, leaving behind the plate from which he had eaten the pie. "Won't you join me now?"

"No thanks," Wagner said. "I never drink much. I have a low tolerance for alcohol."

"So have I," said Sandra, pouring whiskey into her glass. "That's why I drink." Apparently this was not intended to be a joke, for she turned to him, glass in hand, and said soberly, "You might have medical problems."

"I just can't drink much without feeling it more than I like to."

"I don't mean that," said Sandra. "I meant the sex thing."

Wagner actually asked, *"What* sex thing?"

She gestured airily with her left hand while drinking from the right.

After an instant it occurred to him that she was referring to impotence, and he said heatedly, "There's nothing wrong with me!"

She smiled benignly. "Except the woman." She stood up and stepped before him, bent, and took his hand.

Sandra led him into a fancy bedroom, a place of satin coverlets and skirts on the vanity, and alternately undressed him and herself. Wagner had no taste for this enterprise, but it was now too late to become invisible without causing more trouble than he was having. Given the situation, he would have liked to be impotent at this moment, but Sandra simply would not permit it. Though having subordinated herself to her husband, she had become, perhaps in over-compensation, almost tyrannically assertive. In any event, she had her way with Wagner and, inconveniently for him, she found the result so satisfactory that even while he was still engulfed, she enthusiastically anticipated their ever more intimate association.

It was obvious that from now on he would do well never to be visible in the public areas of the building.

7

SANDRA WAS MOST RELUCTANT TO LET HIM ESCAPE.
It appeared that her original invitation to dinner had tacitly
comprised plans for breakfast as well, for which she had
provisioned her larder with crumb cake and sticky caramel
rolls. But though Wagner had been docilely led to bed, his
panic on learning of her assumption that he would spend
the night there, wearing the late Miles's striped pajamas, as
well as the golden terrycloth robe and heelless calfskin
slippers — these garments were handily laid out on the
nearby chair, demonstrating a shameless premeditation —
gave him the strength to be very firm in insisting he must
return to his own apartment and remain there till morning.
You see, he expected a late phone call from his sister, who
was in transit someplace, unreachable. His situation must
be known and fixed, since hers could not be. There could
be no argument against him at this point, and as to his
returning to Sandra after the call, Nancy was an inconsid-
erate nightowl: she might phone anytime at all, and he had
to go to work next day.

An extraordinary thing happened: what had been said as
a polite and somewhat elaborate lie became truth: Nan did
indeed telephone him, and furthermore at 2:15 A.M.

It had been ever so long since he had spoken with his sister, and her voice was now contorted with rage, but he knew no other female who would have called him in the wee hours and therefore recognized her immediately despite her failure to provide identification or, for that matter, greeting.

"You've really done it now, haven't you?"

"Hi, Nan," said Wagner. "How are you and Steve and all?" He could never remember all the names of her children and had to look up this information at Xmastime, when he sent each a piece of paper money enclosed in one of those cards made for the purpose, with an oval cutout through which the engraving of the appropriate President can be seen: in the case of those sent to extremely young people, he included in the holiday wishes a suggestion that the money might be banked for later use.

She now ignored his attempt to be civilized and more or less repeated, "You've gone and done it, haven't you?"

"You received my letter?" She had not awakened him, for as yet he had been unable to get to sleep, what with the amount of food in his stomach, not to mention the session in bed with Sandra.

It was typical of Nan to say nothing of his letter and not so much as acknowledge any of the argument within.

"Apparently she finally had it up to here, is that it?" she was asking, and because it was hardly a sincere question, went immediately on. "It might interest you to know, and if it doesn't, I'm going to tell you anyway: I saw this coming from the first. Carla was obviously too good for you, Freddy. I'm not being cruel: you know me too well for that. I wouldn't be saying this if I thought you lacked the ability to make something of yourself, but you don't, or anyway you didn't in college. You were an honors student, if you can remember that far back. We had reason to expect a great deal from you. Frankly, never till now had I given up all hope."

"I wish you'd actually read what I wrote," said he, "instead of, a continent away, arriving at a conclusion of your own. I told you she and I remain close. Only last night, for example, we went to dinner at a favorite restaurant of ours. Today I visited her at the gallery. Don't talk as if we're divorced. I explained the whole thing carefully, but of course you dismiss it, as usual."

"I've had your number for many years, Freddy. For example, I know it was you, and not Carla, who if she were permitted to be herself would be quite maternal, it was you who didn't want children. Carla's Italian: God, she's a natural mother, yet you —"

"Babe's not Italian," Wagner said in exasperation. "Where did you get that idea?"

But Nan, talking on through what was therefore not his interruption, continued. "And don't tell me her heart wasn't broken when you turned down that magnificent offer Steve got for you, at some cost to himself."

The reference here was to the editorship of the house organ for the corporation of which his brother-in-law was legal counsel. A four-page monthly, printed on a shiny stock from which they took the courage to call it a magazine, it consisted of photographs of the employees' bowling team, which had once again whipped all competitors from factories of a similar size and had all but held its own against the county championship squad from the sheriff's department. Aside from the relevant captions identifying the persons by department, and a headline, "Go, Hewco Keglers!" the only text in the specimen copy furnished to Wagner had been an encomium on a vice-president of marketing. Notwithstanding the breezy tone — "Ken's golf might not be quite up to the National Open, but he sure has fun at it" — this was a composition informed by little but rank obsequiousness. The fact was that Wagner's existing job did require the exercise of a gift for verbal expression; one had to write with precision. He might have been joking irreverently when he referred to Flaubert in his remarks to Mary Alice Phillips, but he had to believe that the great master, more than most, would have appreciated what was at stake in any use of language however humble the end to which it was directed.

"You know very well," he told Nan now, "that all of our professional connections are here. I won't go into that again."

"Ha!" jeered his sister. "And just what are *your* professional connections? When Grammuh Wilkie was a girl they had an outdoor privy where mail-order catalogues were used as toilet paper."

The reference was to their maternal grandmother. Wagner always winced at Nan's affected pronunciation of "Grandma," which she had assumed only since marrying into Steve's family, who were or pretended to be regionally genteel.

"All right, Nan," Wagner said, "once again you've proven unworthy of being sent any serious information. In future I'll confine my messages to those synthetic printed comments on commercial greeting cards. . . . For God's sake, I'm a writer. Why can't you *ever* just read what I've written?"

"You've been making that claim for years, and yet I have never seen a word of yours in print — I don't count that kitchen-appliance catalogue you sent me once! I'm afraid you're a phony, Freddy, and now Carla has confirmed that fact by walking out on you. How long can you keep telling yourself the same old lie?"

It was not a baseless question, and it found its mark in Wagner. Therefore he could survive only by compounding the falsehood.

"Goddammit, Nancy, I had intended to keep this a surprise for a while, but you're really forcing me to lose patience. *My book has been accepted by Burbage.*"

His sister was silent for a long moment, and then she said, "That means nothing to me, Freddy. Who or what is that silly name?"

With a derisive stage laugh, Wagner said, "Only the most distinguished publishing firm in the country. Their authors include Theodore Wulsin, who's widely considered a living classic."

"Uh-huh," grunted Nan, who had never, so far as he knew, read a book whose primary purpose was not didactic. "Does he make a living?"

"For God's sake, of course! He's won all the prizes, visits the White House, and so on. You know, Nan, someone at your well-to-do level of society really should be more conversant with the serious culture of our time."

He wasn't getting far. She responded to his gibe by groaning, "So says the voice from the cheap seats! Tell me this, Freddy: why were you keeping this so-called news as a surprise? On what occasion did you intend to reveal it?"

"As soon as the movie deal was finalized," said he, so desperate he was able to use, without a tremor, that word he had always thought an abomination. But perhaps it was the very term that evoked Nan's credence now: "finalized" of course was one of the basics of the jargon of her milieu. And when he added another — "hopefully" — he had begun to hold his ground.

For the first time a note of other than self-righteous certainty could be detected in her voice. "You're kidding now, Freddy, aren't you?"

"Would I joke when I finally have a good answer to the vicious attacks you've been making on me for years?"

"You have sold this story to the movies?"

"I'm being cautious," said Wagner. "I haven't signed the contract yet." He hastily added, "*They* have, though, so the deal is up to me to accept, but there are some clauses I want to think about awhile."

Nan cried, "You rush a copy to Steve before you sign a thing, you hear? Make use of this wonderful legal expertise at your disposal!"

Wagner sighed audibly. "Don't you think I have my own movie lawyer? These contracts are very special, require an expert." What a good time he was having now!

His sister's tone was softening as she spoke. "I suppose a thing like this can be profitable, Freddy?"

"Very," said Wagner. He then coolly specified an outlandish figure.

Nan obviously heard this, but had an emotional need not to acknowledge it directly, saying instead, "Malcolm's the one with the writing talent: the other day he produced his own newspaper with those letter-stamps and a stamp pad. It was all about the life of the family, including Spunky naturally."

Wagner could not remember whether Malcolm was the youngest or the middle child. Spunky was probably a dog or cat.

"Of course," he said, "the share of the box-office receipts could be a lot larger than that, providing the picture is a commercial blockbuster. Sid thinks it can be, but who knows?"

"Sid?"

"Sidney Guttman," he said. "The studio head."

"I'm sure I've heard of *him*," said Nan, who was now even prepared to swallow this invented personage.

Having done so well thus far, Wagner went further. "And Bill Fontina loves the script. He's dying to do it, if Sid will meet his terms, which are just about the stiffest in the Industry."

"Who?" Nan's question was respectful. She did not keep current with the cinema.

"William Z. Fontina. He won the Oscar last year."

Her breath could be heard. "Well," said she, "this is certainly good news. Tell me, Freddy, this book of yours: it's make-believe?"

"In a sense," Wagner said easily. "It's fiction, after all."

"What I mean is . . ." Nan paused for a moment, and then she blurted, "Freddy, might I ask if your story has anything to do with our family?"

Wagner was briefly silent: his ad hoc fantasy had as yet made no provision for plot or theme, for he had not been thinking of the fragment of novel he had called his own for some years and had apparently (for he had no memory of so doing) mentioned to most of his co-workers. That project could in this new light be dismissed. There should be no limitations on an imaginary narrative.

"There are certainly families in it," said he. "But lots of other things as well. It's a broad canvas. I suppose it's really about life, lives, in our time."

"Because," said his sister, still occupied with the matter of her question, "real people could be hurt, even if you weren't being malicious on purpose." She cleared her throat. "Dad's gone now, of course, but it would be too bad to hurt his reputation even so, and it certainly would be embarrassing to us out here."

"Dad? What are you talking about, Nan?"

"You know, that thing at church, when he was treasurer. After all, he returned most of the money, and it was hushed up at the time. Why reveal it after all these years?"

This was news to Wagner. After a moment, he said, "I agree, and I haven't referred to it."

"Good," said Nan. "You're a decent man, Freddy. I'm sure I don't have to ask if you have used the unpleasant incident involving, uh, you know George Monrovey."

Wagner vaguely recognized the name as being that of a high-school teacher of long ago, but he had no other associations for the name, Monrovey having gone before he himself had reached high school.

However, some instinct now restrained him from assenting too readily to whatever Nan was pleading. "Well, not quite. Maybe I've used certain elements in, uh, a montage, a rearrangement of course —"

"Oh no, you can't," Nan all but wailed, though in a voice with lowered volume, indeed almost a whisper. "He's an old man now, if he's alive at all. Look, he lost his job and his wife of twenty years. Isn't that punishment enough? Let it stay under the rug, I beg you, Freddy. It would sound so sordid at this late date, but it wasn't that ugly at the time. George was a sensitive man." Her voice had become tender.

Wagner had never suspected that his sister could have been sexually attractive to anyone at any age: without consciously thinking about it, he somehow assumed that Steve had been interested in her organizational abilities and had fathered her children as the performance of his role in a rite.

At length, having enjoyed the suspense, he said, "OK. But I wouldn't do it for anyone else but you, Nan." For the first time in his life he now found it possible to say, "I owe you a lot. I haven't forgotten how you stayed behind till I grew up. Thanks, sis."

Nancy was sobbing: another thing he had not suspected she had in her was tears.

After an assurance by Wagner that the family must certainly assemble for the premiere of the movie, the conversation reached its end, and when it had so done, Wagner's heart made a breathtaking descent. Alone in a bedroom that without a partner seemed vast as an empty gymnasium, he was left with only the truth, in which there was no place for anything he had said in the foregoing remarks except perhaps the expression of gratitude to his sister, but denied the pretext for such expression, *viz.*, a personal success, he could not even maintain that feeling for long. Indeed, within an instant his resentment towards Nan had compounded and returned: his outlandish lies were all her doing.

He spent a sleepless night, in the course of which he at one point rose, went to the little desk in the corner of the room, found his so-called manuscript in the bottom of the lowest drawer, under the rubber-banded bundles of canceled checks preserved for years should he be challenged to confirm routine payments made long ago, and taking what existed of his "novel" to the bathroom, tore it page by page into strips and sent it into the maelstrom of a flushed toilet.

When the last fragment had been devoured by the gulping water closet he knew a moment of liberation — this was a beginning; the new could not have got under way so long as the route was blocked by the old. As the Orientals know, creation and destruction are symbiotic, if not synonymous . . . but the moment was left behind as he stepped over the threshold of the bathroom, as if across an abyss, and he returned to bed with haste, so that he would not be tempted to go back to where his cutthroat razor was housed.

Sleepless and still dyspeptic at the time he would ordinarily have begun to prepare to leave for work, he decided to stay home. The company was intolerant of employees not sufficiently ill to enter a hospital: migraines, lower-back aches, flus with temperatures under 100, nonbandaged unslung limbs however bruised or strained, these were officially assumed to be but symptoms of the proscribed disease of malingering. He was well aware that if he phoned in to Jackie Grinzing he would be challenged to defend himself, and the fact was that he would not be staying away from the office had he not felt peculiarly defenseless this morning.

Therefore when the time came, about a quarter after nine, allowing Delphine to get through half the first cup of coffee and to light a second cigarette, he placed a call to his nearest office neighbor.

After an extra ring, the extension was answered by a voice that said, "Delphine Root's phone."

"She's not there?"

"She went to the toilet, I guess. Any message?" asked the person Wagner had now identified as Mary Alice Phillips.

"Mary Alice, Fred Wagner."

"That's a coincidence. I was just over here looking for you, Fred."

"Well, yes, I'm ill, Mary Alice, much too ill to get in there today: headache, fever, and so on —"

"Vomiting, diarrhea?" asked Mary Alice.

She could always provoke a wince. "No, no, not that."

Even though his plea was designed to be forwarded to Jackie Grinzing, Wagner could not resort to ugliness. "Double vision, and my head is throbbing with each word I speak. Tell Jackie for me, will you please? Her phone was busy last time I tried. I can't keep calling. I have to try to get out now and see my doctor." He added the last note to forestall Jackie's trying to reach him as soon as she received the news.

"Sure," said Mary Alice. "I'm really sorry, Fred. I hope you feel better soon. I'd volunteer to write your copy today, but in fact I'm having a lot of trouble with my own and wanted *your* help — which is how I happened to be in your vicinity." She would have talked more, and despite the banality of the subject, Wagner might have hung on awhile, for Mary Alice's telephone voice was very gentle, even sweet, qualities that struck just the right note for him at the moment, but he could hardly stay on the line interminably and sustain the simulation of illness. He therefore produced a groaning thanks and hung up.

The call he expected from Jackie, however, was not quick in coming. Therefore he did not dare fall asleep, for if the telephone rang while he was unconscious he was likely, with his instinctive tendency to respond to the peremptory summons of a bell, to pick up the instrument. He could not have held his own with Jackie in the ensuing exchange. There was no precedent for his claiming to a sudden indisposition: in six years he had never before been sufficiently ill to stay home from work. To make a performance believable now he must be incommunicado all day. Then, on his return the following morning, he would have to bring along a supporting document from a doctor, say an illegible prescription for a placebo, which could be easily obtained from his physician, a hurried practitioner who was never offended by the simple disorders that could be treated by capsule.

However, he could not call Dr. Leprak's office at a time when Jackie Grinzing might be trying to get through: a busy signal would nullify his alibi. There was nothing for it but to beg admittance at Leprak's office after 1 P.M., if the doctor's schedule remained the same as it had been during the previous year, when Babe had visited him several times with regard to a menstrual irregularity that proceeded to correct itself as soon as she proved to be nongravid. Wagner could not see what was so deplorable about having a child, though true enough he would not have been the one who bore it.

Until Jackie called, he had a morning to kill in another fashion than by sleeping. It would have been too easy to regret having destroyed the manuscript of his novel: good taste forbade him that bogus emotion. The story he had been trying to tell therein was essentially an autobiographical account of the period between the onset of the illness that kept his mother an invalid for many months and her death. What was wrong with this for purposes of fiction was that it had already taken place in time: to write about it was either to be a reporter or a liar, in either of which roles he would have felt as though he were corrupting private histories. Yet he had little gift for impersonal literary invention: he could not put himself inside supposititious skins, feel the heartbeats of fancy as if they represented the circulation of his own blood. . . . Invisibility was his proper medium.

Wagner arrived at this conclusion while in a state of somnolence, not fully conscious but not asleep either. Indeed it was the same state in which, utilizing the flashlight-pen, he had scrawled out those incoherent dream-thoughts.

But this one survived his full awakening, perhaps was what had awakened him.

He stayed awake when he heard the sounds of an incursion into the outer room of the apartment. It was someone bold and by no means stealthy, no doubt Glen the super or a professional admitted under his auspices: the roach-exterminator or perhaps a plumber in quest of the origin of the water that dripped mysteriously onto a lower floor. If such people appeared at times on Saturday, surely it was standard for them to work on weekdays: an apartment could never be considered one's castle, especially with an attendant functionary like Glen.

Wagner was somewhat annoyed now — perhaps irresponsibly so, for his own well-being might not be immune to some general menace like escaping gas — but certainly not apprehensive about burglars, Babe having taken with her the few objects of value they had possessed, including the miniature TV with the postcard-sized screen, the little netsuke baboon brought back by her father after a sabbatical in Japan, and a pair of sterling asparagus tongs, for all these had been her own before marriage. However, Wagner did not relish being seen, even by a janitor or a man whose job took him elbow-deep into toilets, in the disreputable nightclothes he had been wearing probably ever since Babe's departure, having no memory of recent alternatives: pale-blue sleeveless summer-pajama coat, stained with coffee and yolk of egg, worn above the jockey drawers of daytime service. The latter were changed occasionally and worn on a body that was often bathed, but in Wagner's solitary existence the pajama top was one of those things to which he was blind except at such a moment as this.

He could have sprung up and found a robe, even quickly pulled on pants and dropped a shirt over his head. But why bother? It was easier, and for that matter more amusing, to become invisible. His intention was sooner or later to wander out and, unseen, identify the purpose of his visitor, should the repair or adjustment, if such it was, leave more problems than it had answered, or if the roach poison had been distributed near an open box of cornflakes.

He inserted his feet into the rubber sandals that served as bedroom slippers and shuffled into the living room. Glen the super was there all right, but it was unlikely that his companion had a role in the maintenance of the building: the sluttish teenaged Todvik girl sprawl-sat on one element of the modular sofa, a cigarette drooping from her sticky red lips.

"You fucker you," she was saying to Glen, who stood before her in his dark-green super's clothes, "how much you really holding back for yourself?" When she moved her head the dependent ash on her cigarette almost let go but not quite.

"Be careful with that smoke," Glen said, putting out a dirty palm as ashtray. "I earn my money: I always got to pick up after you. You won't flush the toilet, and I've found used rubbers on the bedside rug." He made a face. "Yuck."

She tapped the ash into his hand. He went to the kitchen and could be heard running the water, presumably flushing his palm. When he returned he brought a fragment of aluminum foil. After fashioning it into a little receptacle, he presented it to Miss Todvik.

She made a face at him. "Where *is* the old bastard?"

"Probably got detained at his place of business."

"He must make a fortune selling furniture," said the Todvik girl. "And he can only pay twenty-five?"

Glen shrugged. "Well, business ain't so good at the moment."

"Naw," said she. "The truth is you're a lying prick. He probably paid you fifty, and you're taking as much for pimping as I get for doing the dirty work."

"Now, come on," said Glen. He looked genuinely hurt, but was probably acting. "I don't see you getting off your big fat lazy ass and hustling for yourself, and you're not the kind to join the stable of some nigger with a white suit and a Cadillac and get the shit kicked out of you if you don't hand all your earnings over. So quit complaining. You can't say I don't bring you clean, respectable guys."

She grimaced. "If there's anything uglier than a potbellied old man, I don't know what it could be."

"How about an old woman?" the super asked resentfully. "I'd hate to see *you* in a couple years. Your tits will be hanging to your knees."

She shook her head. "What can you expect from a faggot?" She got up. Glen was right: she did seem awfully flabby for such a young woman. She swaggered across to the Early American dry sink that served as liquor cabinet and swung open its doors. "Doesn't that stingy asshole *ever* buy a bottle of anything?"

"Cunt!" cried Glen. "I'm not queer. I'm getting into half the broads in this building, and you know it. If you don't think Kinney is paying you enough, then gimme back the money and get out. I'll find him somebody better-looking, which won't be hard."

"You mean you'll blow him yourself," said Miss Todvik, trying simultaneously to slam shut both parts of the double door, but the compression of the internal air prevented this from happening, and she kicked the panel on the right.

"Goddammit, didn't I just say be careful?" shouted Glen.

"Wagner ain't going to notice. He went around in a dream even before his old lady walked out. I practically rubbed against his dick one time on the elevator, and he never got the idea. No wonder she left."

"Good riddance," said Glen. "She had too high an opinion of herself."

"You mean she wasn't one of the ones you were balling?" asked the Todvik girl, and added with heavy irony, "*According to yourself, that is.*"

Glen was stung. He pursed his thin lips and said, "Oh, yeah, let me tell you something."

Wagner moved between them, intending to kick him savagely in the groin if he proceeded to stain Babe's name. But at that moment the two-toned chime of the doorbell was heard.

"Get in the bedroom and in the sack," Glen said in a loud whisper. "If he sees you undressing, he'll think you're thirty years old. *And put out that motherfucking cigarette.*"

She stuck out her tongue at him, gave him the red-smeared, smoldering butt and the foil ashtray, and went towards the bedroom with an exaggerated, hip-swinging walk.

Wagner had to leap aside, or Glen would have collided with him on the route to answer the chime. The super opened the door on a man who in addition to being the old and protuberant-waisted specimen the girl had foreseen, was also baggy-eyed and pouchy-throated.

While stepping across the threshold he asked, "And the young lady? Has she arrived?" He removed his felt hat and held it respectfully against the chest of his topcoat.

"Don't you worry about that," Glen said. He jerked a green shoulder in the direction of the bedroom. "She's waiting for you, hot as a firecracker."

The comment did not please the old man. He frowned. "She's just a young girl like you promised? I didn't pay you no hundred bucks for some worn-out old bag from off the street."

Glen put a finger to his own lips and lowered his voice. "Let's not talk business details now, Mr. Kinney. Get in there and go to town. She's just a little schoolkid."

The only attractive expression available to a man of Kinney's age was the paternal, but in reaction to Glen's promise his was hardly that. He all but showed his tongue as he hastened down the short hallway and into the bedroom.

Wagner followed in stupefied horror: he had no idea of what to do.

The Todvik girl had moved quickly. Her clothes were in a heap on the bedside chair, and she was sitting up in bed, propped by both Babe's pillow and Wagner's, the sheets and blankets lately vacated by Wagner drawn up to just below her large, spongy breasts. Though having surrendered the cigarette to Glen, she already had another in her sticky mouth. She now withdrew it so as, with lips in fake-prudish compression, mockingly to chide her superannuated customer.

"Why, Mr. Kinney! Ain't you the dirty old man!"

Kinney stopped just inside the doorway, still in his overcoat and holding his hat as if during the unfurling of the flag.

"Polly Todvik," said he, with a disapproval of his own, and not sounding as though it were mock, "what are you doing, smoking like that, at your age? I should tell your daddy!"

Polly shrieked more in amusement than in indignation, "Why, you old fuck you!"

Kinney shouted, spraying spittle, "Me? I come here to measure for the new bedroom set, you dirty little pig-girl." He whipped a tape measure from the pocket of his coat. "Filthy little hoor, don't you stick your naked boobies out at me! You cover up, you little tramp, and take away the smoke from out your mouth." He was thrusting a fore-finger at her now, jabbing the air to make repeated points.

Glen ran in from the living room, Wagner stepping aside just in time. "Why you giving Mr. Kinney trouble?" he shouted at Polly. "Sorry, Mr. Kinney." He turned solici-tously to the old furniture merchant. "You just go ahead and get your clothes off. She'll do what she's told. She's just being temperamental, you know? She's just a dumb kid."

Kinney's face was colorless, except for his lips, which looked blue. "Oh, yeah?" he shouted. "What you got going here for yourself, you criminal, a hoorhouse? I only come about some furniture. You think you can shake me down, you two pieces of turd? I'll see you in jail!" The hand holding the hat was now crushing it against his heav-ing left breast. He was gasping for breath.

"Jesus sake," cried Glen. "You having a heart attack?" He called to Polly, "C'mon, we got to get him outside before he dies here."

She sprang naked from bed to take Kinney's left arm, or rather to try to pry it away from his chest, for the old man resisted her strenuously.

Wagner moved to stamp out the burning cigarette Polly had dropped on the rug.

Glen was shouting in Kinney's face, "You got pills?"

Kinney's response was a munching movement, which was eventually proved to be a gathering of saliva when he spat into Glen's face.

"Shit," said the super, "now he's frothing at the mouth." He leaned over and wiped his cheek on Kinney's shoulder, then sought to take the old man's other arm.

But the merchant pulled it free and slapped the side of Polly's head. "Get off'n me, you dirty slut."

Glen was still obsessed with the need to remove Kinney from the premises. "We got to get him inna hall. Then he could of died for any reason. Nothing to connect him with us."

"He ain't dying," screamed Polly. "He's beating me up." She kicked Kinney with her bare foot. "You old cocksucker!"

"Are you insane?" shouted Glen. "Going to kill him here?" He was trying without success to draw Kinney out the bedroom door, but whether or not the old man was dying, he was not cooperating in the effort. Indeed, he was fighting more savagely than ever.

Wagner feared that at any moment now someone might damage what was left of his possessions. Of course at this point he could have made what would seem to be a supernatural intervention: could have said something from thin air, taken them one by one by the scruff of the neck and the seat of the pants in a frog-march to the front door, for though Glen was young and fit, Wagner would have had an advantage that might have stunned a giant. But he was not yet ready so to challenge the natural state of affairs, and anyway the purpose here was to get rid of all three intruders in the neatest and most decisive manner, not to provide futher complications that might, by inspiring wonder, delay the general exit.

The problem was one for which Wagner could find no help in experience. All the same, in a trice he had let himself silently out of the apartment into the hallway, where he banged on his own door and in a simulated voice of loud and heavy authority, cried, *"This is the police. You in there, quiet down."*

After a moment Glen answered. "Sorry, officer. We was just arguin' about furniture."

"Just keep it down," said Wagner.

When enough time had elapsed for the policeman to have left, the door opened to emit Kinney, who appeared to have recovered to the degree that he could leave under his own power. He continued to shake his hatted head and murmur bitterly as he went down the hall to the elevator.

Wagner had caught the door before it closed and slipped in. Glen and a fully dressed Polly stood nearby.

"You stupid cunt," Glen was saying. "Whyn't you tell me you knew the old bastard so well?"

"What difference would that of made?" she asked indignantly. "He wanted a young girl. So he recognized the one he got! I used to play on the sidewalk outside his store when I was a little kid."

Glen scowled at her. "You don't have any feelings at all. Something's wrong with you."

"I'm not a fucking crook like *you*," Polly said. "That was more than five bucks you added to my money when we gave it back."

"Yeah, well, the pity was we had to give him a refund." He threw his thumb at the door. "Go ahead, you first."

"*I* wouldn't have returned the money, it been up to me," she said. "He wasn't in no position to tell, with what we got on him, looking for a young girl to ball."

"What you don't know is he gives cops a discount on furniture. He could put them onto us, see, and who'd they believe?"

Polly cocked her hip and slapped the substantial right buttock. "You don't think a cop'd like some of this?"

"Get going," Glen said with disgust. "You got an exaggerated idea of your charms. Cops can fuck anybody they want."

He waited until a few minutes after Polly's departure to make his own. After Glen had left, Wagner went on a tour of inspection and found that the bed had been neatly remade and the cigarette butt removed from the rug, leaving only a little place of charring. This cleanup was not however sufficient to mollify him. Glen had obviously made previous use of the apartment as a brothel, perhaps even while Babe lived there. And what was perhaps worse, the wretched super knew very well, as did the sluttish Polly, that the Wagners were separated, and if Glen knew, so did the entire body of tenants, which among other things meant that the comment of Max the doorman, the evening before, had been not innocent but knowingly malicious.

Indeed it must be the case that he was being secretly jeered at by many, including the attractive young women whom simply as a matter of male pride he especially did not want privy to his shame, Ellen Mackintosh and Debbie Fong.

It was almost noon before the telephone rang. Why Jackie had waited so long was a mystery. In any event he would have his alibi for not answering. He showered and dressed and left the apartment to go to the doctor. He now had more reason than ever not to be seen, and therefore he made himself invisible just before stepping out the door.

8

ക WAGNER MET NO ONE IN THE ELEVATOR, BUT A
stout woman took up most of the space in the mailbox-
alcove off the lobby, and finding a sizable quantity of enclosures in her box, she stayed there to peruse each.

When he was finally able to reach his own mail, and
become visible in order to read it, he found he had received
none that bore a stamp, but already there was another pink
envelope from Sandra, this one so pungently scented as to
perfume the entire nook.

> Darling —
> Silly me, I tried to phone you about 11:30 today.
> Don't know what it's like to have a man who earns a
> living!!! Darn, should have gotten your office no.,
> don't even know name of your company. . . . I got
> to work til 8 tonite, so hope you can wait for a late
> dinner. Pick me up at the hotel, please. That's the
> Tally Ho English Lounge, remember, not the
> Montezuma Room which is on the same floor, other
> end, easy to mix up, but remember I play harp and
> not the marimba!
>
> > Your my boy,
> > S

Wagner could not believe he had given the woman any
reason whatever to assume he would be dining with her

tonight. His parting from her had naturally been genial but no more: the confident implication of the note was that they had established a permanent arrangement very like marriage. He could not allow her to labor under such a erroneous assumption. Remaining visible, he rode a bus to his doctor's block. Before going into the building he stopped at an outdoor telephone and tried to get Sandra's number from Information. It turned out to be unlisted. He would have to reach her later at the Hotel Pierce.

As luck would have it, Wagner was not forced to undergo the usual interminable wait to see the doctor. He was shown into the inner sanctum on arrival at the office.

Dr. Leprak's head was lowered over a medical file. "Oh, hi, Fred," said he, raising his pale eyes but not his sandy-haired head as yet. "Better start getting 'em off."

Wagner had had time to think of a reasonable pretext for the visit. He complained of sleeplessness. "I've been under a lot of strain, Doctor: changes at work, and so on."

"The real problem, though, wouldn't you say?" asked Dr. Leprak, "would be the failure of your marriage."

Wagner was unfastening his shirt. "You know about that?"

"Remember, Carla's my patient too."

"She's been in? She's sick?"

"You know I can't tell you those things," said the doctor, but he smiled thinly. "I wouldn't worry, if I were you."

"We're just separated," said Wagner. "We're not divorced."

"OK," Leprak said. "You can let the pants go while I listen here." He moved the stethoscope from around his neck to a connection with his ears and pressed the free end to Wagner's upper torso. Almost immediately he pulled it away to say, "You've obviously lost some weight, Fred.

We'll see how much, on the scale. Have you been missing meals?" He returned the little cup to Wagner's chest and listened at various points. As he had throughout his life, Wagner felt tickling sensations and had to restrain himself from chuckling.

"I'm OK, though," he said. "I feel fine."

Leprak proceeded to give him a complete physical examination, taking blood samples and X-raying his thorax. Finally he put Wagner on the scale.

"Mm, you *have* lost some weight," said the doctor, squinting at the chromium cylinder he had moved along the horizontal element of the balance. He whisked it away with a finger before Wagner could bend and look, went to his desk, and wrote rapidly. "Here you go."

So Wagner got a legitimate prescription without asking. "What is this for?"

"Something to stimulate your appetite."

"But I seem to be generally all right?"

Leprak was scribbling in the file. He glanced up as if he were already vague as to Wagner's identity. "We'll have to see what the tests say."

Now that he had a genuine excuse for his absence, Wagner decided to report to his own office even though more than half the day was gone.

He had to pass Jackie's lair anyway, so he stopped there before proceeding to his cubicle. She was editing someone's copy, rapidly and with bold strokes of the vermilion pen with which she had replaced the traditional blue of her predecessor. Before she looked up through the outsized saucer-lenses, she groaned and said, "You're going to have to rewrite this completely, Mary Alice." Her look of exasperation became hostile when she recognized Wagner. She lowered the pen and asked coldly, "What do you want?"

"Your line was busy, so I left a message." He extended the prescription blank. "In case you need evidence."

"I don't," said Jackie.

"Just trying to do the right thing."

She produced an ugly blurting laugh. "That's your specialty, isn't it? The gall you've got! You just go collect your check over at Accounting. It's waiting for you."

He could not believe what he was hearing. He waved the prescription at her. "You think I forged it? Then call his office, Dr. Howard Leprak . . ." He squinted at the phone number printed next to the doctor's address. "Six-one-two, three-four —"

Jackie stood up and pointed the red pen at him. "Sneaky little skunk. What did you do, shadow us?"

"What?"

"Couldn't face me like a man, could you? At least you could have made the accusation face to face. Instead you write that poison-pen letter."

What a complete misinterpretation of his obvious intent. He was so upset as rashly to forsake anonymity. "Please, Jackie, don't say that. You can't possibly believe I was out to damage you. The letter seemed the best way to handle it."

"My husband read it." Jackie sat down. Her fury was replaced by a deeper emotion. "How do you think he felt? He's been sick for a long time. He's not able to —"

"But how could that have happened?" Wagner asked. "It was internal office mail. Furthermore, I sealed it and marked it 'personal.' " He would have been angry now at the injustice of it had not Jackie seemingly laid claim to all available feelings.

"I threw it into the case with some other papers I was taking home to read. My husband likes to hear about my day: I let him look at the stuff I bring home. The worst of his existence is the boredom. He was once an active executive." Sadness was softening the usually harsh lines of her chin.

"God, I'm sorry, Jackie. I didn't know about any of this. My whole idea was to be discreet. What can I say?"

She reacquired her previous look. " 'Goodbye,' " she answered.

He grimaced at the floor. "I can certainly understand how you must feel. But with all respect, a terrible mistake of this kind doesn't have any bearing on how I do my job."

"You're being treated more than fairly," Jackie said. "Three months' severance pay. Morton's already okayed it. And I won't bum-rap you on a recommendation anyplace else."

Wagner pinched his lip between thumb and forefinger, hurting himself before he realized what he was doing. "How about this: you got that note by accident. It had been intended for someone else. There wasn't any name in the text, as I remember: it could have applied to any woman in the office. I'd be willing to call up your husband and swear to that, or even go see him if you'd like."

Jackie stared at him, again with that new suggestion of vulnerability. "I told Howard the truth," she said. "I owed him that much." She curled her lip at Wagner. "What do you take me for?"

He was contrite. "Obviously I underrated you. I humbly apologize for that too."

She lowered her head and seemed genuinely to be reacting to his self-abasement. "All right, Fred. . . . But you still have to leave."

Of course he knew she was right. She had lost face before a subordinate. He said no more but left her and went

164

quickly along the little corridor to his cubicle. Delphine was on the telephone. In his own chair he saw Gordon's person. The former office boy remained oblivious to his arrival until addressed.

Wagner coughed to open the constriction in his throat. "I've got some personal possessions in the middle drawer. . . . If you don't mind. It won't take a moment."

Gordon swiveled himself around. "Oh, hi, Fred. Listen, all your stuff is in a big manila envelope being held at the stockroom."

"*Terry* has it?"

Gordon was no longer nursing his grudge. With a sweet smile he said, "That's right."

Wagner stuck out his hand. "Good luck to you, Gordon — in everything: the promotion and of course the poetry too."

Gordon languidly shook hands. "I'm leaving here in a couple of weeks myself," he said. "I'm just doing this for a few days till Jackie hires somebody. I'm taking that post at the *Critical Edge*. I'll be losing money, but it's worth the sacrifice, I think."

"I can understand," said Wagner. "I've been reading it for years: it meets a real need."

"Maybe you're thinking of another publication," Gordon suggested. "*CE* was just started last May."

"Oh, sure." Wagner scraped his lower front teeth across the moist undersurface of the upper lip. "Gordon, may I ask your advice? You know about that novel I'm writing. I —"

"I know nothing *about* it," said Gordon. "All I have ever known is that you told me once you were working on some such."

"I stand corrected once more. But what I wanted was to

165

ask you for your advice. Supposing I had enough of a manuscript which, perhaps augmented by an outline or detailed notes on that part of the story yet to come — uh, making a package of this all, would it be legitimate, do you think, to show it to a publisher at that point? I'm aware it would be quite a tentative thing at best, but —"

Gordon's voice was chilly. "I haven't the foggiest as to *what* is done with fiction. All I can say with authority is that I *never* read it. Sorry, Fred." He turned the chair, and himself, back to a working situation.

Yet Wagner persisted: at this point he was desperate for any kind of assent, however faint.

"I know this is an imposition." He spoke to Gordon's perfectly barbered nape. "But do you suppose I might just mention your name if I wanted someone at Burbage to take me seriously?"

Gordon apparently wrote the first draft of his catalogue copy by hand. His moving pencil did not stop now.

"It wouldn't do you any good." But then impulsively he dropped the pencil and spun around. "Now, Fred, if you'll reflect you know I'm right. Please don't take the easy way out and call me mean."

The swine had effectively blocked him in all directions. To maintain any pride at all, Wagner had fervently to disavow all feelings of resentment and furthermore to provide Gordon with better reasons than the contemptible young man probably had. "No, I understand perfectly. The novel people are completely different from the poetry department, so your intervention would be irrelevant at best. At worst, it might be taken as an offensive piece of cronyism."

Gordon said drily, "Yes, something like that." He went back to work.

With blood in his eye Wagner looked for Pascal, the one

person whom he could punish without fear of reprisal. As he had always made it his purpose to avoid the man, he had only a vague sense of just where the appropriate desk could be located, and had to peep into a series of cubicles occupied by persons whom he usually saw only at staff meetings in Jackie's office or at drinking fountains and snack machines. When he had begun, six years before, the Xmas party had provided an annual opportunity for intramural fraternization, including some decorous foolery under a sprig of mistletoe at the end of a string tied to a ceiling sprinkler ("Watch out you don't set it off!"), but on coming to power Jackie had substituted the universally preferred half-day off, and thus Wagner knew few of his remotely situated co-workers as unique human beings.

For example, for a good four years he had had Meg Mulhare as a colleague, yet if asked to characterize her could have said nothing but that she was extremely fat. He passed her cubicle now.

"Hey, Fred, I hear you're leaving us," she cried. With her little eyes and pouchy cheeks it was difficult to assess her expression, and her voice was flat by nature.

"You know already?"

She made some movement of the flesh which was perhaps a shrug. "It's a secret?"

"No, certainly not. Uh, so long to you, Meg. It's been nice working with you."

Her frown was easier to identify. "I don't think we ever actually did, though. We just worked at the same place, not really with one another."

"I can see why you're a good copywriter," said Wagner, spiteful all at once. "You use words with care. However, when speaking of only two persons, preferred usage calls for 'each other,' not 'one another,' which is reserved for three or more."

Meg's little mouth quivered. "You better watch your dangling participles, Fred. I don't believe you mean that Preferred Usage is doing the speaking."

"The only reason I'm here, Meg, is that I'm looking for Roy Pascal's desk."

She disdainfully pointed, with a swollen finger, at the fiberglass partition the west face of which made the east wall of her own niche. And hard thereafter came Pascal's voice.

"Come on over, Fred!"

Wagner went to him, and even before speaking saw the 24-inch steel rule lying at the top of Pascal's desk, otherwise a barren place sans photos, writing implements, even any notes stuck into the sides of the blotter-holder.

"That happens to be my personal property." He pointed angrily at the rule.

Pascal smiled. "I know. That's why I kept it out. So I wouldn't forget."

"In the unlikely case I came to say goodbye. Is that your story?"

"Come on, Fred. There's no argument."

"And what about the pen with the different colors? That was mine. It was given me by Harwich House. I mean it was not just the sample. They specifically said it was a gift. They are out of business now, but before your time they were a big client of ours."

"Fred," said Pascal, "it wasn't before my time, and — or should I say 'but' — I didn't take the pen." He lifted the steel rule and handed it to Wagner. "Here."

"Keep it," Wagner said with heat. "Add it to the other

things you stole from me over the months, while I was away from my desk."

Pascal blinked, as if to clear his eyes for the look of pain that entered them now. "I assume you're joking, Fred. The only time I ever touched your desk in your absence was yesterday, when Jackie asked me to stay late and do a rush rewrite of the copy for the Perpetual Faith Calendar. She said you must still have the research. You had already gone, so I looked for it in the desk. I couldn't find it."

"Naturally you didn't consider the file cabinet."

"I looked there first of all." Pascal stood up and put out his hand. "Let's not make this the occasion of a fight."

Beyond the thin partition Meg complained, "Keep it down! I'm trying to work!"

"You bastard," Wagner said to Pascal. "Don't try to pretend you're my friend. You *never* were."

Pascal lowered his hand and said soberly, "All right, Fred. But it seems to me you could use one."

He was right, of course, but it enraged Wagner further that such a truth would be uttered at such a place and time. *"Pascal —"* he began, but was interrupted by Meg Mulhare, who had lifted her bulk from the chair and waddled to the threshold of her cubicle.

"You're creating a disturbance, Wagner. Just get the hell out. You don't work here any more."

"If you still want to maintain the illusion that you're a man," Wagner said to Pascal, "you'll go with me to where we can have some privacy."

Pascal shrugged. "You know I'm always somebody you can talk with."

Wagner led the way in quickstep. As he passed Meg he answered her. "Go to hell, you tub of lard."

She screamed at his back, "Shit on you, Wagner!" This

could be heard throughout the department and heads began to appear around other partitions. Until this time Wagner had had no reason to suppose he was not the most respected copywriter in the firm. An awful thing was happening, and he suspected he might be only making it worse by what he was doing now. Nevertheless he could not or perhaps would not arrest the thrilling progress towards destruction.

He led Pascal to what by now seemed the unique piece of nonhostile turf at hand: the landing just behind the door to the stairs.

"Why are we out here?" Pascal asked, his complexion sickly in the dim light that was wasted on the deserted staircase. "Can it be *that* private?"

"I didn't want to embarrass you," Wagner lied. Without further preface he threw a roundhouse punch at the other man, which however the intended recipient easily dodged.

"What are you *doing*, Fred?"

"You son of a bitch," Wagner said. "I never liked you even when I thought you were sincere. But then I finally saw the light: you were sucking up to me in public while sabotaging me behind my back." He sent a violent jab Pascal's way, but once again it was effortlessly evaded. Wagner believed it was his overcharged emotional state that caused his punches to be so ineffectual: it was like being drunk. He must try to exert command over himself without losing any of the healthy rage that had brought him this far.

Smirking, Pascal said, "Very funny. Now why are we *really* out here?"

This time Wagner managed to connect, if not quite solidly: he gazed the man's cheek and struck the right ear, but the blow was sufficient at last to erase Pascal's smile.

"You're not kidding," Pascal said in quiet astonishment, rubbing his ear.

"You scum," said Wagner. "You sent that poison-pen letter to Wilton."

Pascal's heavy eyebrows rose. "I'm afraid I don't get the reference at all."

"You're slime," said Wagner. "You've been uncovered: might as well come clean. I'm going to punish you anyway."

Pascal said calmly, "I assume you mean our very own Morton Wilton. I have never been in any direct communication with him whatever. I haven't even ever said hello to the guy. I've only seen him at distance. I doubt he even knows I work here. Why would I write him a letter?"

"*Why?*" cried Wagner. "Why? You told him I was regularly meeting some queer in the stalls of the men's room. I ought to kill you for that!" He threw a flurry of blows, but Pascal quickly stepped out of their range.

"Now, you listen to me, Fred. I did not write such a letter. I have always been your friend. At least I have always intended to be, whatever your feelings towards me. I certainly haven't ever denounced you anonymously or otherwise, and —"

Wagner rushed him, but Pascal parried his punches and then, when he would not desist, struck him lightly in the midsection and, as he bent, somewhat more forcefully in the upper chest. Wagner was hurled off balance, and he sat down hard on his behind. After a moment, seeking to rise, he took Pascal's proffered grasp in a thoughtless reflex, then of course despised himself for it once he was on his feet.

"Now, Fred," Pascal said levelly, "just let it go at that. I boxed a lot in college, and it's obvious you did not."

"All right, you're a boxer and I'm not. What does that prove? I'm leaving this place with no regrets. I have nothing but contempt for all of you. I'm going to do something glorious."

He glared at Pascal, but the other man nodded calmly and said, "I'll bet you will, Fred. I've always thought you had it in you."

Wagner hastened down the stairs, lest he burst into tears: he had singlehandedly given Pascal the opportunity, after all these years, to humiliate him absolutely.

Someone above was calling his name. For a moment he supposed it was Pascal, who had become so vile as to assume a falsetto, but when he heard the subsequent sound of hard heels on the flight of steps just over his head, he paused. Could it be that Jackie was pursuing him, determined to get in one more thrust of the knife?

But on the instant Mary Alice Phillips came around into view at the turn of stair just above him.

"Fred, wait up!"

It was a relief to recognize her — Wagner was exhausted by the various phases of his strife — but what he ached for at this moment was to be alone.

"I'm really in a hurry."

"No, Fred," said she, arriving at his side. "You just slow down. I'm not going to let you just wander off into the wilderness."

He realized he would probably miss her ingenuousness. "I'll probably get another job in town somewhere. I'm not thinking of moving to the Gobi Desert." He even tried to smile.

"Fred," said Mary Alice, "should we sit down right here and talk, or should we slip out to a quiet bar or tavern?"

"I've got to get going," said Wagner. "I've had enough talking for the day."

"It's been the wrong kind, if you ask me," Mary Alice said, suddenly taking him by the arm.

He saw this action as having to do with power and not affection. Now that he had hit bottom, even a former inferior could get familiar. Yet neither was he in a state to resist. So she conducted him down the stairs and through the lobby and into the street, where she walked shivering against him. He had never taken off the topcoat in which he had left the doctor's office, but Mary Alice was wearing only a figured dress in some thin fabric.

He asserted himself. "You shouldn't be out here, dressed like that. It's chilly, and this breeze!"

"It's only two steps," Mary Alice said, her hair going wild in a burst of wind. And then she pulled him into the doorway of a bar.

In all his years of working just next door, he had never before penetrated this establishment. Indeed, he had hardly noticed it. Swan's, the office hangout, was in the next block. Wagner was even ignorant of the name of this place though he had passed it several thousand times in six years. Its interior had no visible character whatever, consisting of a routine back-mirrored bar tended by a nondescript man in an open-necked shirt, and a sequence of murky booths all of which were now deserted. Three persons, each exclusively self-concerned at the moment, sat on bar stools widely separated each from each.

"A vodka and tonic," said Mary Alice. "I don't want to smell."

She proceeded to the remotest booth while Wagner stepped up to fetch the drinks.

"I do serve tables," said the bartender. "But I won't knock ya if ya do my work."

Mary Alice had left Wagner the seat that faced the door. This was contrary to Babe's practice with him — but not with Zirko.

"Now, Fred," Mary Alice said, leaning so that her breasts met the tabletop. "It's an awful mess, isn't it?"

Wagner did not wish to discuss his troubles with her. Sandra would really be helpful at this point. He now welcomed the date she had set up without consulting him; suddenly he saw it as almost maternal generosity and not as obtrusive arrogance, and was pleased that he had not been able to reach her to cancel.

"It's the result of a misunderstanding," he told Mary Alice.

She was intense. "It can be straightened out!"

He did not intend to establish just what it was she knew. "I think we'd do better to let it go."

She took a drink, staring at him over the rim of the glass with enlarged brown irises. "I know Jackie will want you back."

"No," said Wagner, "she couldn't. And I wouldn't."

"She'll have to," said Mary Alice, "when I explain."

"You don't understand, Mary Alice." Wagner took a drink from his own glass. "It's a thing of authority. You know, I trained her as I've been training you."

"Oh, God."

"It was nothing dramatic. It's just that the shift of power is always a fascinating process, especially when the different sexes are involved."

Mary Alice spoke with intensity. "I'm sure you'll always be an authority to me, Fred."

He knew a slight discomfort. "Let's not make too much

of it. You're by now almost ready to train someone of your own." This was scarcely true; perhaps it would never be. But he really found her gratitude embarrassing, and he wanted to limit it.

"You've been a lot more than a friend," said she, staring at him in exaggerated approval.

He put up a hand. "Please."

The bartender misinterpreted the gesture, no doubt through greed, and in a moment brought them two more drinks. Mary Alice was still working on the first half of her original glassful.

"You're just feeling blue right now," said she. "But there's also someone else who's fond of you: Roy Pascal."

Wagner struck the table with his glass. "He's a skunk!"

"I don't like to disagree with you, Fred, but to be fair —"

"He called you a lesbian," Wagner said brutally. "Then right afterwards jumped on the elevator to feel you up."

But Mary Alice's reaction was an almost saintly smile. "It wasn't him, I mean he, on the elevator, Fred. It was that guy from the art department, that short fellow with the red hair and bad skin. As for the lesbian so-called accusation, well, we have to consider the source, don't we?"

The bartender arrived with still another round. As he paid him, Wagner realized that the man had considered the banging down of the glass as a reorder.

He squinted at him. "All right this time, but don't come again until I definitely ask you to in clear English."

The bartender clucked merrily and said, "I hear you talkin'."

All this while Wagner had been thinking about the last sentence in Mary Alice's latest speech.

"Are you implying that Pascal may be homosexual?"

"Well, that's no secret, is it?" She maintained her smile. "I don't condemn him for saying what he did about me. I realize it was just jealousy. In practice he's been as sweet as he could be. He's even spoken well of me to Jackie: she told me as much."

Wagner was draining the glasses before him.

Mary Alice continued to smile. "He's *very* fond of you, Fred."

Wagner grimaced and said, "I suppose you won't believe it if I say he's never made a move towards me, uh, of that nature. *Never.* He's hung around, but there was never that."

"I know that now. Yes, I do."

"Does that mean you didn't always?"

She took an outsized swallow of her drink. "I know," said she, "it was pretty silly, but then you guys seemed inseparable, and then I heard your marriage was on the rocks. . . . I'm really sorry, Fred, and will do whatever I can to make it up to you."

Wagner all of a sudden recognized that he was drunk, a state he had seldom experienced throughout his life. He also had to go to the toilet.

When he returned Mary Alice was tracing designs in a drop of tabletop liquid with a forefinger whose ragged nail gave evidence of nibbling.

She smiled up wryly at him. "You must think I'm the dumbest person alive. Can you forgive me? *Ever?*" Again she said she'd try to make it up to him.

He plunged to a seat in the booth.

Mary Alice said, "I'm not *that* drunk. I can certainly feel it, though. One's usually my limit." She was leering at him.

Wagner considered becoming invisible, but before he could make a decision Mary Alice was clutching both his hands.

She was speaking in a low, hurried voice. The beginning of her speech was inaudible to him. He picked it up at ". . . nerve, but I *know* it's right." She gave his hands one more squeeze and then was somehow out of the booth while still holding on. Under these conditions he had to come along too or exert sufficient force to break her grip, which might even require violence, so powerful were her fingers.

The bartender uttered some final ironic sentiment as they left, but Wagner could not decipher it. Indeed he was in a general quandary and devoid of will.

In no time at all the girl and he were in the expectedly shabby but surprisingly clean room of a little hotel that he had probably passed thousands of times obliviously. To be sure, by the time he had recorded this fact they were in bed. He seemed to be thoroughly naked, but Mary Alice retained her brassiere, no doubt because she was shy. After all, she was very young.

She was safe enough under his protection. For example, he was so drunk he could hardly molest her. . . . He actually was still saying that to himself while the act was under way, perhaps because there was a savage, and incredible, feature to this hallucination: before he had penetrated her, Mary Alice had been a virgin.

9

WHEN WAGNER WOKE HE FELT AS THOUGH HE HAD
been mauled by a large animal; its feral, musky odor stayed
behind. There was bright sunlight behind a pull-shade with
a gaping tear just below the roller. This could not be his
own bedroom.

Nor had he been sleeping with Babe. An unrecognizable
head of hair lay on the adjoining pillow, face averted. He
had been drugged and dumped into bed with a corpse,
whose murder would be easy to pin on him: a hackneyed
plot.

Of course when forced he could remember the late afternoon and evening of the day before. He simply rejected
it. He had hardly known Mary Alice Phillips. Therefore it
was unlikely that it would be he who had made her a
woman. He was not a lascivious man, was in fact notorious
for his moderation in all things, just ask his estranged wife.

Then too: if Mary Alice was so modest as to wear a
brassiere while in bed with a naked man, how could it be
that she had willingly surrendered her virginity, if not
downright imposed it upon him?

He could recall a sharp image of the desk clerk who wore
a blue shirt with the button missing from one point of the

collar, which therefore was lifted as if in greeting. Later on, someone had gone out for pizza and Coke: he could remember the event, and the protagonist had probably been himself, but he could not yet certify this as a fact. By that time he should have been sobering up rather than becoming less aware, but the deflowering had been a shocker — far more to him than to the person uniquely immediate to it. Except for a certain gingerliness at the outset, and a brief loss of color at the mouth, Mary Alice had proceeded so wholeheartedly as to distract him from the moral implications of the deed until it had been accomplished, and in fact compounded. Her one reference to the most critical phase of their conjunction — "So *that's* what it is" — was scarcely in the idiom of shame. But whether or not the experience had been a mere novelty to her, Wagner was hard hit after the fact. If the physical particulars of the encounter had been less troublesome than he would have anticipated, the strain on his spirit was heavy. What seeds of degeneracy might he not have planted in this young person hitherto respectably fallow? Would that she were weeping! Was it natural to display so much smugness?

He remembered now: surely it had been he who had gone for pizza. He was not at all hungry but had needed a breather. He did not relish being seen by the desk clerk, who might well suppose that if the john was finished the whore'd better come down soon or get the old heave-ho. But when he reached the cage and saw the man with the wayward collar-point staring vacantly out into the very area through which he was passing, he realized that he was invisible again, this time as the result of no volition whatever.

There being no convenient means by which to get a cooked pie while invisible, Wagner materialized at the counter of the branch of the Pizza on Earth chain just around the corner from the hotel and also the office. He might have been recognized here by members of the daytime staff, but that was out of the question now: the wall clock, in the form of a pizza, with imitation-pepperoni-cylinder hands, informed him that the time was 1:12.

On the round trip he was accosted by two streetwalkers and saw three more. One, leading a wiry little bowlegged client, entered the hotel just ahead of him on his return. He had never before been in the neighborhood of his office this late in the day. Apparently it was a sort of Tenderloin after business hours. The desolate bar in which he and Mary Alice had got into the condition to visit the nearby hotel was now turning raucous. Laughter and clinking could be heard from within. Coming back, he encountered a truculent drunk who staggered out the door in a rush of noise and beer fumes.

"Gimme that pizza pie," this man demanded, clawing towards Wagner's flat box. Wagner found it politic to vanish until he returned to the room.

"Well," said Mary Alice when he had folded back the lid of the pizza box, "you've already succeeded in making me unhappy. I distinctly said all cheese, and yet what do I see on the top? Mushrooms!"

Having, with all his worries, forgotten her instructions, he had produced an invented explanation to the effect that the mushroom was ready to go, whereas had he waited for "plain" he would have been kept away from her for more painful minutes. But there was nothing coy about Mary Alice, and at this point she no longer sought reassurance. Her annoyance proved to be genuine. She turned over, buried her face in the pillows, and went immediately into a resentful but sound sleep.

Now he had awakened and was staring at her tangled back of head. Though he was sober and the day had just begun, he was lacking altogether in a spark of enterprise. While none of his recent misfortunes had been properly the result of his own errors — the malice of chance had simultaneously been operative everywhere — his amour propre had never been feebler. It was absurd that a man who could become invisible at will was not able quickly to take dominion over his existence but instead must go from one predicament to another. Invisibility might seem an overwhelming advantage to have on other mortals. If what you wanted to do was make an ass of your fellow man, tormenting him from an impenetrable hiding place, then you could not do better. And of course it was incomparable for snooping on the most private of events. An unseen personage could be privy to all manner of shame. For criminal activity, from espionage to the snatching of purses, it would be the ultimate technique. One invisible assassin, for example, might single-handedly bring down a nation. A Wagner without conscience could have sold his services to any one of a host of international brigands and been instantly rich. A heroic Wagner might save common decency from its many enemies domestic and foreign.

Instead he lay here, head supported on a fist (for Mary Alice had appropriated his pillow the night before), staring at the stained ceiling, remembering how one such had allegedly fallen on Miles Elg. All his current problems were associated with women: to the list of Babe, Nan, Sandra, and Jackie must now be added the name of Mary Alice. What a reckless thing for him to have done; he should have resisted her; he had no character at all.

He touched her shoulder. "Mary Alice."

"I'm awake." And, judging from the clarity and strength of her voice, had been for some time.

"We'd better get up."

"Why? I'm sure I don't have a job to go to now."

"I'm the one who was fired," Wagner said.

Mary Alice rolled over. Not being one for much makeup when wearing office attire, she provided no morning disillusionment. "I just stepped out for a word with you on the fire stairs," said she. "I haven't returned yet."

"I see," Wagner said. "But I'm sure it can be explained to Jackie: you suddenly took sick or something."

She made a resentful chin. "And it was me who was going to explain to her about *you*."

"That was a generous offer, Mary Alice, but what Jackie has against me is not something that another person's intervention could help, I'm afraid. I made a mistake. With the best will in the world, but still a mistake." His body was embarrassing him: the proximity of a naked woman was arousing his appropriate part. This seemed to be an isolated phenomenon: at first he had not taken mental notice of it, and now, trying consciously to ignore and then to resist the burgeoning assertion, he was being defied.

"Oh, come on, Fred," Mary Alice said irritably, "it was because of that anonymous letter." She shook her head. Another woman might long since have arisen and combed her hair. "I'm sorry, but I got tired of waiting." She grimaced at him. "So look at the pickle I landed up in."

"Oh, you haven't lost your job," Wagner said. He found her statements cryptic but was not impatient to have them deciphered. "I'll blame your absence all on myself. What do I have to lose? I'm out anyway."

Mary Alice propped herself up on an elbow and looked down into his face. "Fred, you still aren't getting it. *I wrote the letter that got you fired.*" She made this confession angrily, as though *he* were the culprit.

Perhaps he was. "I don't know where you got that funny idea," said he. "It was the letter *I* wrote to Jackie that did it. I never heard of any other . . . unless you mean —" No, that was impossible: how could Mary Alice speak of what went on in the men's restroom?

"Of course, that's exactly what I mean," said she, glaring down at him. "You hadn't made a move toward me in all those weeks, and I happen to know your wife walked out on you, and you and Roy were always together, you have to admit that."

Wagner at first felt more curiosity than anger. "Then you didn't actually know there *was* some depraved activity going on in there?"

She wrinkled her blunt little nose at him. "You're not saying you're bisexual?"

"Certainly not." He told her about "Artie." However, by now he was experiencing the onset of resentment. "It's decent of you to admit your error," he said, "but it was an awfully reckless accusation, and it could have —"

"Now, don't you dare *attack* me," cried Mary Alice, "when I'm *admitting* a lack of judgment, not to mention that I'm offering to go to Jackie and make a clean breast of it."

Which was more than she had done with him, Wagner reflected in a moment of perverse humor: she had yet to reveal the contents of her brassiere. But what he said was, "I guess it doesn't matter now."

"It certainly does!" Mary Alice said with urgency. "She might fire me, but I don't want her to go on thinking my lover is queer."

For a moment Wagner despaired of setting her right. She

had not listened to him at all. Furthermore, he was now incongruously at full, imperious distension. It would seem to be the moment for a dramatic move.

Suddenly he rolled over on top of her.

She cried, "Hey!" and suggested resistance, but when his hand swooped behind her back and unhooked the brassiere she went limp.

Her bare breasts were undersized. The cups of the garment were stuffed with material that though inorganic must have felt natural enough the night before.

It was too late to hook her up again. He didn't mind small breasts at all, and after a moment of mental adjustment these seemed more appropriate to her slender body than had the twin melons, but how to convey that to her without offending? His way with words would seem peculiar to the written language. And he sensed that by penetrating her the night before he had lost the authority and respect that had been his as the veteran who had trained her in their profession.

"So now you know," said she.

"You have a beautiful body." He had an unexpected inspiration: "You're like a silver fish."

"That's one way to say I'm flat-chested," Mary Alice said. "Listen, *you*'re not exactly well-built."

Funny, he would never have said he was, but she was being gratuitously insulting. Nevertheless, it had been he whose action had humiliated her.

So he said, "Don't argue. You have an exquisite body." He caressed her delicately.

"I wish you wouldn't poke at me like a pork chop," she complained, sliding out of bed onto her feet. Now that she had nothing more to conceal she displayed not even that routine modesty that had seemed natural to every woman with whom Wagner had ever been intimate: perhaps not that extensive a roster, but presumably enough to make the point. A few had on occasion proudly paraded in the nude, but none had ever simply forgotten she was naked, as Mary Alice gave evidence of doing now as she trudged in an almost slatternly stride to the window, to pluck back a piece of the shade and peer down at the street.

"All the creeps are going to work," she said, making a face as she turned away. "Well, I never did like that stupid job. Good riddance."

Could the act of love have so altered her character? Nobody at the office had been more eager to please than Mary Alice. Her application to the task and her complaisance had done much to compensate for her lack of ability.

"Please," said Wagner, having drawn up the bedclothes to cover his groin. "Mark my words, you can walk right back in there this morning and nobody will oppose you."

She went, slumped, to look at her peevish expression in the mirror over the washstand. Wagner studied her buttocks, which were on the spare side, with proprietary smugness. In one limited but essential way, she was his product. But that was surely another truth he could not effectively have expressed to her, at least not while she was in this mood. Yesterday he could not have imagined a querulous Mary Alice, but neither could he have supposed that he would have shattered her hymen by nightfall.

"Christ," she said now, at last having looked down, "I'm a mess. Couldn't you at least have gotten a room with a bath?"

Again this was unfair. It had been she who pulled him towards the hotel, but again he was placating. "I was so drunk yesterday I can't even remember registering here."

"Thanks a lot!"

He showed a smile that was intended to be endearing. "I haven't forgotten you."

Despite her youth Mary Alice could look aged and downright ugly by means of one scowl. "I bet my parents haven't forgotten me, either."

Wagner raised his eyebrows at her.

"Well," said she, "when would I have had the time to call them? You were *screwing* me all night."

"That's not fair." He found the language as offensive as the charge.

"Then who was it?" she shouted. "An unidentified rapist? Dragged me into this fleabag and brutally forced me to do his bidding?"

"Oh, I see. You mean, that's going to be the story you tell?"

"Who would believe shit like that?" cried Mary Alice.

"We can invent something better." Wagner's own voice was now raised. "Haven't you got a girl friend with whom you might have spent the night?"

"You idiot," she barked in her new coarse voice, "in that event why wouldn't I have phoned home?"

"I wish you wouldn't take it out on me," said Wagner, making the effort to lower his own volume. "I'm your friend, and I'm in this with you."

"*Some friend*," Mary Alice said bitterly. "You just used me for your own pleasure. How often do you come across a fresh young girl in that old folks' home?"

Wagner now believed he could recognize it was anxiety that worked the extraordinary alteration in her. She was like the callow male youth in the war movies who panics in battle. Perhaps she needed the slap of a grizzled sergeant.

"Get hold of yourself, Mary Alice, and get washed and put on your clothes."

"You just hate my body."

He welcomed her return to the self-deprecating. "Don't say that." He got up and went to embrace her.

But she dashed to put the bed between them. "Don't touch me!" She bent over crossed hands. "Don't put that thing in me again!"

He raised his arms as though he were being held up at gunpoint. "All right, all right. I don't know what to say when you're in this mood. But I tell you your fears are exaggerated. You'll still have your job and I'll dream up a good story to tell your parents."

"Just you take care of me," said Mary Alice. "Just you promise."

"I just told you I was going to get you out of what you call a pickle, but I don't think the situation is that grave."

"You're going to have to do a lot more than that, if you expect to get any more of *this*." She made a very coarse gesture.

Wagner felt a chill, though not on the skin. Surprisingly, the room was well heated by an old iron radiator in the corner. "Let's get out of here first before we formulate our plans," said he, now speaking towards the mirror. He leaned forward, his genitals sliding into the washbowl, where he washed them and his hands with a sliver of tan-colored soap that had no doubt been used by a succession of harlots and their clients. There was but one towel, thin as a handkerchief.

Mary Alice was sitting on the far edge of the bed, bent forward, with her spine all bumps. He had an awful suspicion she might be weeping, but in an instant she had risen, gone to the dresser, and begun to chew at a limp triangle of the cold pizza found there.

Wagner decided to limit his conversation to the minimum until he could get away. It was difficult for him to think coherently in Mary Alice's presence.

She finally got perfunctorily washed and quickly dressed. When she again looked as she had before he had possessed her, he found it easy to believe she still was full-chested and untouched by man. But if he therefore assumed her old manner would return as well, he was in error.

"I trust you're good for a taxi, anyway," said she when they had reached the lobby, where the cockeyed man now on duty in the cage contemptuously disregarded their departure.

Wagner just wondered whether he had enough cash with him to pay for her ride home, wherever that might be, perhaps in an outlying district or suburb. He had taken the young lady's maidenhead without even knowing where she lived: such lack of care was unprecedented in his history. Perhaps he was on the threshold of a new existence, where precedents would not be all that important. Yet he had felt vulnerable as they passed the desk clerk — even though such a room was paid for on entrance and had no telephone or room service for which extra charges could be assessed.

The taxi hailed by Mary Alice from curbside was already occupied, but she seemed prescient, for as if in answer to her summons it pulled to a stop directly in front of her.

The door was flung open, and Jackie Grinzing stepped out of the vehicle. She ignored Mary Alice to smile sardonically at Wagner.

"At least I had the decency to find another hotel than the nearest one to the office," said she.

Mary Alice had caught the door of the taxi. "Go fuck yourself, Jackie. Come on, darling." She climbed in.

Had Wagner had his wits about him, he might have done something before it got this far, but obviously there was nothing left to preserve now. He climbed into the cab after Mary Alice.

He shrugged at her. "I guess it's pretty certain *now* that you've lost your job."

"I told you it was a foregone conclusion." She leaned forward to give the driver Wagner's home address.

Wagner was both flattered and worried. "How do you happen to know where I live?"

Mary Alice settled back in the seat. "I made you my hobby, Fred. You really succeeded in fascinating me. You're brilliant, but there's no getting away from the fact that you're getting older and life has not brought you the rewards your talent deserves. That could be either *your* fault or life's, and guess which one always has the upper hand?"

This was still another phase: Mary Alice as girl-philosopher.

"I'm not that old," he said.

"I don't call six years at that dumb place getting anywhere. And anyway except for Roy everybody else is a woman."

She had forgotten Gordon, but then he was soon to leave. Wagner tried to change the subject. "I've been thinking about what to tell your parents, Mary Alice," he lied. "Your friend's phone was out of order; you assumed it was a temporary condition, and by the time you realized it couldn't be repaired till morning, it was too late to go into the street to a public phone. Anyway, by then they'd have been asleep."

"Fred," Mary Alice said, patting his wrist, "you've been letting your potential go to seed. It's ridiculous that a person with your command of the English language should be in harness to some second-rate catalogue-writing business

189

for the best years of his life." She glanced over his shoulder. "But here we are. Pay the man." She was already out the door.

Wagner could not believe that in such a short time they had made the trip for which the record by bus could be no less than thirty minutes, but he saw the correct house number over the double entrance doors and below it the dour morning doorman.

The taxi driver, a toothy, long-jawed man of about Wagner's age, accepted the fare with a wink. "Boy," said he, "they can sure bitch you up sometimes. My old lady —"

Wagner was on the sidewalk. He realized only now, when he saw Andy the doorman sizing up Mary Alice, that she clearly showed the night's wear and tear. He was embarrassed, he who had hitherto been seen only in the company of the well-groomed Babe. Mary Alice looked for all the world like a girl who had been filled with liquor, screwed all night, and now was still with her user only because no convenient moment had yet appeared in which she could be dumped.

He made the best of a bad job, and introduced her to Andy as "Miss Phillips. We work together."

This did not erase the scowl from Andy's face. What did, however, was Mary Alice's contribution. "We just both got fired!" She clamped a proprietor's grip on Wagner's arm. Wagner had never before seen Andy's grin, which proved vulpine.

Just as they arrived at the elevator, its doors opened and Debbie Fong and Ellen Mackintosh, the roommates and co-workers, stepped into the lobby. By contrast with these sleek young ladies, Mary Alice might have been his charwoman.

Wagner muttered a hello. As if Mary Alice were a

190

stranger, he made a gallant little bowing gesture the implication of which was that she should board the elevator before him. She did not comply. Instead she positively gawked at Debbie and Ellen.

"Hi, Ed!" Ellen cried enthusiastically.

Debbie poked an elbow at her. "It's *Fred*. Hi, Fred. We're going to a seminar."

"I see," said Wagner. "Well, enjoy yourselves."

"That's why we're off today," said Ellen. "Sorry I called you Ed. I knew it was Fred." It looked as though she had subtly lightened her hair; Debbie of course retained the glossy black bangs of her heritage.

Thus far it seemed as though he might be getting away with it, but now Mary Alice said, in a voice with an identifiable edge, "I'm Fred's friend."

The roommates were affable as always when introducing themselves, but Wagner could not doubt that they would despise him now.

Once he and Mary Alice were on the elevator, she asked, with an implied groan, "*Who* were those two characters?"

Wagner had both keys ready, and as soon as the car reached his floor he dashed for the door of his apartment and opened it with dispatch. Mary Alice however took her time, staring up and down the hallway, apparently with interest, bleak though this prospect had always seemed to him.

Standing inside the doorway, he motioned to her.

"What's the hurry?" she asked, grinning disdainfully. "Don't you want to run into any more call girls?"

He brought her inside and closed the door. "You're joking. Debbie and Ellen both have junior-executive positions at a big downtown bank."

"Oh, *sure* they do," said Mary Alice, glancing around

the living room. "How long have you been living in this apartment, Fred?"

"Three years. We —" He caught himself. It seemed wrong to allude to Babe in any way at this time, lest Mary Alice seem even more of an invader. "Three years, take or leave a little."

"Don't you think it's time then to get drapes that fit the windows?" she asked, turning abruptly away from the articles in question. "Oh, so there's how you got so smart." She nodded at the small bookcase in the corner, which in point of fact held few books, with its empty shelf-and-a-half forlornly awaiting Babe's return with her potted plants, and then some more of its space was occupied by horizontaled magazines and newspapers, all outdated. There was probably a total of no more than two dozen volumes on the lowest shelf of all, which sagged midways thereby, and it would have been fruitless to seek literature as such amongst the classified phone book, a no doubt useful but never used tome on the removal of stains, and a thick-spined *Who's Who in Private Country Clubs*, in which his sister and brother-in-law had paid to have themselves listed ("but you have to be invited").

Along with the houseplants, Babe had taken away all the pictures, which of course were her property, and the only decoration on the walls at this time were rectangles of pale plaster outlined in the soot that must always be in the air but otherwise goes undetected: an unpleasant thought. Only now did it occur to Wagner that it must be a shabby-looking place: the irony was that the dusty-gold draperies were the most attractive item on hand, having been sewn to order by the appropriate department of an expensive store and installed only a year ago.

In an officious stride Mary Alice went back to the

kitchen, followed by Wagner, who asked, if only to remind her who was host, "Would you like some coffee?"

"Oh," said she, "I'm capable of *that*." She seized the kettle from the stovetop and went to fill it at the sink.

Wagner hastened to fetch the jar of powder from a cabinet which was otherwise empty except for a teabag without a string and a can of Petite Marmite Henry IV, imported from Portugal and given to Babe by Cleve Guillaume after breaking up with a boy who had cost him a fortune in exotic canned goods. The tin was slightly deformed from, probably, a fall; fearing botulism, the Wagners had never broached it. In any event, Wagner did not want a stranger to see how pitiful was his larder.

Yes, despite their excruciatingly intimate association of the night before, Mary Alice now seemed, in the environment of his own home, the slightest of acquaintances.

Deaf to direction, she quickly ransacked two drawers before she found the spoons. Then she sloppily shoveled too much instant coffee into each of the cups.

"When I get some of this in me, I'll use the phone," she said, indicating the wall-hung instrument next to the refrigerator. "My father will have gone to work by then, and I can talk to my mom."

Wagner sighed in relief. "Oh, good. I'm sure you can explain it all." He was not sure in the least, but he wished this whole matter could be concluded without delay. He had to give himself to the really important issue: namely, what he would now do with his life. Surely it was all to the good that he finally had no alternative to sitting down and writing that novel. It was no longer the thing he would eventually do when the time came. The moment was here; he no longer had a source of income.

He went on. "And when you've got that straightened

out, we'd better think about returning to the office, unpleasant as that might seem. But you left your coat there,
I believe. And I have to pick up my check."

"I'm never going back to that shit hole," Mary Alice
said, plucking away and dropping to the counter the little
blue plastic bird from the spout of the teakettle. Wagner
had always found its whistle useful as well as homey, but,
not wanting to be provocative, made no complaint now.
"They can mail my check. And they can keep the coat. I'm
sick of it. It's the kind of clothes you wear as one of the
jerks who have to go to work at an office every day."

Wagner moved quickly to make the coffee as soon as it
seemed sufficient time had gone by for the water to have
heated, but no doubt owing to his impatience he miscal-
culated.

Mary Alice made a face and lowered the mug. "This is
cold."

"Sorry," said Wagner. "But that's why the bird was
there."

"I can't stand cute kitchens," Mary Alice said. "At least
you don't have twine coming out of a ceramic French chef's
lips or a duck's-head towel rack."

"Better call Mom," Wagner advised.

She grimaced at him. "She's my mother and not yours."

"What I meant was she'll be worried."

Mary Alice went to the wall phone, where she turned
and asked, "Do you mind?"

"Oh, sure." He left the kitchen and went into the bedroom. That's where his real library was: one whole wall of
it. Babe had not been too happy about giving up that much
picture space, but it was the only wall he claimed of the
many. The bed was impeccable: he had to admit that Polly
Todvik and Glen had made it up tightly before they de-

parted. He reminded himself that he must have the locks changed. After a long while he went out into the living room, expecting to find that Mary Alice had concluded her phone call, but he could still hear her remotely speaking from time to time. He could not distinguish the words, but the tone seemed calm enough. After all, she was no longer a minor. She even had a BA. Staying away all night should not be an occasion for parental outrage.

It turned out to be fortunate that she was so longwinded. A susurrus was heard at the door. As he looked there a pink envelope came sliding through the slit at the threshold. He went hastily to take and — to pocket it, for out in the kitchen Mary Alice had suddenly raised her voice.

"All right then," she cried. "You'll never see me again!"

Immediately she came marching out. "Bad luck," said she. "My dad was home, refused to go to work with me missing. We tangled, as I was afraid we would. I don't know if you heard just now."

Wagner nodded lugubriously. "I'm sure you'll both settle down, though, before long. My sister and I have always fought a lot, but we always soon make peace." He gave a hollow laugh. "We have to. We don't have anybody else."

"Don't minimize this," said Mary Alice. "I'm a stubborn cookie. If I say I'll do or not do something, I don't back down, whatever the consequences."

Wagner kept nodding, like a certain kind of spring-necked toy figure. "Gosh," he said eventually, for she was staring fixedly at him, "friendship with me hasn't helped, has it?"

"Fred," said Mary Alice, "I just intended to stay with you till this thing blew over. I didn't spell that out because I didn't want you to be disappointed. But now it looks a whole lot like I'll be moving in for good. My father is as stubborn as I am." She looked around. "Now where's your bathroom? I need a good hot tubbing."

Wagner believed the time to discuss the matter would be after her belated bath, so he politely found a clean towel for her and a thicker piece of soap than that snottily deliquescing in the niche above the tub.

Once Mary Alice closed the door behind her, he read the pink letter.

> DEAR FREDO —
> I admit I was darn mad when you stood me up. I still am some. But I'm getting a little scared by now. It doesn't seem like you at all to not get in touch all this time. You wouldn't be likely to stay out all night without informing me of all people. I'm going to try to find where you work — I bet Glen can tell me — and call there. But if I don't find you by noon, I'll bring the cops in. So *please* if you come back meantime, let me know.
>
> Your devoted but worried
SANDO

The affectionate diminutives were new since he had last seen Sandra. Unless the one assigned him were to be pronounced "Fraydo," shouldn't it be rather spelled with two *d*'s?

10

ʕʕ WHILE MARY ALICE WAS BATHING WAS A GOOD time to get straight with Sandra, and therefore he called the latter on the bedroom phone.

"Thank God," Sandra said. "I'll be right over."

Wagner had been sprawling across the bed. He sat up now. "Please, listen," he said. "I'm calling you from a public booth, downtown. I'm sorry about last night, but on leaving work yesterday I was seized by two husky men and pulled into the back of a limo, bound and gagged and held hostage in a secret place. Apparently they believed me a spy or agent of some group with whom they are adversaries. It was morning before they were convinced they got the wrong guy, and let me go."

"Miles told me every cock 'n' bull story in the book," said Sandra, "so I wouldn't bother if I were you. I just talked to your boss, one Jacqueline Rinsing. She told me you were seen leaving a hotbed hotel this morning with some little tramp."

"Does that sound like me?" Wagner asked. "Jackie's nursing a grudge, Sandra. Anyway, I quit my job yesterday, and she's just being vindictive."

"Wish you'd have discussed that move with me first,"

Sandra said. "Sounds as if it wasn't as well planned as it might have been. But come on home now. I'm not gunning for you."

For wont of a better response, Wagner said, "You're not?"

"Listen," Sandra said, "a little sowing of wild oats before making a change in your life is not a crime in my book, as long as hygienic procedures are observed, of course." She chuckled. "But that doesn't mean you can keep getting away with it. Next time I lower the boom."

He wondered why this woman was so attached to him, and he could not think of any reason except convenience. He was the nearest male neighbor of a suitable age and seemingly suitable situation.

Mary Alice, wrapped in an outsized towel, came into the bedroom, having cut the bath short for some reason. Wagner hated himself for feeling guilty towards both women.

Meanwhile Sandra was saying, "You certainly owe me one tonight. Name an expensive restaurant."

"I'll call you back," said Wagner. Mary Alice was advancing on him with an odd smile. "Someone has been waiting for the use of this telephone."

"You just get back up here on the double, Freddo," said Sandra. "I'm off all day."

Mary Alice bent and began to unfasten his fly.

"OK, Sandra."

"And Fred?"

"Yes?" Mary Alice's hand was in his trousers up to her wristbone.

"You should know you really had me worried. I even got Glen to let me into your apartment, on the chance you had passed out and were laying helpless there. . . . Fred?"

"Yes."

"You know what? I had to bribe him," Sandra said indignantly. "I guess he was just being responsible, though. But suppose something would have been wrong with you?"

"I'm all right," Wagner said dully.

With her free hand Mary Alice took the phone from him and hung it up.

"It's funny," she said. "As soon as I sat down in that warm water I got full of love." The big towel was tied across her breasts, but it was loose at the bottom, and she opened it now and straddled him. "If I had known it wouldn't hurt that much, I wouldn't have waited so long."

"I understand," said Wagner. He would have preferred to have his pants off or at least down farther.

"I *read* all about it," said Mary Alice, who looked from below as if she were riding a trotter. "God, how I read about it!" She was pink and damp from the bath.

Wagner wished he had gone to the front door and turned the knob that operated the deadbolt for which there was no outside keyhole. Sandra might barge in again on some pretext, or hearing that he was missing, Glen might even bring back his harlot.

"But nothing you read," Mary Alice continued, "really prepares you for the way it feels." She was beaming down on him. "There's something words can't do, Fred! So you see they have their limitations."

Wagner nodded. He could easily grant the point. He had never before copulated during a partner's monologue.

Mary Alice seemed to have recovered fully from her abhorrence of him on awakening. He saw no sense in bringing up that matter now and providing even more pretext for talk. Though she needed none.

She was shouting down at him. "I could go on forever."

Wagner was performing adequately, but to have matched her energy he would have had to simulate a glee he did not feel.

He answered, "Yeah. I know what you mean." This was the second and more serious occasion on which his marriage bed had been recently profaned. He could hardly be blamed for Polly Todvik's incursion, but here he was as Mary Alice's unresisting victim. Being in sudden sexual demand by both her and Sandra should have improved his morale more than it had. Instead he seemed to have more doubts about himself, not sexually but as to what might be called existential substance: was he really an independent entity? If he fell in a remote forest with no one about to hear the crash, would there be one?

He was summoned from this sentimental inquiry by the realization of his proximate fear: namely that someone was about to enter the apartment. That he heard the distant sound of the key was remarkable, for Mary Alice now was singing and in fact not badly: her voice was deeper and more supple than when speaking. Also she had an almost professional command of the lyrics of what Wagner recalled as a popular song of a season or two back. But with the turning of the lock he was out from under her and on his feet in one flowing movement that made her gasp, it appeared, with pleasure: she probably took it for a highly skilled sexual maneuver. She fell back on the pillow as if satiated.

In another efficient sequence Wagner seized his robe from the closet and donned it while closing the bedroom door behind him. However, rising from even a licit bed is never a firm foundation for a display of self-righteous indignation, even though it should have as good a claim as any, and in this case it was not quite that. Also, he was certain it was Sandra, on some pushy mission. Perhaps, for she seemed capable of it, with an idea of surprising him by being in bed when he returned from his supposed jaunt downtown: again she had suborned the corrupt Glen. Wagner had time to give this supposition some detail because whoever it was at the door was lingering there, with bumping noises.

It was Babe.

She had her back to him at the moment. She was fooling with a bulky object on a little flat truck whose rollers were being detained at and by the threshold. Surely its load was a stack of her personal possessions, which she had brought along because she was returning to him. This of course meant that he would have to get to the bedroom, hurl Mary Alice out the window, and get it closed again before Babe penetrated that far. The alternative was to activate the old joke, "Do you believe me or your own eyes?" Wagner's fancy could be as ruthless as it wished: it was utterly harmless to all living things. The reality of the coming moment would be the worst he had ever experienced, and there was no means of escaping it.

But then he had a wondrous inspiration. Babe had not seen or heard him: the truck had stuck a wheel, and she was bending to free it. He went quickly back to the bedroom and fell onto Mary Alice, who looked as though she were already asleep, carrying out the traditional role of the man to the limit.

"Mary Alice," Wagner said into her ear. "I'm going to roll you over on top of me so that you are not in contact with the bed at any point. There's someone in the living room whom I don't want to see at this moment: a person who's making a delivery. If we stay perfectly quiet, they won't know we're here! Won't that be fun?"

201

Mary Alice acquiesced. She was still in a mood in which she welcomed new experiences. When her body was separated altogether from the bed by that of Wagner, he was able to turn them both invisible. Mary Alice made no suggestion that she was aware of her new state. He was hugging her so fiercely she had probably closed her eyes.

He had left the bedroom door ajar, so that he could hear Babe's noises. He could not imagine what she was doing or why she was pulling the truck. That she had retained her doorkey was gratifying to him. However minor, it was a positive fact. Thus far Mary Alice was behaving well: staying quiet and only wriggling a little, which indeed had a friendly feeling. Wagner loved it when everything went right and everybody got along with one another, asking only what it was possible to provide. He didn't know what he'd do if Babe came into the room and sat down on the bed to take a pebble from her shoe.

. . . Or simply entered and glanced at the bed, for it occurred to him that the weight of two bodies would be making a visible impress in and of the bedclothes and mattress.

"Let's try another thing," he whispered into Mary Alice's ear. "Keep your eyes closed: this is fun!" He climbed out, then bent and, with an effort, managed to pick her up in his arms. She was no heavyweight, but even so he might not have had the strength to move while holding her, had she not relieved his arms of half the burden by swinging around to clamp her legs about his waist. Mary Alice was behaving better than he had a right to expect.

He was able, if awkwardly, to move to the door, to edge it farther open with an elbow, and peep down the little hallway into the living room. He now viewed Babe in profile. She was staring at something beyond his line of vision. Being invisible, he could have gone all the way out there to stand alongside his estranged wife, but that was taking quite a chance while giving Mary Alice a ride: the girl faced backwards at the moment, but who could say when the novelty of the game would wear thin for her and normal curiosity would return?

It soon appeared that such a change was not imminent: Mary Alice was utterly distracted by the opportunities afforded by their new situation. He was both helped and hindered by her avid belief that his purpose in holding her so was to make possible another genital connection, and now she was groping for him importunately.

In no time at all it became impracticable for him to move except in place. Despite his impatience, Babe had turned and left the apartment before Mary Alice lowered her feet to the floor, stepped back, and said, "Wow. I love it when you're kinky."

Seeing her blink, he materialized.

"Wow," she repeated, hugging him. "For an instant there, I thought screwing had made me go blind." She staggered back and exhaustedly spread-eagled herself on the rumpled sheets.

"Excuse me for a moment, Mary Alice," Wagner said politely, and he finally went out into the living room.

Babe had delivered to him a large television set. Singlehandedly she had hoisted it to the top shelf of the bookcase, where her geranium, coleus, and potted ivy had once sat. Scotch-taped to the screen was an envelope. Wagner peeled it away and found the doorkey and a typewritten note inside.

FREDDY,
When Cleve really *thought* about my leaving to open a gallery of my own, he decided to make me a full partner in his. Anyway he wants to spend more

time in Marrakesh. So, for a while anyhow, it will be the Guillaume-Morgat Gallery. Maybe eventually I can buy him out.

Replacement plants would have been nice, but I know you're no gardener and didn't want to give you a new chore. I think the time has come for you to relent and look at *some* TV. There are live operas and concerts and foreign films and book-talks and nature shows. One really can't stay contemptuous forever.

You'll be hearing from my lawyer soon. Please don't take it amiss. The terms won't be hostile. Nor am I.

Your old friend,
C.

Morgat was Babe's maiden name. It was the only thing about her he had never liked: something, from a different terminal consonant to perhaps an entire syllable, seemed to be missing from it.

But was it not typical of her to attempt at least to soften the blow of a formal filing for divorce? Perhaps he would, in the same spirit, look at some television. Babe had taken with her the tiny set on which he had sometimes watched routine news reports. This set looked gargantuan by contrast. The irony was that while living with him Babe would have thought it unspeakably vulgar. Still, it was darned sweet of her, so kind that he was almost moved to tears.

Mary Alice was sleeping soundly. After showering he put on some clothes and slipped down the hall to ring Sandra's bell.

She wore a fancy housecoat, frilly-trimmed, and quite as much makeup as she habitually used after dark.

"I can't stay," said he, stepping inside. "A lot of things have come up. I no longer work where I used to. Everything's in the air. I'll just have to take a raincheck for tonight."

"Now, now, calm down, Freddo: that's what I'm here for." She led him to the couch. "I want to hear all about it, and then we'll work everything out, I promise you."

He sat down, but he said, "I'm afraid it's not that simple, Sandra. There are complications in my life that I haven't revealed to you. Believe me, you've seen only one phase of my existence. You'd be surprised at some of the others, maybe even appalled."

She had remained standing. "Know what?" she asked. "I've got some Heimat."

"What?"

"Just the most famous chocolate cake in the world," Sandra crooned. "No matter how bad things looked for Miles, a piece of Heimat would make him feel better."

"That's awfully nice of you, but . . ." Wagner said uselessly, for on concluding her speech she proceeded inexorably to the kitchen and soon returned with a wedge of flat dark cake.

Wagner was at least relieved not to have to grapple with a towering hunk of many layers, for though having had nothing to eat since the lukewarm pizza of the wee hours, he was not in the least hungry.

He took a bit on the end of the fork. It proved to be the quintessence of chocolate, so intense as almost to sting his tongue.

"This really is good," he told Sandra.

She moued, an expression of some magnitude given the bright lipstick. "That was Miles's trouble. He had perfect taste in everything. But the only way he could indulge it was to steal the necessary funds."

Wagner took more of the cake, which was really like

candy. A small portion once in contact with the palate seemed like a mouthful. When he spoke it was in a voice altered by the sweetness. "Everything with me is in transition at the moment, and —"

"There's a bureauful of cashmere sweaters in the bedroom," Sandra said. "He was huskier than you, but I bet some of the things would fit. And the sports jackets with the double vents, and there's a beautiful one in fawn suede — they might be altered to fit you. I'd hate to see them just go to charity."

Wagner lowered his plate to the coffee table. Sandra was still hovering over him.

"Come on," said she. "I want do something about his stuff. I didn't have the nerve during those weeks all by myself."

That being the kind of plea one could not in decency reject out of hand, Wagner followed her, but when they reached the bedroom he said, "I really can't stay long. I've got a lot of serious problems, and I have to attend to them."

Sandra put her hands to his shoulder and stared first into one of his eyes and then into the other. "We'll meet them together, darling. You are not alone any more."

How difficult this was! He despaired that anything non-violent could be done to get her attention.

She now hurled open the door of a closet full of hangered male garments. "Look at this collection. It could do credit to a movie star! Select anything you like."

Wagner soon found himself enveloped in what there could be no denying was an exquisite piece of buttery suede. However, the mirror told him that the garment would have to be ripped apart and reconstructed before it could come anywhere near to fitting his figure. You had to try on the man's clothes to appreciate what a splendid physical specimen Miles had been, whatever his moral failings. It was chagrining to Wagner that though only his fingertips were visible below the jacket's sleeves and he could have put another of himself into the chest and shoulders, the waist was not all that voluminous, even given his current underweight.

The jacket still reeked of an intensely scented aftershave lotion.

Wagner took off the beautiful piece of hide. "Thanks anyway," he said to Sandra. "Too bad." He was prepared for her resistance, but was surprised when she sighed and nodded in agreement.

"Look at it like this, Freddo," said she. "You've got it all over him in other ways. You're steady, you're reliable, you earn an honest buck, and you're proud of it. You don't bite off more than you can chew."

The more she said, the more Wagner resented her sense of him. "Well," said he, "I'm not all that steady."

Sandra patted him with an owner's hand, then rehung the suede jacket on the shaped wooden hanger. "I told you I am willing to overlook your antics of last night. I don't ride herd on a man. So you had a few too many and helplessly went home with the trash from the next bar stool." She winked at him and suddenly punched him lightly in the belt buckle. "Just never do it again or I'll murder you."

That she could so easily rise above such a coarse act amazed him even more than that she had accused him of committing it — because the brief synopsis, if the rude characterization was omitted, did cruelly approximate his experience with Mary Alice, with the condition that she had not really begun to manifest tramplike symptoms until they had come to the apartment in the morning at hand: who could have anticipated her voracious appetite?

Suddenly he began to wonder whether Sandra, though having embarrassingly little in common with him, might not save him from Mary Alice. He had no idea of how, but she was surely forceful and probably ingenious as well, and if she so generously forgave him for the hypothetical episode with a stranger, how tolerant she would be when a professional colleague was the female who had ensnared him. . . . Perhaps she'd be willing to impersonate Babe, whom Mary Alice had never seen, and pretend to have returned to him. But then who could be found to pry him loose from Sandra?

"Anyway," Sandra was saying, "we've got more important matters to straighten out. Keeping both these apartments makes no sense. I want you to think about that. My lease doesn't run out till the end of next month, so we've got a little time to plan. What about yours?"

"Oh," said Wagner, who, weary from the activities of night and morning, lowered himself to the edge of the pink bed. "Another year, I think. I'd have to look it up."

"They're about the same size, I guess, so at least some of somebody's possessions would have to go." She sat down alongside him. "As you can see, my things are quite expensive: Miles insisted on that."

It took a while in his exhausted state for the implication to take effect. She was the second woman within an hour or so to threaten to share his domicile, and of course Mary Alice had apparently carried out the threat.

He rose abruptly. "Thanks for offering the clothes. Also thanks for the cake. I have to get going. I just stopped off to explain about last night." Which he had not done, but it sounded credible.

Sandra extended her fleshy lower lip. After a moment he understood that she was pouting. "I've got a *big* problem," she said, making the enlarged eyes of reproach. "I've been neglected."

Wagner had no patience with this style, of which however he had never had experience except as witness of movie scenes, where he had always seen it as tiresome.

"Well then, Sandra," he said, as if she were not doing this, "I'll be on my way. Oh, about tonight: I'm sorry to say that once again I can't make dinner. It's, uh, family business. You couldn't *believe* how many prob—"

Sandra had lain back on the bed and, with a scream of zipper, opened the entire length of her housecoat. The last thing he wanted at the moment was more sex, but he simply couldn't walk away when she said fervently, "Oh, honey, I really *need* some loving."

Given his exertions of the previous night and those only within the last hour, Wagner at the outset doubted whether he might once again rise to the occasion, but he must have so done, for Sandra was profuse in her display of satisfaction. To be seen as a stallion was new in his career, and though he was capable of male pride, exhausted as he was he hardly felt like whinnying in triumph. His big problem, how to earn a living now that he was unemployed, remained — unless he were to open a one-man agency for the depucelation of mature maidens and the servicing of lonely widows.

After he had performed the task at hand he expected Sandra to permit him to leave, but she was no Mary Alice. Quenching her sexual thirst freed her to exert her considerable energy in other areas. She sprang up and beat Wagner to the shower, then in a damp robe, hair cocooned in a towel, shouted, en route to the kitchen, "Waffles and sausage patties!"

Wagner was worried about what Mary Alice might do if she awakened and he was not at hand, but on stepping into the tub he decided to take a sit-down bath so as to put moist heat on those parts for which months of inaction had been replaced by frenetic demand, and hardly had the level of the affectionate warm water reached the bottom of his rib cage when he fell asleep.

When he awoke, Sandra was kneeling on the bathmat, a loaded plate in her left hand, a laden fork in the right.

"Open," said she, nodding at his mouth, and he obeyed the command and shortly was chewing on a forkful of waffle, butter, and syrup followed hard after by one of sausage patty. Actually, while he could have taken or left the chocolate cake, he found himself genuinely hungry for this traditional breakfast provender once it was between his lips. Sandra proceeded to feed the entire plateful to him, alternating the solid food with a mug of coffee which between trips rested on the tile floor.

When he finished the last morsel, the final sip, Sandra took away the crockery but returned immediately to scrub his back with a textured washcloth and a creamy soap.

This was all unique in his experience, and he could not deny it was pleasurable, but a certain uneasiness would not be dislodged: he was not the person Sandra took him for, and would never be. She was no more like Babe, his ideal, than he resembled the late Miles: a truth he alone seemed in possession of, for now once again she was trying to encapsulate him in the robe her husband had left behind: an almost furry terrycloth, of an old-gold background onto which were superimposed glossy black stripes, far from the traditional faded blue and threadbaring one Wagner had owned time out of mind. Not to mention that Miles's robe exuded the same strong reek of aftershave that had been smelled on the suede jacket: inhaling with the nose buried in a lapel might well cause asphyxiation.

Wagner found the will to oppose Sandra's attempt to towel him dry, a process to him more intimate than back-scrubbing or, for that matter, coitus. Nor did he even like to do it while she stood by, so he asked for privacy by pretending to need to use the toilet.

"Go ahead," said she. "I always think it's so homey."

So much for Miles's perfect taste. Wagner hastily dried himself and went out and reclaimed his clothes.

"Now, Sandra, I absolutely must go about my business. Thank you for a delicious breakfast and your other gener-osities. I —"

"I wish you wouldn't talk like I'm the Salvation Army," said she. "I *am* your woman, after all."

This was the kind of talk that made him shudder, but he preserved his composure. "You're a very kind person," he said. "And I owe you a dinner, but I'm afraid I can't —"

She was gently pushing him towards the apartment door. "OK, then get going. The sooner you do, the sooner you're back. Pick me up at seven. That should give you more'n enough time for your business. You know what would be nice? Have you got a tux? Let's go formal! What does it matter? You can wear Miles's, with the cuffs pinned up. After all, we've got a lot to celebrate."

Wagner was in the hallway before he would have had a chance to ask what, and anyway he dreaded hearing the kind of answer Sandra would have given.

He had no idea of how long he had been gone. He just hoped that if Mary Alice had awakened she had not been induced by his absence to manifest extreme behavior. When he unlocked and opened the door to the apartment he was gratified to see her seated on the living-room sofa, staring at the illuminated screen of the TV set lately delivered by Babe.

As it happened Mary Alice was attired in *his* old robe, which looked even more shabby than he had remembered it to be. She sat slumped on the small of her back, and her bare feet were propped on the plate-glass top of the coffee table.

"Shit," was her greeting to him, "they get the dumbest people in the world as contestants on those quiz shows. I'm sure it's an intentional policy, else *you* might try to get selected. You could make a year's income from one program. The questions are pathetic. Listen . . ."

From the TV set came a voice that said, "Henry the Eighth?"

"Sorry," was the baritone answer. "I'm afraid it's Kaiser Wilhelm."

"*Shit*," squealed Mary Alice, lifting her feet and banging them down on the glass. "Can you believe it?"

Wagner could see the screen only at an extreme angle. "Yes," he said dolefully. "Too bad. . . . Come on, Mary Alice, let's go down to the office and get our checks."

"I told you I'm not going back to that fucking place."

He really hated her new idiom. He also despaired over how he was ever going to dislodge her from the apartment. He would have felt more hopeful had she asked him where he had been.

It was almost to taunt her that he said, "I had to step out for a while."

After a pause in which she listened to the TV quizmaster, who was saying, "King Gustavus Adolphus," Mary Alice gave Wagner a roguish glance. "If we really get hard up, we

can make a nice living renting this place out by the hour."
She returned to the screen, from which issued an uncertain
voice that said, "War of Eighteen-twelve?"

Mary Alice grimaced. "Now, that's actually a tough
one."

"Thirty Years' War," Wagner said, only an instant before the same answer, preceded by the routine "I'm sorry,"
was heard from the television set.

"See," said Mary Alice. "It's just too bad you can't make
your vast knowledge pay such dividends."

"May I ask what you meant about renting out the apartment?"

"Oh." She crossed her ankles the other way. Plate glass
was not made to bear the weight of human limbs. "That
super showed up — Glen? He's quite a case, isn't he? He
was looking for you. I didn't know where you had gone,
so I told him to tell me if it was important, because you and
I are on confidential terms."

And she had been wearing his robe over her naked body.
Glen was a vigorous gossip: by nightfall her presence would
have been made known throughout the building.

Wagner tried to look on the bright side. "Good you
were here. He takes advantage of the tenants' absence to
snoop around."

"He had a proposition for us," Mary Alice said, smirking though keeping an eye on the TV proceedings. "In so
many words, what he wanted was a place to bring whores."

"Next time I really will call the cops," Wagner said, with
inadvertent reference to the episode of the day before.
"You'd think after his experience —" He stopped there.
"How dare he speak that way to you?"

"He didn't actually. I had to draw him out. I got the
idea, though. He definitely is a pimp of some kind."

"That swine," Wagner said. "I'm going to make a formal complaint to the management." This was sheer bluster, but he had to say something as he desperately searched his imagination for a means by which to get Mary Alice out of his home. "Well," he said next, though he was surely not hungry, "it's getting on to noon. We'll have to get lunch someplace."

"Let's call for takeout," Mary Alice said. "I don't want to put my clothes on again." She winked at him. "In case I get another attack of the hornies."

Wagner couldn't really understand this. "You don't experience any discomfort?"

"Not me! Who would have guessed?" She then cried at the screen, "The War of Jenkins' Ear! . . . I finally got one!"

"That must have been the toughest question thus far," said Wagner, who had not heard it. "I wouldn't have known that one: it's always been just a name to me." Mary Alice had hitherto unsuspected resources — like everyone else at the office; perhaps she too was about to publish a book.

His wonderment was superseded by a banging on the door.

"Don't answer that," said Mary Alice. "That pimp was amusing the first time, but I think maybe I ought to be insulted now."

"That won't be Glen," said Wagner. "He just barges in. I'd better open it. Why don't you go into the bedroom?" He extinguished the TV.

"In fact I'll get in bed," said Mary Alice, with a conspicuously suggestive smirk.

Wagner opened the door to see a small middle-aged man, with a sandy mustache and eyes genially crowsfooted, who carried a leather-trimmed canvas golf-club bag though his attire, a brown suit and green tie, seemed not designed for sport.

"Sir," said this man, "would you be Frederick Wagner?"

"Yes," said Wagner. "That's exactly who I am."

The small man pushed into the apartment, kicking the door shut behind him as he went. He then removed a long-barreled gun from the golf bag.

"I'm Alwyn Phillips, father of Mary Alice, the young maiden you have abducted. I am trying to control myself, but I am quite capable of using this weapon."

Phillips brought the muzzle of the gun to bear on Wagner's chest. Wagner was not conscious of feeling fear as such, yet he could not force his voice to become audible. He could however point vigorously into the corner beyond Phillips' left shoulder.

Mary Alice's father whirled and stared there. When he turned back, Wagner was invisible.

Phillips dashed down the little hall and into the bedroom, Wagner following. The armed man opened the closet and poked amongst the hangered clothing with the barrel of his weapon, then knelt and peeped under the bed. Both he and Wagner, at much the same time, next took note of the closed door of the bathroom across the hall. Phillips went out there and threatened loudly to blast away the lock.

The door opened and Mary Alice emerged. She was fully dressed in her street clothing.

She said prissily, "Dad, you're making a fool of yourself."

"Where is he, Maywee?" asked her father. "Is he in there, hiding behind your skirts?"

"He's not in here," said Mary Alice. "He hasn't mistreated me, either, as I assured you on the phone. Why don't you believe me?"

"Because you're too indulgent of human frailties," said Phillips in the intense way that contrasted with his appearance as a reasonable person. "I demand that you step aside and let me search the bathroom."

"Go home, Dad!" Mary Alice wailed. "I'm twenty-three years of age. I'm legally responsible for myself."

"Maywee," Phillips said sternly, "this isn't easy for me to ask, but I must: are you still *intacta*?"

"Is that any of your business?"

"Then you're not, pure and simple. And I know you. Such a venture could never be your own enterprise."

As always when an unannounced kibitzer on the private moments of others, Wagner felt some shame now — until he remembered that both father and daughter assumed he was listening from a place of concealment, and then he began to develop an indignation against them both. Mary Alice could easily cancel this emergency by simply answering the question in the affirmative. Why must she continue to compound the trouble that she indeed had begun the day before?

"Dad, you'll just have to accept the fact that I can't stay a little girl till I'm old and gray. Now put down the thirty-aught-six and go home."

"Not before I put a round or two into him," Phillips said in a dispassionate voice.

"How come you didn't bring the nine millimeter?" asked his daughter.

"Why, you ought to be able to figure that out. The permit's premises-only. It would be a violation."

"But, Dad, my God, isn't it also against the law to shoot somebody?"

Both of these people seemed to know the specialized jargon of firearms enthusiasts. Listening to them, Wagner felt even more out of his element than when in the company of Sandra. Any prolonged connection with Mary Alice was out of the question. No doubt her father would be overjoyed to hear such sentiments, but how to get the message to him without being shot first?

Alwyn Phillips answered his daughter now with a contemptuous laugh that sounded like the bark of a miniature dog. "No danger at the moment, it seems," said he. "Your admirer has fled the premises. Went out a window and down the fire escape, I suppose. It seems he is a poltroon." He lowered the weapon, banging the butt on the bare wood of the hallway floor. Babe had taken away the little rug, handwoven by peasants in the mountains somewhere. Wagner would rather have had that back than get the TV set: when one was barefoot it had been a welcome island in the straits between bedroom and bath.

"Oh, maybe you had to take the step eventually," Phillips was saying, "but why with this dog-eared example of the opposite sex? Why not with a fine lad of your own age, Maywee, and not this poor specimen of manhood?"

Making every allowance for Phillips' emotional state, Wagner was annoyed by the slurs, especially when made by such a runt.

Mary Alice spoke. "Don't judge by exterior impressions. Fred cares nothing about his appearance. So his posture is awful, he's skinny, his clothes are rumpled, his shoes scuffed, et cetera, et cetera. He'll even wear socks of different colors. So? But he has quite a mind."

"Oh, yeah?" her father asked defiantly. "And what has he invented for the betterment of humanity?"

Though of course he was flattered by her tribute to his

other gifts, Wagner had not realized that Mary Alice so despised his person. He was tempted to point out, from thin air, that it was not his mind that she had been over-using during the last twenty hours.

Phillips added, "That's my definition of brilliance: does it contribute to the welfare of humankind. I can scarcely find anything to admire in some cheap cleverness that has no purpose but to delude the naïve into buying that which they do not really want."

"My gosh, Dad, you can't expect everybody to be another Archimedes. Fred's not the only person never to have discovered a principle as far-reaching in its consequences as the lever."

Mary Alice continued to reveal new facets of herself, but none thus far that Wagner found especially fetching. Of course, one is always otherwise with members of one's own family than with even the closest of friends: indeed, just thinking about his sister could make Wagner feel like a ninny.

"The important point," said Mary Alice, "is that when it comes to words, he hasn't met his master." This was too outlandish an overstatement to be at all pleasing, unless of course it was confined to the preposterously literal: no, he had never sailed with Capt. Joe Conrad or gambled with Dusty at Roulettenburg or met Chuck Baudelaire at Mallarmé's *mardis*.

"If that were the case," said her father, his weedy mustache quivering in derision, "then how can it be we are not reading his byline on dispatches from the tinderkegs and flashpoints across the globe, or seeing his Burberry outside some chancellery on the cathode-ray tube? Answer: he's nobody, Maywee. He's simply used his seniority at the office to win your favor."

"You're wrong, Dad. He's publishing a book with Burbage."

The statement had an uncomfortably familiar resonance, but Wagner had no memory of ever making it to Mary Alice. Apparently he could not be trusted when it came to the matter of his unwritten novel.

Phillips looked as if he were impressed by what embarrassed Wagner to hear. "Can it be true?"

"Sure it is," said Mary Alice. "Same publisher as your favorite, Theodore Wulsin."

Phillips peeped at the ceiling, hand at chin. "You certainly know how to fetch me up short," said he, under the finger that was across his lips. "Mightn't you have imparted this information at the outset?" He lowered one eyelid. "But look here, he's married, isn't he?"

"That's a technicality," said Mary Alice.

Her father plunged a finger into his collar. "Well, you know you can count on me to apologize if I'm wrong," said he. "I won't be deterred by a narrow concern for amour propre." He glanced up and down the hall with an air of drama. "But if he's a man of probity, where *is* he? He disappeared without an argument."

"He's shy," said Mary Alice. "Not to mention you came in muzzle first."

"Indeed a slippery customer," her father said, not unkindly. He and Mary Alice drifted along the hall to the living room, where Alwyn found his golf bag and returned the firearm to it. Now, thought Wagner, would be the moment to jump him, but it was too base an impulse to survive. Caring about the fate of one's offspring was not a contemptible emotion: this was a lot more than Wagner's own father would have done, and though it might not have been his mother's fault as such, she *had* died when he was yet a boy. Suddenly he felt an unprecedented access of affection for his sister. After all, she was kin. But in the next moment he remembered that in his latest conversation with her he had made the outlandish claim that apparently he repeated later on during some sexual transport with Mary Alice, and he found himself resenting both women for believing him.

However, if he could only get rid of Mary Alice and then somehow elude Sandra except for carefully scheduled meetings, there was now no procedural reason why he could not sit down and write that novel. He had no job to deter him. And why did he need Gordon's permission to use the poet's name to make contact with someone in power at the Burbage Press? Things often seem impossible only because one has not tried them. Invisibility was a case in point.

. . . It was ridiculous that he continued to be on the retreat long since perfecting the process of becoming invisible. In the latest exercise of his power, when Phillips pointed the gun at him, he had disappeared in a millisecond. His potential was unlimited: by invisibly manipulating orders at headquarters, he could exert his will on an army. He could saunter unseen into the White House and, monitoring the President at close hand, learn all the secrets of state. From the Bureau of Engraving and Printing he could in one visit take away enough high-denomination bills to make him immediately rich, then go again at any time for replenishment.

But his moral principles had not changed. He had no intention of being a spy or a traitor, and as to stealing money that was not yet current, if he did that those responsible for it would be placed in jeopardy. Surely the sheets of newly printed greenbacks were tallied at every phase of their production. He could not prosper by the ruination of the innocent.

Thus despite his extraordinary gift, Wagner was still as much at the mercy of events as he ever was. Perhaps he lacked the basic stuff to be a legendary invisible personage, one of the pioneering titans of the tradition, on whose shoulders all future unseen practitioners would stand. Perhaps he was a poetaster, not a poet, of invisibility, his experiences a mere doggerel of the ability to elude the eye.

He found himself standing between father and daughter now, near his own front door.

"I am big enough to reconsider, Maywee," Alwyn Phillips was saying. "But I really would like the opportunity to converse with the gentleman."

"Undoubtedly you shall have it anon, *moan pear*," Mary Alice replied, continuing to manifest her father's stylistic influence though perhaps with an edge of parody.

Wagner stepped aside so that they would not collide with him when they embraced, but in fact they shook hands, not even with much apparent warmth. Reflecting on Mary Alice's newly awakened appetite for fleshly contact, Wagner once again felt an uneasy sense of responsibility.

Phillips and golf bag made their exit. Mary Alice stood before the closed door for a moment, then lifted her shoulders and sighed.

She lifted her chin, and shouted, "Where *are* you, Fred?"

Wagner went quickly to the sofa, lay down, and materialized. "Hi."

"You were there all the while," Mary Alice stated. "You were counting on Dad's being distracted." She gave him a look of brief vulnerability.

"It's just that I didn't want to be wounded," said Wagner.

221

"I suppose you'll tell me now his shotgun didn't have any bullets in it."

This time she sighed in another fashion. "Finally found something I know and you don't. All wrong. It's a rifle, and it *was* loaded with cartridges. Dad had blood in his eye."

"Then you saved my life," said Wagner, but without a genuine feeling of gratitude.

Mary Alice screwed up the corner of her mouth. "Does that surprise you? Seems little enough." She began to leer at him.

Wagner put out a finger. "Now, Mary Alice, I absolutely must go down to the office and get my check."

Her underlip rose to cover the upper. Then she opened both to say, "You don't care for me."

Though he found this display exasperating, Wagner did acknowledge that he owed her an explanation. "But you see, Mary Alice" — he had to restrain himself from using "Maywee" — "I need money to buy paper to complete that book of mine you told your dad about."

Her eyes displayed incredulity. "You mean you've really *got* such a book? I assumed you said that last night merely to get into my pants." She grinned brilliantly. "And it worked!"

At this point the telephone rang. Wagner stepped into the kitchen and answered at the wall-hung instrument.

"Mr. Wagner, this is Miss Brink at Dr. Leprak's office. Could you come to the office at your earliest opportunity?"

"Is something wrong?"

"How about this afternoon at one P.M. sharp?"

Wagner looked at his watch. "It's already eleven-forty. I've got some errands to run."

"Put them off," said Miss Brink. "Get over here."

"If it's that important."

"Please."

"I'm not supposed to be dying or anything, am I?"

"It's hardly my place to say," said Miss Brink.

Wagner felt no sense of doom as such; it seemed simply as if he were in another state of being as he hung up.

When he emerged from the kitchen Mary Alice was watching TV again. Now he might have welcomed a sexual advance from her as being an affirmation of his healthy life force, but she had changed in just that short a time.

She looked away from the screen to say, "Tell *them* I'm doing all right."

It took Wagner a moment to understand. Had he not taken her virginity he might never have been aware of how much resentment Mary Alice felt towards their former colleagues. But whatever the milieu, at any given time someone must always be the most newly arrived.

11

⌘ "I'M FREDERICK WAGNER."

Miss Brink consulted her appointment book. "I just don't see your —"

"*You* called *me*."

"I'm sure I did if you say so." She gave him a look of disapproval through the tops of her eyeglasses, chin remaining down.

"If you don't remember, then there's hardly the emergency you implied on the telephone," said Wagner. "I've got to do some important errands. I'll drop back later."

"My, oh my," blurted Miss Brink. "Now I recall. Doctor must see you immediately."

Waiting in a physician's office is not an occasion for joy in the best of times, but one could always take comfort in the assumption that if it was anything really bad, you would hardly be sitting there, leafing through outdated magazines: you'd already be in Intensive Care if not the grave. Only now did it occur to him that there could be a banal beginning to a fatal disease. Indeed, no doubt that was more characteristic than one for which the houselights were dimmed, the curtain opened, and the orchestra struck up. Now that he forced himself to remember, his own mother had eventually died from what had started as mild indigestion.

But in his current case he was not aware of manifesting any symptoms of disorder. His being underweight was due simply to missing so many dinners since Babe's departure. Under the right conditions, e.g., at A Guy from Calabria before the appearance of Babe and Siv Zirko or in Sandra's bathtub, it was proved he could eat a proper meal with relish. And his organs of generation had certainly been proved to be in superb condition. One thing to be said for Dr. Leprak's summons was that it served to get him away from Mary Alice for the moment. Wagner wondered whether he would have the nerve to return and quote the doctor as having urged him to have no traffic with women until the condition cleared up.

He had no time for further deliberation. Leprak came in from outside. Wagner had never before seen him in street clothing: it seemed he actually dressed like a physician in a play, i.e., in homburg and velvet-collared chesterfield. Seeing him on a sidewalk, Wagner would have thought: he looks too much like the legend to be living it.

Miss Brink told the doctor to call his wife. He vanished into his inner office, from which he soon buzzed for Wagner.

"Hi, Fred," said he belatedly, no doubt because he had had to consult Wagner's folder to get the name. "I don't want to call my wife, because I'm sure it would be only to hear that my boy has caused some kind of trouble at school. He's a scallywag."

The quaint term was noted by Wagner, who had previously heard it only in movies, but uneasy as he was it did not elevate his spirits.

"I've run out of ideas," said the doctor. "He's not quite

225

old enough to send to sea in a square-rigger." He lowered his head to study the papers before him. "We have a mystery here, Fred." He rose and walked to the long panel of backlighted milk glass on which were hung several X rays. "According to these you have no internal organs. Look for yourself."

But the best of X rays would have been untranslatable to Wagner. He confessed as much to Dr. Leprak after only a glance at the murky pictures.

"Take my word for it then," the doctor said. "And I've checked the machine, which works perfectly in every other case. Take off your clothing above the waist. Let's look through the fluoroscope."

Wagner was soon enclosed in this device, Leprak squinting at the screen in front of his thorax.

"By George, there you have it," said the doctor.

"My entrails?"

"A figure of speech," said Leprak. "In fact your internal organs are still missing and now your rib cage has joined them. Lean over and look down and you'll see what I mean."

Wagner did as directed. The screen was blank above his belt buckle.

Leprak stuck his own left hand between Wagner's thorax and the screen, and switched on the brief flash of power. The fingers were seen in skeleton form.

Wagner had never given thought to how he might eventually reveal his unusual ability to become invisible. He had assumed that such a revelation might bring more trouble than it would be worth. There were people extant for whom another's ability to become invisible would simply be a pretext for resentment.

Dr. Leprak took Wagner from the machine and placed

him on a treatment table, where he kneaded his midsection. "Yet they seem to be there," said he. "Anyhow, you'd hardly be going about your business without those vital parts." He slapped Wagner's stomach. "Well, old fellow," he cried, though Wagner was obviously much younger than he, "I'm going to book you into General for a more thorough examination than I am equipped to do here."

"Why?" Wagner asked. "I feel all right, and I gather you haven't found anything out of order in those other tests you made."

The doctor frowned into his face. "Come now, Fred. You are a man of reason. It simply doesn't make sense that your viscera are invisible to the X rays. You know we can't let that go and escape the charge of obscurantism." He chuckled in apparent self-approval. "By George, we'll find the cause and pin it to the cork. We're scientists!"

"All right then," said Wagner. "I saw no need of mentioning this earlier, because it might be confusing to hear, but lately I have been able to turn altogether invisible as an exercise of the will. Undoubtedly that state of affairs has something to do with this situation, wouldn't you say?"

Leprak was studying his own knuckles. "It wouldn't really *explain* it though, would it, Fred? Wouldn't it simply expand the existing mystery?"

Wagner had certainly not anticipated this kind of response. He had assumed he would be confronted with disbelief, no doubt derisive.

"I'm no scientist, I grant you," said he. "I'm just telling you what happens."

"Forgive me if I say you aren't doing a good job of it," Dr. Leprak said. "Come here and sit down and start over." He led Wagner to the chair before the desk, and went himself to the one behind it.

"I don't know what else to say," said Wagner, "than to repeat that I can turn invisible at will."

"Are you invisible now?" asked Leprak, the fingers of his left hand gathered into a kind of claw with which he picked at his chin.

"Well, certainly not!" Wagner was annoyed. "As you can plainly see."

"Let's not be hasty," said the doctor, with a rolling motion of his head as if to relieve a stiff neck. "Let's move step by step from what we can establish as veritable fact and try to avoid epistemological tricks by which *je pense* can pretend to be proof that *je suis*."

"Wouldn't you say that if you can see me it means I'm visible?" Wagner asked in exasperation.

"Now we're quibbling about terms," Dr. Leprak said, leaning back in his chair. "I'm no match for you there, I'm afraid. Don't you write lexicographical definitions or the like?"

"Yes, the like," said Wagner. He became invisible. "Is this sufficient evidence?"

"Now, that's not fair," the doctor complained, looking around the room. "Come out. I wish you'd stop treating this as a game. You remind me of my son. That's his trouble, you know. He's not a bad boy, but he tries to make everything a competition: that rubs people the wrong way."

"I'm still here where I was," Wagner said. "Only invisible." He felt silly having to explain something that was self-evident.

Leprak said, "I assure you I am not going to make an ass of myself and come over there and poke into empty space while you jeer at me from hiding. As your doctor, Fred, I'm asking you to submit yourself to further examination. Now is that unreasonable? If it turns out you are suffering from some disorder, I don't want you to say I was derelict in my professional duty."

"It sounds to me as though you are refusing to admit that I am invisible," Wagner said. "You are ducking the real issue. That's hardly science."

"On the contrary," said the doctor, "that's precisely what science does: reserves judgment till a preponderance of incontrovertible evidence has been provided. And all I contracted to do was to pursue the matter of the missing internal organs — remember that."

"You will grant that at least *they* are invisible."

"Not at all!" cried Leprak. "I will 'grant,' to use your term though it's hardly apropos, only that I was not able to see them just now with the fluoroscope."

Wagner got up and went to a little white-enamel table on which stood a jar full of cotton swabs. He lifted the jar and shook it at the physician.

"Look here!"

But as soon as it lost contact with the table, the jar vanished. Having nothing to see, Leprak continued to stare expressionlessly into the middle distance.

Wagner refused to be so vulgar, and so destructive, as to hurl the jar at the wall in the fashion of the protagonist in trick-photography invisible-man movies.

"I'm waiting," the doctor said after another moment. "But my time is not my own to squander, you know."

Wagner was exasperated. He wished he could reappear partially; that would certainly prove his point . . . but as it happened he possessed no technique for fine-tuning his state. He became visible all at once and in toto.

The doctor had blinked at the appropriate instant, or had been distracted, and therefore put no great value on Wagner's reappearance — unless it was for him some matter of face not to admit that he had been confronted with a phenomenon he could not begin to explain: in ex officio situations doctors outrank even the emperors and dictators of the laity and cannot afford to admit a loss. Wagner decided that delicacy was called for.

"I'll try to go through it more slowly," he said with a smile.

Leprak rose. "I'm sorry, Fred, we just don't have time for any more shenanigans. Mind you, I'm not worried, but I do want you to go over to General on leaving here. Now, it's not going to hurt, for golly sake." He had arrived at Wagner's side, and he patted him in the small of the back while grasping with his right hand at Wagner's fist. "They'll give you a milkshake and take some pictures." His mustached chuckle was designed to dismiss all menace from this projection.

"That's a GI series, isn't it?" Wagner asked, remembering the earliest phases of his mother's last illness. "I'll have to be there overnight?"

The doctor leered into his face. "If you'll reflect, Fred, isn't that what hospitals are for, and aren't we lucky that surgery is no longer done in barbershops?"

Wagner left the treatment room and spitefully became invisible during the short trip to Miss Brink's desk and slipped out of the office without paying. Of course the bill would be mailed to him, but he was anyway evading compliance with Leprak's pay-as-you-go policy, announced in prominent black type on a white card that stood atop the little counter provided as a surface for check-writing.

Once he reached the street he found that his exasperation with the doctor was replaced by worry. Until now he had avoided looking at his situation in that way, but of course it could not be denied that his ability to become invisible had to have a cause; perhaps it was a pathological condition, as was said to be the case with the husky voice of certain popular singers. And it might not be good news that he now was able to disappear instantaneously, whereas only a day or so ago it had taken him a few seconds to complete the process. What had at first seemed such a useful change might instead be seen as an advanced stage of disease. His internal organs had disappeared permanently from detection by X ray. Obviously they remained in place and were functioning, else he would be dead, but it was clearly not an acceptable state of affairs even if it went no further, but the worry was that, like many human progressions, it would be degenerative.

And if the innards went, could the carapace be far behind? To be permanently invisible would have little to recommend it — Wagner was by now sufficiently experienced to know that.

He decided to go to the hospital. From a street telephone he called both Mary Alice and Sandra to tell them as much. Neither answered. It was likely that the former had gone back to sleep, so he hung up after not too many rings, but he persisted in Sandra's case, determined to force her to hear what he was saying for once and inclined even to attempt to bring their affair, though not necessarily their friendship, to a halt by confessing that another woman had moved in with him. At this point Mary Alice was the greater problem. But he succeeded in speaking with nobody.

It was now too late to pick up his check and get it to the bank before closing time. As it happened, he had counted on collecting some cash by that means, and had left the remainder of his ready spending money at home with Mary Alice, should she want to send out for food before he returned. In the cab, within a block of the hospital, he discovered that he carried too little cash to meet the fare recorded on the meter. He became invisible and as unobtrusively as he could left the vehicle while it was stopped at a light, yet the driver did not miss the sound made by the closing door and jumped cursing into the street to look for him in vain. A day or so earlier Wagner would at least have pretended to himself that he would memorize the number of the cab and the name of the firm which owned it, with a purpose of sending the fare along by mail, but now he had become too desperate and therefore too spiritually coarse even to consider such an exercise in conventional morality.

He materialized to be admitted as a patient in the hospital. Despite the astronomical price he signed up for a private room, for conversing with a stranger in another bed would have been unacceptable at this time.

As soon as he reached his room he again tried to telephone Mary Alice & Sandra, of whom he was beginning to think as a team; it might soon get to the point that having reached one, he would ask her to take a message for the other. As it was, he still could not rouse either.

But as a patient in a hospital he assumed he had gained the right to break the rule against calling Babe at work, and he dialed the number of the Guillaume Gallery. The phone was answered by Cleve. Wagner did not want him to know who was calling, so he lowered his voice and also assumed a style of speech other than his usual.

"Hiya. I wanna talk to Carla."

"Who's this?"

"Don't you mind about that," Wagner said. "Just you put her on the line."

Guillaume said, "Pardon me, but I don't think you have to be rude."

Wagner's patience was fraying. "Goddammit," said he, "is she there?"

"Is it really Carla you're after?" Cleve's voice had gone very arch.

The last thread parted, and Wagner said, "Do you think I'd be calling for *you?*"

The gallery owner sounded full-throated laughter. "What a bitch you are, Ralphie! I trust you didn't think you were fooling me. So where are we eating tonight?"

Wagner hung up in chagrin. He must wait awhile before placing a call in his normal voice. And now that his demon had been temporarily appeased, he was able to regret the manifestation of bad feeling against Guillaume, who was not the world's worst, and he began to think about making it up to him, along with performing an act of atonement with respect to Roy Pascal, by perhaps bringing the two of them together in view of their common interest. However, Guillaume never seemed to lack for friends, well-to-do as he was, and Pascal was not all that attractive. It must be tough to be in his situation with so few resources.

On a generous impulse Wagner now phoned him at the office.

"Roy, Fred Wagner. Let me say this before I run out of nerve. I apologize for yesterday. I hope you can find it possible to disregard what I said: I realize now it was contemptible nonsense. You've always been more than decent to me."

Pascal was obviously moved. "That's awfully nice of you, Fred. It takes a lot of character to say such a thing. How are you?"

Wagner said flatly that he was OK. Squaring the account was one matter; he didn't want the man to believe he was offering close friendship.

"I hope you'll continue to keep in touch," Pascal said. "This place's not the same without you. In any event, I hope you will come to the reception next month. The invitation's in the mail."

"Reception?"

"I told you," said Pascal. "I'm getting married. But now, please, no gift is expected."

"What's his name?" Wagner asked, fortunately in a voice that must have been so contorted as to render the possessive pronoun incomprehensible, for Pascal answered with no special emphasis.

"Dorothy Kilbride," said he. "My childhood sweetheart. She got sidetracked for a while and married somebody else, but they're divorced now and we're getting together at last."

Wagner's annoyance now switched itself to focus on Mary Alice. How irresponsible she was! He had all but disgraced himself with Pascal.

"My congratulations," he now said with shy heartiness. "I hope you'll be very happy."

"I trust we'll be seeing a lot of you and Carla," Pascal said. "I've certainly told Dorothy about my best friend and the terrific woman *he* married, and she can't wait to meet you both."

Wagner made some additional congratulatory comments and got away from him. This time he at last made telephone contact with Mary Alice.

"I'm in the hospital, of all places," he told her. "I have a mysterious condition: that is, I mean I'm *in* one. Now, Mary Alice, with all respect, I am aware that in view of what happened last evening, you believe we are in a special sort of association, but you must realize that it had to happen eventually with someone of the male sex. Perhaps it was just by chance that I was at hand."

"I don't know what kind of crap you are pulling now," said Mary Alice, "but I won't buy it."

Irritated by this response, Wagner asked, "Why did you say Roy Pascal was homosexual? He's not. He's getting married."

"Now, let's not go into that again. I *told* you: you and he were inseparable. He didn't have a wife, and you had just lost yours. Neither of you seemed to know I was alive — in that way. *Fred?* When are you coming home? I *need* you, if you know what I mean: I don't want to spell it out on the public wire."

"Didn't you just hear me say I am in the hospital?" He had originally intended to play down his "condition," whatever it was, but now decided to exploit it. "I've got my doctor worried. I might have a serious disorder. In any event it looks as though I'll be here for a while."

"A *while?*" Mary Alice asked in whining incredulity. "You say that just as if it doesn't mean anything to you at all. What about me in the meantime?"

"Aha," said he. "I left some money in the blue bowl in the kitchen cabinet on the right of the fridge, for groceries and other household needs, or you can eat out. I've got a charge account at the deli two blocks down and also at the bakery around the corner: just mention my name."

"I don't care about *food*, for Christ's sake!" Mary Alice's voice had turned nasty. "You just get back here pronto or I won't answer for the consequences." She hung up.

After a moment Wagner realized that this had ended better than it had begun. The "consequences" were just what would be welcome: *viz.*, that Mary Alice would walk out on him. As to Sandra, he decided not to try again to reach her. He would simply stay out of touch so long that she would eventually have to infer that he was indifferent to her. It was unpleasant medicine to prescribe in the case of someone who had given him nothing but kindness, but he saw no alternative.

He refused to abandon a belief in the possibility of a permanent reunion with Babe, though no hope might be more unreasonable.

He now phoned the Guillaume Gallery again, and when Cleve answered he said, "Hello, Cleve. This is Fred Wagner. How are you?"

"I'm so sorry," said Guillaume. "Do I know you?"

"Carla's husband," Wagner said. "We met once at an opening several years ago. No reason for you to remember."

"I'm sure that's true," Guillaume said abstractedly. "But husband? Shouldn't your name be Morgat?"

"That's her maiden and professional name."

"I'm so pleased we've got that cleared up," said Guillaume. "Would you like to leave a message?"

"She's not there?"

"She's holding Siv Zirko's hand. This show has him all frazzled. He's an *artist*, you know. I warn you: never let one in your house."

Wagner asked, as if with polite curiosity, "Isn't the show sold out?"

"Of course," said Guillaume. "And that's just the trouble, you see. Siv feels he's done it all, shot his wad with nothing left, never to sculpt again."

" 'Sculpture,' " said Wagner. "The verb is 'to sculpture.' There is no such word as 'sculpt.' "

"Why, sure there is," Guillaume said enthusiastically. "I use it all the time."

Wagner took a lungful of the medicinally scented air of the hospital and said quickly, "Siv is a titan."

"Why so lukewarm?" asked Guillaume, making what Wagner at length identified as a joke.

"He's changed studios, hasn't he?"

"*Nobody* ever tells me anything," Guillaume complained. "But I just saw him two days ago at the old place."

Wagner got the address by pretending to want to verify an invented one: he had learned this technique from a movie. He hung up just as a tall nurse entered the room.

"Afraid you don't get dinner, Mr. Wagner," said she, prognathously inspecting the chart that hung at the foot of the bed. "We've got to take a look at your tumtum and the other things in its locality, and everything's supposed to be emptied out by tomorrow morning."

"Fine," said Wagner.

She peered at him. "You can't mean that."

"Oh, but I do," said Wagner, and then feigned drowsiness. As soon as the nurse left he found his clothes in the closet and put them on. Invisibly he left the room and the hospital, materialized to catch a cab, and then once again beat a furious driver out of the fare by disappearing: the difference this time was that Wagner felt no sense of triumph.

Zirko's studio was in a sizable building in a district of wholesalers. A carpeting business occupied the ground floor, and a truck was pulled across the sidewalk at a loading door. Alongside stood three stocky persons who were airing contrasting opinions, one punctuating his remarks with the tiniest butt of a cigarette.

The board in the little lobby to the left of the carpet firm said a company with "Belting" in its name was on 2 and "SZ" was on the floor above that. Wagner used the iron stairs, for he assumed that the outsized elevator opened directly into Zirko's studio.

On reaching the third floor he went to the available door, which was made of battered, dun-colored metal and unlabeled. Still invisible, he turned the knob and entered. He was in a large enclosure, which obviously had been designed for industrial use. It was now empty up front, near the wall of large, iron-framed windows, one of which was open on the street. At the distant rear were collected, in a crowded corner, the furniture and appliances pertaining to quotidian life: sink, fridge, stove, and not far from that cuisinatory complex, a couch, a canvas sling chair, and a kind of coffee table of which the base was a metal milk case and the top a rectangle of unpainted plywood. No works of art were in evidence throughout the vast loft, but that it was Zirko's studio was confirmed by the artist's presence on the couch.

Babe sat in the canvas chair. Wagner approached her, walking quietly on rubber-soled shoes.

The loft was so long that it took him a while before he was near enough to hear what Zirko was saying. The artist was barefoot. He sprawled on the couch in such a fashion that the protuberant crotch of his tight denims was projected towards his vis-à-vis.

By the time Wagner got there, Zirko was rounding off his latest comment with a sequence of "shits."

"Oh," said Babe. "I've heard all of that before. Bet you've already forgotten your depression after the last show. You'll feel differently when your creative reservoir has been refilled, just as you did then."

"But I didn't jack off into a plastic bubble that time," said Zirko. "That's *all* of me down there, doll."

"But now you must give even more," Babe said with a

piety that of course could have been bogus. "Isn't that what we expect of the artist?"

Zirko sat up. "What bullshit you talk, lady. Why don't you do something really meaningful? Come over here and sit on my face."

Babe spoke as if he had been silent. "And, if we must be practical, much as you've made from this show, given taxes, et cetera, et cetera, the money goes, and you like money, Siv. I want to show as much of you as I can while you're so hot."

Wagner's regard for her was returning after this nonsentimental speech. If making a profit was the point, then her obsequiousness towards this little rodent was probably permissible. But whatever Zirko spent money on, it obviously was neither his studio-home nor that of his wardrobe thus far seen by Wagner.

"That's right, I *am* hot," Zirko said petulantly. "I want to get laid."

"Of course," said Babe, "it *is* true that having too frequent shows can cause a critical backlash. You know for all the impression he gives of irresponsibility, Cleve is actually a master of timing. I've learned an awful lot from him. Underneath it all, he's a natural businessman. That's not apparent on the surface, but you should see him handle the museum people — and sometimes the private collectors are even tougher. You have to agree that he's really done a fantastic job with you, Siv."

"Oh, I don't know," Zirko said, depressing both his heavy eyebrows and the corners of his mouth, "I always do well, whatever dealer I got. Now what Guillaume's got going for him is the faggot connection: that's who buy the pieces like 'Artist's Cock' and my plastic ass: rich buttfuckers." He made a seated bump-and-grind. "Hey, open us a bottle of champagne. Chilled glasses in icebox." He pulled up his legs and stretched out full-length on the sofa, left wrist over his eyes.

Babe went to the refrigerator. When the door was open Wagner could see that, aside from several wide-mouth glasses on the uppermost shelf, there was nothing in the fridge but foil-necked bottles of champagne. Yes, to maintain that supply Zirko must obviously continue to have frequent shows.

Babe removed one of the bottles and struggled with the little wire cage that enclosed the bulbous head of the cork. On the rare occasions when she and Wagner had had a bottle of bubbly, it had been his job to open and pour, and Babe had paid no attention to the process. At the moment she was on the verge of breaking a nail on the wire.

Wagner was at her side. Without thinking, he said, "Take hold of the little loop and twist counterclockwise."

"Oh," said she and followed his instructions. She apparently took his voice for that of Zirko, though to his ear there was little resemblance. When the wire was off she worked at the cork. Suddenly, with a smart report, it popped out and struck Wagner in the forehead, for just at that moment he had been standing in a situation from which he might offer more help if needed. The metal cap had remained on the cork top, and the blow was medium-painful. Wagner rubbed vigorously at it as Babe poured a glassful of champagne and took it to the now apparently somnolent Zirko.

"Siv," said she, speaking down, "are you asleep already?" She waited for a moment, but the artist displayed no sign of life. "I'll put it right here on the floor," said Babe, bending to do that. As she was on her way back up,

Zirko's forearm left his side, where it had been paralleled, and in a trice it was up under her skirt to the elbow.

She shrieked in surprise and kicked the champagne over; it foamed on the floorboards. Yet she did not appear to be outraged.

"Now look what you've done," she chided. She retrieved the glass, which had not broken, and returned to the sink, where the bottle had been left.

Wagner was aching to do something violent to Zirko, but because his concern for Babe must always be preeminent, he restrained himself. Obviously she believed every indulgence must be offered to an artist so essential to the livelihood of a gallery owner. To recognize that truth was to embrace the kind of realistic morality for which Wagner had hitherto frankly lacked the stomach. But it seemed to be the fundamental way the world worked, and not even being invisible had any effect on it.

Babe brought Zirko a fresh glass, and this time he sat up and accepted it. She then poured one for herself and sat down in the canvas chair. In response to the sculptor's salute with raised glass, she took the slightest sip of the champagne. Babe had never been much of a drinker.

"C'mon!" cried Zirko. "Get some of that drink in you. It'll warm up your twat."

Wagner stepped to the couch and slapped the artist's face as hard as he could swing. Zirko's head snapped to the side, and immediately a handprint in subcutaneous blood began to form on his left cheek. Yet he did not lose a drop from the glass he held. He drank the champagne down now in one draught, then shook his head as if to clear it.

"Damn," he said, "I might be coming down with something. Maybe I'll have a stroke and die without ever getting into your pants, but it won't make you sad, right? My work'll just go up in value. You parasite dealers are all the same." He gestured at her with the empty glass. "Life is short, and art is my dong. Bring the bottle and leave it, and open the next one. I'm going to get you dead drunk, lady, and then I'm gonna give you the stuffing of your life."

Babe gave him more champagne but took none for herself. As commanded, she left the bottle on the floor near him. He reached for her again as she put it down, but she evaded his fingers and went back to her chair, where she sorted through the interior of the soft briefcase she had long carried in lieu of a purse. "Aha, here it is." She glanced at the sheet of paper. "Amsterdam. They're enthusiastic." She looked at Zirko. "The retrospective. So that makes Munich and Stockholm and —"

"I can't seem to get it through your fuckin' head," said Zirko. "My career's over. It's the late Siv Zirko. The artist is deceased . . . only his royal red American pecker is alive." While speaking he had been opening his fly.

With gentle reproach, Babe said, "Siv, please! Be serious."

Wagner went invisibly to the sofa and, though he was not an exceptionally strong man, seized Zirko by the collar and lifted him to a standing position, at which point he clutched the seat of the sculptor's jeans with his remaining hand. At a running frog-march he took Zirko down the entire length of the loft to the wall of windows, and when they arrived before the one that was open, he hurled his captive through it.

At last he had committed a criminal act that could not be undone. He was now a murderer, but having been invisible at the time of the crime, only he could have identified himself as the perpetrator.

12

&ce2; WAGNER BECAME VISIBLE AND GREETED BABE.

"Fred," said she, frozen in the canvas chair, "something terrible has happened. Siv just jumped out the window. He didn't give any warning at all." She was so distracted by Zirko's defenestration as not to notice anything remarkable in Wagner's sudden materializing in a place in which he had never before been seen.

"Oh," he said cruelly, "I'm sure there's a never-ending supply of his kind in the world."

In her current state she was not quick to take offense. "No," said she, "all the critics agree that Siv Zirko is one of a kind, one of the talents that come once in an era, and he had only just arrived at the threshold of what could have been his major period. Oh, my God." She put her face into her hands.

Wagner did not want to appear insensitive and therefore he sought to give Zirko a justification for committing suicide. "I heard he believed he had lost his gift: that of course could make a man desperate."

Babe's blanched face came into view. "He said that after every show. It was meaningless."

Wagner was cruel again. "Well, not quite, Babe. He

really did go out the window." He might have felt guilty had he acted from Philistine motives, but his negative feelings towards Zirko were personal; considerations pertaining to art did not really apply. Suddenly he remembered his humanitarian obligation. "Where's the phone? I better call an ambulance." But as he asked he saw a telephone on the wall, up front by a fire extinguisher, and he walked towards it at a measured pace.

Before he got there, Zirko lurched through the intervening doorway. He looked only slightly shaken, not visibly bruised or battered. His fly was still open.

He glanced at Wagner, whom he had never seen before, without surprise or indeed anything but the usual self-obsession. "That did it," he said. "I'm productive again."

Wagner could not have defined his own reaction except as a complex mixture of both relief and regret. Therefore nothing seemed appropriate but an introduction.

"I'm Fred Wagner," said he. "Carla's —"

Zirko brushed him aside and lurched towards Babe, shouting, "I'm back on track!"

Babe rose. "My God, Siv! It was all a joke?"

"Far from it," said Zirko. "It wouldn't have worked if I hadn't been dead serious. I threw myself out that window with every intention of being spattered on the street below. I tell you, stimulating my faculties demands more extreme measures as the years go by."

Babe asked with awe, "But how did you survive the fall?"

Zirko grinned. "An open truckful of discarded mattresses was at the curb below at just that moment! Now can you doubt that I am a man for whom Fate has something special in mind?"

Wagner certainly could not, else he would have been

244

sorely tempted to try another defenestration. As it was, he realized that he was up against something opposed to which his own powers were nil.

"The real point of this episode, however, *is*," Zirko was telling Babe. "I now know where to go from here. I get a suit of coveralls, you see, with helmet and face mask, and I cover myself with pigments, and I leap through the window and plunge down into a canvas mounted horizontally in the bed of a truck — no, wait a moment, onto a canvas lying on top of one of those safety nets used by firemen to catch people jumping from burning buildings."

"*You're developing a new style*," Babe said with low volume but great intensity.

"Babe," said Wagner, "would you mind introducing me?"

"Siv, this is Fred Wagner," said she. "He's a . . . writer."

Despite the hesitation, Wagner was grateful to her for using the honorific term.

Zirko winked at him. "This is going to make your career, a scoop like this: Zirko has never worked with color." He lay down on the couch and said, "Please try not to misquote me, and include the salty language, or it can't be authentic Zirko. If I say 'cunt,' don't write 'lady,' or there ain't gonna be nobody who will buy it."

Wagner tried something new, at least in this context. "You prick," said he, "anyone can defecate in a jar and call it art, but can *you* become invisible?"

"The unseen," said Zirko, "is always a part of any work of art. What's visible is only the tip of the iceberg."

"For a change the subject is not you, you bastard, but me! I can disappear right before your eyes. Babe! I want you to see this." But his wife was speaking with energy into the telephone. He became invisible anyway, and shouted at Zirko, "Look here! Can you see me?"

"As a painter," Zirko said, "I must forgo the tactile. I will be denied an entire dimension. But I'm counting on the sheer drama of the act, that is, the vault through the window, the plunge to the truck, the trampoline effect, et cetera, et cetera, to supply what would otherwise be missing. What I seek is no less than a synthesis of ritual, dream, and gymnastics."

Invisible, Wagner said, "I preferred you in the foul-mouthed phase. Go back to making obscene overtures to my wife. You'll get no more resistance from me." He went to Babe. "I'm leaving now," he shouted. "I won't bother you again. But you were *wrong*, Babe, to ignore me. This is really a unique power, and furthermore I can control it. I could use it to accomplish something remarkable, if only someone would believe in me."

But Babe continued to speak into the phone, oblivious to him. Wagner could have tried something obvious, like tapping her on the shoulder, but he deplored vulgar effects — and after all they had not succeeded with Dr. Leprak.

Therefore, having no means by which he could do more to make his point, he returned to the hospital, where the same nurse who had previously told him he would be served no food dropped by to taunt him with a repetition of that announcement.

Again he disappointed her by a display of indifference.

"Man does not live by bread alone," said he. "Bring on the barium."

But now Miss Hogan, identified by the nameplate high on her gaunt left chest, delivered a telling thrust. "They've changed their minds: they've got to dig a bit deeper."

"Do you mean surgery?"

246

"Not exactly," said Miss Hogan, who had a mouth that fell naturally into negation.

"You're lying, aren't you? They intend to do exploratory surgery."

"Well, there you are. You didn't say the magic word first time."

" 'Exploratory'?"

"Why sure: they're not going to take anything *out*."

"If they'd only pay attention when I became invisible," Wagner said bitterly. "They're not going to learn anything by cutting me open."

Miss Hogan put her hands on her straight white hips. "Look who knows more than the people who spend their lives in medical practice. I'd think you'd be grateful."

"I would if I were sick. But I don't think there's anything wrong with me. I just have a remarkable gift."

"Which is — ?"

"The ability to become invisible." He extended a petulant chin. "For a while I did my best to conceal it, and I don't know why. I guess I was afraid it would bother people. The fact is, now when I reveal it no one seems to care. Which makes this hospital business hard to understand. Doctor Leprak refused to take me seriously when I made myself completely invisible in his office. Yet he wants to cut me open because my internal organs don't show up on the X rays."

"That's easy to explain," said Nurse Hogan. "One thing is just private. Whereas the other's *medical*."

"Would you do me a big favor?" Wagner asked. "Just watch me become invisible and then tell me what you think."

"Now, Mr. Wagner," said Miss Hogan, rapidly leaving

the room, "you should realize I don't have time for that. I've got patients here who might die at any minute."

Of course she was right. But the whole truth was even more devastating: it wasn't only people concerned with mortal illness who lacked the time to do justice to him. In all the world there was no one who would willingly and with more than a polite interest serve as his audience.

He simply had to take the courage to accept the truth that the old life had arrived at its logical end, that to persist in trying to make a go of it would be as fruitless as his attempts to get some serious acknowledgment of his ability to become invisible.

He slept well and he rose early, before they came to take him to surgery, and wrote a farewell note with writing materials to which he invisibly helped himself at the nurses' station.

TO WHOM IT MIGHT CONCERN:
I intend to drown myself as soon as I can reach the river after concluding this message, the purpose of which is not to posture but rather to allay all possible doubt as to the nature of my death: it will definitely be self-inflicted and not a crime for which anyone else can be accused. I accept all responsibility, and not only for this act but for all else I have done or failed to do, and for those who believe I owe them an apology, please take one from this text, which is as compromising as I shall ever again find it possible to be.
FREDERICK V. WAGNER

With a water tumbler he anchored the note to the bedside table, dressed in his street clothes, and left the hospital invisibly. Arriving at the promenade along the river, he saw with approval that he was not alone, despite the earliness of the hour. Still some distance away, what appeared to be the figure of a young woman, probably out for her morning constitutional, was striding vigorously in his direction. It was essential to his scheme to have at least one witness, in full view of whom he could remove his outer clothing and plunge into the water. She would never see him surface. His identity would be established by the wallet to be found in the discarded jacket. Wagner was proficient enough at underwater swimming to travel downstream to a point at which he could emerge from the river invisibly with nobody the wiser. There could be no real impediment to his being declared legally dead, and what a lot of matters would thereby be resolved, to, so far as he could see, universal satisfaction, for surely both Sandra and Mary Alice would be no less capable of dealing with the loss than they had been in fitting his presence into their arbitrary fantasies. Babe's way would now be without obstacle, and his sister might eventually realize that she was better served by a dead brother whose success had been imminent than by one who had actually achieved renown.

What could not be as confidently projected was his own future, but that was the very excitement of it. He would emerge from the river fully grown but otherwise in much the same situation as at his first birth: wet, (very nearly) naked, and with no possessions and no means for independent support. To maintain his new life he could never use any part of the old identification. He must go to an altogether different part of the country, and not one which any of his old associates would have a reason to visit: which would eliminate from consideration anyplace with a shoreline, a colorful history, sporting facilities, or dramatic vistas. He could probably expect foul weather, the fumes of industry, and neighbors of low culture, perhaps even

249

benighted bigots who would naturally resent a man of mind like himself . . . but was he such, after all?

In any event it was high time to step off the path and materialize behind one of the stouter treetrunks in the bordering park, for at her smart heel-and-toe pace the young woman was drawing near — and now to her witness could be added that of the large man who had emerged from a thicket in the grove into which Wagner was just withdrawing and who moved rapidly to intercept her.

With two citizens to confirm his bogus watery suicide, the success of Wagner's plan was assured. He must now move to execute his own role in it, and let the future take care of itself. He would be a new man: surely opportunities would find *him*. He might even go so far as to write his novel.

He checked the situations of the only two other human beings with whom he shared the early-morning landscape: if they were friends, lovers, they might be too distracted by each other to observe him.

But their conjunction, which occurred now, was anything but amiable. The man, a husky specimen, had seized the woman from behind. Her struggles were ineffectual within his grasp. He carried her to the very cluster of trees where Wagner invisibly stood, hurled her to the earth, displayed a long-bladed knife, and addressed her with intense hatred.

"*Bitch*, I'm going to take your money, come in your mouth, and slice you up."

Wagner found a rock the size of a fist, and clamping it in his fingers, he swung it as hard as he could against the skull of the prospective thief, rapist, and murderer. But the man was in motion at the instant of the blow and thus inadvertently escaped the full force of it. He was hurt and bleeding; but seething with increased energy, he spun about and slashed the air with his blade and cut a slit in the sleeve of Wagner's jacket, though he could not have known that. In fact he knew nothing, for he could see nothing, and he cursed violently and continued to stab the air.

"Go *on*," Wagner shouted at the woman on the ground, "run away!"

But she failed to act on the advice, which perhaps was unconvincing without a visible source, and her attacker, with flashing knife, turned back to the business for which he had come, not in the least deterred by his bleeding head.

Wagner had to strike him twice again before the man reluctantly buckled at the knees, slowly fell as it were in sections, and at last lay prone and unconscious.

Wagner seized the fallen knife and hurled it into the river. Then he knelt by the woman, who as it proved had not responded to his earlier directions, because she had fainted.

He remembered to become visible before gently agitating her to consciousness. She had exceptionally beautiful eyes.

"My name is Fred Wagner," said he. "This thug is out of action at the moment, but I urge you to get up and leave before he comes to. Even though I got rid of his knife, he looks like he still could be an ugly customer."

She sat up and stared at the recumbent form of her attacker. Then she gave Wagner her wonderful eyes once more. "You did that?"

He shrugged. "Yes. . . . If you think you have the strength, maybe you could go up to the street and call the police. I don't want to leave this guy."

"But what about *you*?" she asked with concern. "Are you armed?"

He considered whether he should reveal that he possessed the ability to become invisible at will, which was really more effective than any weapon, but he decided against doing so, for the result might well be that regardless of the circumstances she would no longer take him seriously.

"I'll be all right," he finally told her. "For all I know, he might even be dead."

As if on cue, the fallen monster groaned and stirred.

"Oh-oh," Wagner said, seizing his rock again. "Please go get the cops."

The young woman complied with his plea, starting off somewhat shakily, but soon she had conquered the short hillside and was crossing the street above. Wagner prudently tied the criminal's hands together in the small of the back, using the man's shoelaces, and with his own belt bound him at the ankles.

When the police arrived, leaving their car up on the street and walking down to the riverbank, they too were impressed with Wagner's performance.

"*You* did this?" asked one of them.

"I guess it was dumb of me to throw the knife in the water," said Wagner. "It's evidence, isn't it?"

"Not deep there. We'll have somebody get it." Though the cops were different in appearance, they had almost identical voices: had they been invisible, they could not have been distinguished each from each. They now lifted the perpetrator to his feet. Despite his wounded head, when the hobble was removed he was ambulatory if pushed.

It was necessary for Wagner and the lady to come to the precinct house to make a full report, and the police considerately radioed for transportation so that they would not have to ride with their assailant.

While they stood waiting on the street corner, Catherine Rider, for such was her name, noticed the slit in the arm of Wagner's jacket.

"You're wounded!"

"No," said he. "It didn't reach the skin."

"It certainly ruined your suit. I'm going to reimburse you."

Wagner protested. "No need for that, really."

"Oh, listen," said Catherine. "You saved my life, Fred."

"I did what anybody could have done."

She continued to give him her intense brown eyes. "Oh, come on, my God, he was *huge*, and a knife besides? You're a brave man, Fred. You're a real hero. Don't they give some kind of medal for doing such things? I'm going to look into it: I want you to be famous." She touched her chest and panted. "My heart's beating like crazy. It's a delayed reaction."

Wagner said hastily, "You're going to be perfectly all right, Catherine. *You're being looked after.* Just breathe as deeply and regularly as you can."

After a few moments she said, "Sorry. I'll be OK." She finally managed to produce a smile. "You know just what to do! You're not an undercover operative of some kind, are you? A secret agent — I mean, for our side?"

Again Wagner considered whether he should reveal the only secret in his possession, but again he decided against so doing: whatever else could be accomplished thereby, the experience would be cheapened.

"Now, now," he said, not really answering her question (whether or not it had been seriously asked), "you just try to put this behind you."

She took his hand. "Fred, I'm *really* grateful. You're too good to be true: fearless, gallant, yet modest all the same."

She shrugged and winced as if in apology and let his hand go. "I'm getting married next week. . . . But Alan will be as grateful as I am. You'd like him, Fred. Maybe you could come to dinner, at least? Alan's a violinist — if you like music?" Her eyes, widening with the question, grew somewhat less lustrous.

A police car was coming. "Here we go," said Wagner. "Look, Catherine, please stop worrying about how to compensate me for merely doing what would be any citizen's duty. Believe me, I have already been richly rewarded."

Now that invisibility had been proved so effective in the prevention of crime, he felt otherwise about disappearing for good. Perhaps it was unrealistic to expect that the opportunity to rescue a beautiful maiden from dire peril would come every day, but obviously his peculiar gift could be used in many ways to further the cause of common decency.

It was only after he and Catherine had discharged their immediate responsibilities at the police station in the matter of the assailant (who was elaborately named Upton Quincy Flippens and was further identified as a mental patient on furlough from a state facility) that Wagner experienced his own delayed reaction to the fight. He had done his best to brain a man. That the man in reference else might have committed murder was now theoretical. His own role had been actual, and now he was feeling by turns chilly and on fire. In this condition it made sense for him to find refuge.

On arriving invisibly at his apartment he was relieved to find that Mary Alice had carried out her threat to decamp, and, according to the note she had left behind, not too bitterly.

FRED —

Maybe it's just as well you let me down before a terrible mistake was made. I see now that despite a superficial physical compatibility (which due to my inexperience I might have been exaggerating), there is a vast difference between our ethical beliefs. To be frank, when you didn't come out and face up to my dad, I guess I began to realize I couldn't continue to look up to you with personal respect. In other words, I came back down to earth, and in fact I called up Jackie Grinzing and apologized, and in view of the fact that training two new people really would be a strain, with Gordon leaving soon as well, she gave me my job back. I'm sorry to say she is not willing to make you the same offer though.

Take care, Fred,
M. A. PHILLIPS

Sandra telephoned him early that evening. "Thank God," she said as soon as he answered. "I've been trying to reach you for days. Was I that awful that you had to go and hide?" But before he could respond, she announced, "The fact is, Miles came home all of a sudden."

With all that he had been through, Wagner was blasé and asked easily, "From the dead?"

"It's not as complicated as it sounds," said Sandra, "and since I'm just calling you on my break, I can't explain in detail, but the man who was killed was carrying Miles's driver's license for some reason. When the ceiling fell on him, his appearance was altered. It was simple to assume he was Miles, and this suited Miles's purpose, for if he was thought to be dead he could get out of certain financial obligations he had to people who were pretty impatient about collecting."

"That makes sense," said Wagner. "But now that he's turned up, won't the mob find out?"

"He snuck in late one night," said Sandra, "and he hasn't left the apartment since." She chuckled shrilly. "Isn't it a good thing I wasn't in bed with you? That's why I've been trying to get hold of you ever since. Miles is an awfully jealous person."

"I understand."

"Do you really, Fred?"

"It was a joy while it lasted."

"You're awfully swell to say that," said Sandra. "I can certainly add, 'Likewise.' Now I'm due back at the harp. So long, Fred, and when we meet in the hall we can just say hi and there won't be any harm in it."

Ignoring his suicide note, the hospital sent Wagner an enormous bill for his stay of one night, and he received separate statements, also for gargantuan sums, from the surgeon and the anesthetist whom he had stood up, and for the visit to Dr. Leprak.

Catherine Rider proved to be persistent in the matter of asking Wagner to come to dinner and meet her fiancé. There was a limit as to how many dates on which he could pretend to be occupied without hurting her feelings, and he finally had to accept an invitation.

Catherine was exquisite in claret-red velvet. Alan, whose last name Wagner did not quite hear, was a dark, wiry, intense-looking man.

"Alan," Catherine said, "especially wanted to thank you for what you did."

"I expected somebody a lot huskier," said Alan. "You took quite a risk for this girl of mine." He gestured Wagner to an upholstered chair rather too near, almost under, a grand piano, and without asking brought him a glass of something colorless without identifying it. It smelled like quinine water.

Catherine disappeared into the rear of the apartment, perhaps into the kitchen. Alan sat down at the end of a green sofa, not especially near Wagner. He bent in his guest's direction.

"Look here, Fred," said he. "We're music people. We're nonviolent. Would you be offended if Katie dropped the charges against this Flippens?"

"The man is a walking terror," said Wagner. "He threatened to kill Catherine, and I gather he has a record of such crimes."

"In this case, it was an attempt only," said Alan, leaning back against the cushions of the sofa, a place Wagner would much rather have been sitting. "The fact is, he didn't succeed."

"He oughtn't get an opportunity to try again."

"That's one argument," said Alan, rubbing the tip of his sharp nose, "but I think we've suffered enough. We don't want to be targets of retaliation."

Catherine served a casserole. Wagner could reflect that it was the first time he had ever found seafood truly delicious. She looked even more lovely by candlelight, with her sleek dark head, hair parted in the middle, and an expanse of bare upper bosom. She taught piano and sometimes performed herself at recitals. She had not been out for exercise on that fateful morning: she had been in transit to a place from which a peregrine falcon's nest could be seen, high in the girders of the bridge.

Wagner, who knew little of music and less of birds, found all of this very romantic.

"I'll come to see you perform," said he. "But I really do think we should get Flippens off the street."

Alan said, "Well, I just don't think we can, Fred — for

the reasons aforementioned. We could too easily be way-laid."

"Not by Flippens," said Wagner. "He'd be in confinement."

"But he got out before, didn't he?"

"We absolutely have to stop this guy," Wagner said, making a fist. "Whatever it takes."

Alan was shaking his head. He poured more wine for himself; he had already drunk a good deal and was showing it.

Catherine offered more French bread in a napkin-lined silver basket. She seemed to be silently appealing to Wagner, though as to quite what he could not say.

"I'll give you my protection," he suddenly told her. "I did it before, when I didn't even know you."

She gazed at him. "You certainly did."

"Who *are* you, Fred?" Alan asked in too loud a voice. "Some karate expert or something? A vigilante of some sort? I tell you: I don't care who or what does the violence, I don't really approve of it, and I don't want any personal part of it." He swallowed some more wine.

"You have nothing to fear, my lady," Wagner told Catherine, who had begun to assume a place in his imagination. "I won't let anyone touch you as you go about your life."

"Oh," cried Alan, "and isn't that a handsome promise! And how do you propose to carry it out, sir? That man is a homicidal maniac. The only way to deal with him is to stay out of his way."

Catherine said quietly, "I believe in Fred."

After a moment Alan rose from the table. His napkin continued to adhere to his suit for a while, owing to static electricity. "All right," he said to Catherine. "All right for you."

Noticing the napkin, he tore it away and dropped it on the tablecloth. He turned and lurched out of the apartment.

"Oh-oh," said Wagner, with fake guilt, "it looks like I've been a troublemaker."

"Alan can't stand it if I oppose him in anything," said Catherine. "But I hope you don't think too badly of him. He's not really a coward. It's just that —"

"I'm in love with you," Wagner said. "Forgive me for interrupting, but I wanted to say that before he comes back."

"He won't be back," she said. "Not tonight."

"Doesn't he live here?"

"No, he doesn't. He'll call back and want to talk it over. I hurt his pride by disagreeing, you see. He won't return till we've got that straightened out."

"Don't straighten it out, Catherine," Wagner said impulsively. "Be mine."

She smiled inscrutably into her wine glass.

"I wasn't lying when I said I was a writer," he went on. "Actually I am, but not really the kind you might think. I have always wanted to be that kind, but now I suspect I won't ever be. At the moment I don't even have a job. You might think I've got my nerve in speaking to you this way at all."

She looked at him. "No, I don't, Fred."

"You're being hospitable," said Wagner. "Yet, if I do say so myself, I am more than meets the eye — by being, so to speak, less. You may not believe this, but I can become invisible at will."

Catherine nodded. "Of course I believe you."

"It's my only real talent when all is said and done. It's the only reason why I could subdue Flippens."

"It must be a marvelous gift," Catherine said. "I sensed there was something very special about you from the first."

"You're not dubious?"

"You saved my life."

"I don't intend to trade on that episode forever," Wagner said. "I think I might well be able to find just the right use for my talent as a career, or perhaps more than one, but I'll need help."

The telephone rang. Catherine said, "That will be Alan." She found an instrument on a table near the doorway, lifted it, and listened for a moment, then said, "I think you are wrong."

She returned to the dinner table. "There have always been a lot of his ideas that I haven't liked. I rarely have had the nerve to tell him."

"Well," said Wagner, "will you be mine?"

"It's awfully soon."

"It's just that I'm impatient right now," said Wagner. "I've wasted so much time. Things have only begun to clear up since I got here to your home. But you don't have to take my word for what I can do. I'll give you a demonstration." He became invisible where he sat.

Catherine sighed in admiration and addressed the chair. "That's wonderful, Fred."

Silently he had got to his feet and crossed the room to the sideboard. "I'm over here now."

"It works perfectly," said Catherine. "It's really a wonder."

Wagner realized he could slip around back of her chair and embrace her from behind, but he was no Flippens.

"You're not frightened?"

She smiled into empty space. "With you looking after me?"

"Oh, good," said Wagner. "I love you, Catherine."

"This whole thing has come about so suddenly for me," she said. "You understand, I'm very fond of Alan, whom I've known for years. And then we have music in common."

Wagner had unthinkingly returned to his chair. Catherine was still looking where he had been. "I'm back here," he said, materializing.

Catherine turned with her usual serenity. "Gosh, isn't that something!"

"Life is going by as we speak," Wagner said. "Great things are waiting to be done, and I sense that you and I could do them. We'll start by getting Flippens put away securely. And if you reflect, only you and I are capable of doing that at this time. But though necessary, that's essentially a negative act. It will just clear the stage for some positive, creative accomplishments. You've seen my potential. What I need is someone who believes in me. I think you're that person. I want you to know it's a lot more than mere sexual attraction: it's important to me that you yourself are a performing artist."

Catherine smiled in the candlelight. She put her exquisite pianist's fingers on the back of the hand he had slid halfway between them. "I'm worried about Alan. Fred, I'm afraid I must ask you to leave, because he'll be watching the doorway from the phone booth on the corner and otherwise won't go away."

Wagner lost emotional momentum. "Then he'll come back up here?"

"No," said Catherine. "He won't do that. He'll still be too sulky."

They moved to the apartment door, where Catherine continued to disappoint him by offering only the most perfunctory handshake. He realized he was still going it alone insofar as a real friendship between them was concerned. No doubt realism was called for here, as in so many other cases, but why must truth always be so banal?

"You will at least think about what I'm proposing?"

"I could hardly help doing that," she said, unhelpfully. "Now, be sure to let Alan see you leaving. Walk in the direction of the phone booth, please, and not the other way."

"That's easily accomplished," said a dejected Wagner. "I just hope you'll let me see you again."

Catherine's smile seemed unusually remote. "Once you're around the corner, come on back."

He experienced an instant of vertigo. "Just a moment," he said, detaining her opening of the door. "Do you mean tonight?"

Catherine said levelly, "I think you can do more or less anything you want. To stop you they'd have to see you."

Wagner regarded this as the first genuine evidence he had ever obtained that being invisible was not, underneath it all, only a self-serving delusion.

For a complete list of books available from Penguin in the United States, write to Dept. DG, Penguin Books, 299 Murray Hill Parkway, East Rutherford, New Jersey 07073.

For a complete list of books available from Penguin in Canada, write to Penguin Books Canada Limited, 2801 John Street, Markham, Ontario L3R 1B4.